# KILLER DESIRE

## KILLER TRILOGY BOOK 2

## ALEXIS ABBOTT

PATHFORGERS PUBLISHING

© 2018 Pathforgers Publishing.

All Rights Reserved. This is a work of fiction. Names, characters, places and incidents are the product of the author's imaginations. Any resemblances to actual persons, living or dead, are entirely coincidental.

This book is intended for sale to Adult Audiences only. All sexually active characters in this work are over 18. All sexual activity is between non-blood related, consenting adults. This is a work of fiction, and as such, does not encourage illegal or immoral activities that happen within.

Cover Design by Wicked Good Covers. All cover art makes use of stock photography and all persons depicted are models.

More information is available at Pathforgers Publishing.

**Content warnings:** mafia violence, human trafficking, murder.

This is part 2 in a 3 part series.

Wordcount: 76,000 Words

Get an EXCLUSIVE book, **FREE** just as a thank you for signing up for my newsletter! Plus you'll never miss a new release, cover reveal, or promotion!

http://alexisabbott.com/newsletter

"*D*rop me off up at that corner, please," I tell the cab driver, leaning forward to point at the crossing of two residential streets. I tuck my hair behind my ear before it has a chance to fall across my eyes as I settle back into the plush leather seat. I'm flanked on either side by glossy shopping bags in various shades of pink, white, and green, and when the hazy late afternoon sun glares through the tinted windows, I tip my designer shades down over my eyes.

The taxi pulls to a stop and I pay him, giving a hefty tip, as I always do. My mother rolls her eyes at how easily I spend money, particularly when I spend it on other people, but Dad is always sure to remind me that there's no use in having money if you keep it all to yourself. And what can I say? I'm a daddy's girl.

I carefully hook my arms through the handles of

my shopping bags and climb out of the cab, giving the driver a little wave as he drives off. I had the cabbie let me out at the corner because our driveway and the street in front of our new house are both crammed with construction trucks and piles of building materials. It's just easier to walk through that obstacle course than have some poor taxi driver try and maneuver through it.

I make my way down the street to the construction site, gingerly stepping over the upturned, muddy bits of lawn and stacks of perfectly-sawed dark lumber. I just know the bottoms of my Manolo Blahniks are going to be caked with reddish mud by the time I make it across the yard to the front door. Luckily, I think to myself with a smile, there's a brand new pair from this season in one of the bags I'm holding right now anyway.

The only part of the house which is even remotely livable at the moment is the first floor den, which is currently serving as a sort of operations base for the construction job. My father spends most of his free time here, having set up a makeshift office in order to keep tabs on how things are going. He's a hands-on kind of guy, and I think there's a part of him that really wishes he was out there helping build the house himself. He's more of a numbers guy, I think, though. I've never been one-hundred-percent certain as to what his work consists of, but I know he makes good money and he goes to a lot of private meetings. He keeps secrets sometimes, and he does everything in his power to keep his work separate from my mom and me.

Occasionally I do worry about him. Despite his attempts to keep it all under lock and key, sometimes I can see the stress of his job bleeding through into his interactions with Mom and me. He tries to be a jokey, good-natured guy and most of the time that's exactly what he is. But now and then I can see something else going on underneath the surface, like maybe things aren't quite as rosy as he makes them out to be. Still, I can't complain. Our life — my life — is amazing. I have never wanted for anything in all my years, and I know at the end of the day my dad can take care of absolutely anything the world throws his way. He's a strong man, that much I do know.

And besides, this whole construction thing has definitely made him happier. I catch him still awake late at night in his study, poring over blueprints and running numbers on his calculator, a look of feverish joy on his face. I think he must have been an architect in another life or something. It's always fun to come with him to the new house and watch him boss the construction guys around. He's never cruel about it, but I can tell he means business. Everyone can tell. He has a booming voice and his checkbook always in his hand, ready to write out another big number and hand it off to whomever he thinks he can trust to get shit done. My mom says he's too showy with his money, but I think he's just honest. Why hide it? Everybody knows we're rich. Everybody knows my dad. I don't know for sure what his reputation is, but I do know that he has one.

I push open the front door and slip inside, my arms starting to ache with the weight of my shopping bags. I squeeze through the skeletal wooden archway and into the den, where a cheap plastic desk and office chair sit in the center of the room. My dad is sitting on a couch on the other side of the room, his cell phone pressed to his ear. His face lights up at the sight of me and he gives me a wink.

"Hi pumpkin," he mouths at me. I wave back before carefully setting my shopping bags down on the desk, covering the mish-mash of blueprints and contracts. I grimace at the state of my expensive shoes, debating whether to try and wash them off in the one barely-functioning sink or just wait until I can ask our maid, Janet, how to take care of them.

"*Si. Bene. Parliamo più tardi,*" my dad says quickly into the receiver, then promptly hangs up and sets the phone down on his lap. His expression turns from vaguely grim to bright and joyous as he grins at me, holding his arms wide open for me to come hug him. I smile and walk over to embrace him, then settle into the couch beside him.

"How is *mia principessa?*" he asks me warmly. "I

see you did a little light shopping," he adds with good-natured sarcasm.

"Fifth Avenue was full of tourists today," I lament with a sigh. "I mean, it always is, but today was especially annoying. I think a couple of people even snapped photos of Katie and me while we were walking down the street. I mean, that's got to be illegal or something, right?"

It happens more often than I would like. Sadly, when you're an immaculately-manicured, fairly attractive young woman wearing flashy designer clothing walking around with your equally well-dressed and pretty friend, people are bound to stare. It's not something I would consider a point of pride. It's just the way it is. There are always photographers out on the street in the city, trying to snap a new, magical iconic photo that might propel their portfolio to stardom. My best friend Katie and I are both exactly the kind of fashion mag street-style editorial muses your everyday Joe Schmoe with a high-definition lens go looking for. And today the lighting is beautiful. It's June, warm, and just the right amount of clouds in the sky to filter the sunlight. All the girls like me, with money and means, are dressed in our best summer dresses, heels, and sparkly jewelry.

I guess I should have expected the attention I got today. It's nothing new. And if I'm being totally honest, it doesn't even really bother me all that much. It's flattering to think that some people find my look photo-worthy, even if it's kind of superficial.

"Don't let some low-life photog rain on your parade," my father says, giving my shoulders a squeeze. "I hope you had a good afternoon anyway."

"I did," I answer truthfully.

"Good. Well, I'm probably going to finish up here in about an hour if you want to just sit tight for a little while, pumpkin. Just got to go talk shop with the crew and set some things straight and then we can go home. Sound okay?" he asks, standing up.

"Mmhm. Sounds fine," I answer absent-mindedly, already trying to figure out what to do to pass the time until we leave.

"Just make sure you stay out of the guys' way, alright? Wouldn't want you to get hurt."

"Okay, Dad."

"Good girl. Won't take long, I promise."

I like hanging out with my father, and going to visit the construction site is always exciting. I enjoy seeing what changes have progressed since the last time I saw the house. Riverdale is a ritzy neighborhood, full of old money and high-class reputations, and I know rebuilding a house in a place like this is a huge deal for my dad. He's always looking for that next step up the ladder, clawing his way to fortune. He wants my mom and me to have comfortable lives and give us the very best, and I know this new house means a lot to him.

As soon as my dad disappears, I get up, too antsy to just sit here in silence for the next hour waiting on him to finish up. I know he wants me to stay out of the way, but I'm sure there's something interesting happening.

Besides, my shoes are already mud-stained. What's a little more dirt going to do?

I creep out of the den and back out the front door, taking note of my dad standing at the end of the long driveway talking to the foreman sitting in his big white utility truck. I sneak around the corner to the back of the house, where the guys are working on building a luxurious, massive back porch and sunroom. The sun is sinking a little closer to the horizon, making its slow, long descent across the sky. I know the sun won't actually go down until much later, because it's summer and the days seem to last forever. But the sun hovers in that orange, lazy space overhead, sinking the world into magical light. The bugs are starting to buzz around a bit more now that the unbearable noon heat has relented. In a couple hours, it'll be evening, and the residential neighborhoods will start to smell like barbecue smoke and domestic bliss.

I'm sixteen, and the world is full of potential at every turn, like I'm standing in a room with a hundred unlocked doors. Behind every door is another world waiting for me, mine for the taking, if I can only choose which door to open first. It's almost overwhelming how easy life is, how smoothly everything flows along from one season to the next.

Sometimes, though, I do wonder if it'll end eventually. Everyone tells me these are the best years of my life, and I'm scared that maybe I'll waste them by being too good, by staying too on-track. After all, I've always made perfect grades and followed the rules to the letter, staying away from drugs and partying and all those dark temptations my parents have warned me about. Katie and some of my other friends go to those crazy rager parties in Brooklyn every other weekend, and even though I'm always invited, I don't go.

I always tell myself it's just not the right time, that next time I'll feel up to it. But deep down I know I'm kidding myself. I'm just not cut out for that kind of thing. I like to shop and hang out with my friends and sometimes I'll go to parties, but I don't get wasted and black out like everyone else seems to. I don't know if I'm just too afraid or if I'm just of really strong moral caliber or whatever. Either way, I'm fully aware that I'm curating a stick-in-the-mud reputation for myself by abstaining from all that crazy stuff. I don't want to be known as the good girl, but as the same time, I don't think I have what it takes to be a bad girl, either.

Most of the time when I do go to the party, I end up pretending to laugh at people's dumb jokes and taking sips of my water while telling everyone who asks that it's vodka and Sprite. In the back of my mind, I'm always just tallying up how many books I could have devoured instead of awkwardly loitering around the kitchen in some stranger's loft in Midtown. According to my mom, my curfew is midnight, but my dad says as long as I keep in touch and look after myself I can come home later than that.

I rarely stay out past my mom's assigned curfew, though. I just get bored and take a cab home before the party even starts to really warm up. There's nothing like the feeling of coming home, changing out of my form-fitting party dress and into soft pajamas, then eating cereal in bed while reading a book and listening to my dad's old vinyl collection until I conk out and go to sleep.

But this summer, I'm starting to feel different. I'm starting to get restless. I want something more to do, something new to try out. It's like I'm outgrowing this version of myself and I'm ready to be somebody else for a change.

I'm so lost in thought that I'm not even paying attention to where I'm going, and as I start idly turning around to walk back to the front of the house I nearly walk smack into a stack of wood coming my way. I jump backward, startled, and realize that there's a man standing in front of me with a half-amused, half-concerned look on his face.

His extremely *handsome* face.

"Whoa," he says, shifting the wood planks on his shoulder and giving me a roguish grin. "Damn near took your head off just then."

"Sorry, I kind of zoned out for a minute," I apologize quickly, feeling my face start to flush pink. The guy seems to immediately take notice, but to his credit, he doesn't say anything. For a moment, time seems to slow to stop all around me as all of my attention zeroes in on the hot guy in front of me. His biceps bulge through the thin fabric of his white t-shirt as he balances the wooden planks on his shoulder effortlessly. His skin is a golden, ruddy tan and he's clearly no stranger to working hard outdoors. He has dark hair and an intoxicating smile as he towers a head taller than me.

And his eyes. Bright, vibrant green eyes piercing right through me, like he can see into my thoughts, into my heart, see it pumping furiously in my chest as I try to get ahold of myself. It's not like I've never seen a gorgeous guy before. Hell, I live in New York City. There are actors, underwear models, musicians of all flavors walking the streets every day. I've been hit on by so many attractive boys at school, and sometimes older men flirt with me when I'm out and about because my makeup and my high heels make me look more mature than I am.

But god, there is just something about this guy that's throwing me for a loop.

"You alright?" he asks, puncturing my thoughts and bringing me back to the present.

I nod vigorously, letting out a nervous laugh as I tuck my hair back behind my ears. "Yeah, yeah, sorry. It's—it's the summer heat, I guess. Making me a little dizzy," I lie quickly.

"Oh, it's definitely getting hot out here," he replies, just a twinge of double meaning in the flash of his smile. "Let me set this down over there and I'll get you something cool to drink."

"Oh no, you don't have to do that," I interject, but it's too late. The guy has run across the yard to deliver the gigantic wood planks to the crew, taken a bottle of water out of a red cooler on the ground, and is now jogging back to me, all rippling muscle and boyish charm.

I try to regain my composure, reminding myself who the hell I am. I'm Serena De Laurentis, new money princess who's moved on up from the Bronx to Manhattan and soon to the affluent neighborhood of Riverdale. I wear this season's designer clothes and I have friends in high places. My dad is a powerful man and my mom is a notoriously snobby socialite.

I should absolutely be able to keep my cool around this construction guy.

But as soon as he gets back and hands me the bottle of water, I nearly forget my own name. It's like he's putting out some kind of dumbing fog which turns me into a speechless, star struck little girl. *Be cool*, I tell myself firmly.

"Thank you, that's so sweet," I comment, taking a sip of the water.

"It'll cool off a bit when the sun finally goes down," he replies, standing with his hands on his hips as he looks me over. Now that I'm starting to chill out a little bit, I can detect an accent bleeding through his words, a faint one, like he's trying his best to suppress it. "So, is this gonna be your house?" he adds.

I nod. "Yea. My father's talking to the foreman right now. This house is kind of like his passion project or something. His baby."

"And how do you feel about it?" the guy asks, surprising me. I didn't expect such a weird question. It's my future house, but it has nothing to do with me. I just go where I'm told.

"Um, I mean, it seems very nice," I answer haltingly. Then, when the guy's green eyes stay locked on me, clearly expecting a longer answer, I go on. "I don't know. I like our apartment in Manhattan. It's close to my school and all my friends and stuff. So moving out here is going to be... different, I guess. I'm a little worried that I might get lonely sometimes. But it is what it is."

I'm shocked at myself for sharing so much with this complete stranger. I'm usually better about keeping my cards close to my chest. I don't let just anyone in, and I'm always careful not to overshare with anybody, even with my close friends. But there's something about him that just makes me feel secure, like anything I say is safe with him. Besides, who is he going to tell? He's not from the same side of the tracks as I am, and I know for a fact he runs in very different circles. Hell, I'll probably never see him again after today.

Weirdly enough, that thought sends a slight pang of sadness through my heart, which is just ridiculous. I don't know him. He doesn't know me. I don't even know his name.

"I'm Luca, by the way," he says, almost like he can read my mind. He holds out his hand for me to shake and I reluctantly take it, feeling his warm, calloused palm against mine. I hope to god my hands aren't clammy.

"I'm Serena," I reply, unable to suppress a smile.

"Well, Serena, I'm going to do everything within my power to make sure this house is perfect for you. Hopefully that will make the move a little less painful," Luca says, without a single note of sarcasm. He's earnest, one-hundred-percent.

"Thank you," I answer quietly, feeling very small and silly all of a sudden. Changing the subject, I ask, "So, what is this back porch monstrosity going to look like when it's finished?"

Without missing a beat, Luca launches into an in-depth explanation of the dimensions, materials, and projected design for the back of the house, using terms I can't even begin to understand as he rapidly paints me a picture I can only half-imagine. Either way, I'm impressed. I expected that he was just kind of a grunt worker following orders since he looks to be about my age and I don't know any guys my age who could even build a birdhouse, much less a house for a person to live in. But he seems to genuinely understand the process of craftsmanship, and even though I can't quite follow what he's saying, I can tell that he feels passionate about what he's doing. Passion. I don't know any guys my age who show the least amount of enthusiasm for anything, much less a job.

But everything about him tells me Luca is different. He's not the kind of guy I'm used to, the kind of dude who sits next to me in chemistry class and tries to throw tiny paper balls down my cleavage and brags about last weekend's keg stand like it's the most impressive feat any human being has ever attempted. Luca is something else entirely, and I am intrigued.

"Wow, you really know your stuff," I comment, shaking my head in awe.

Luca shrugs. "It's my job to know it. Plus, now that I know this house belongs to a beautiful girl like you, I'm gonna work extra hard at it."

I open my mouth to respond, but no sound comes out. It's not even that suave of a pickup line, and yet I'm literally speechless. I look down at the ground, my heart racing.

"Come with me," Luca says suddenly, reaching out to take my hand. I glance back up, startled at this intrusion, and meet his vivid green eyes. He's smiling at me brilliantly and I realize there's not a cell in my body that can refuse him. It's stupid, but it's true. He's got me hooked, and even though I don't know a thing about him, I will follow him anywhere.

"Where are we going?" I ask as he pulls me along.

He looks back over his shoulder. "Shh. Just be cool. You finished off that water so fast, I'm just gonna get you something better to drink. It's a balmy summer evening."

I have to laugh a little at the ridiculous wording. What a weirdo. He leads me to the back of one of the utility vans, glances around surreptitiously for a moment, and then slides the side door open, gesturing for me to follow him inside.

"You know, I think this definitely feels like the start of some cautionary tale I read as a child. Something about not getting into a van with a stranger," I remark, lifting an eyebrow.

Luca chuckles. "Okay, I can see how this might be weird. But I swear, I'm not about to kidnap you or anything. Although judging from the house your dad is building, it looks like I could probably get a pretty sweet ransom for you."

"Yeah, that definitely makes me more likely to climb into this van with you," I joke, crossing my arms over my chest stubbornly.

Luca shrugs, still grinning. "Fine, fine. You can hang out there. I'm just going to mix a couple of drinks. Something to cool off with. Better than water."

He starts digging around in a couple of coolers, taking out different bottles of what looks to be liquor and mixers, concocting a drink he pours into two red Solo cups, handing one off to me.

"So now I've gone from following a stranger back to his van to now accepting a strange drink from the back of the stranger's van. Great. My mother would lose her shit," I say, rolling my eyes. "I don't drink, by the way. Not usually. I'm only sixteen."

"I'm seventeen," Luca says, casually taking a sip of the mystery drink. "But who cares? Nobody has to know but you and me, and I'm sure as hell not going to tell anybody."

"This better not have anything funky in it," I warn, sniffing the drink hesitantly. It smells vaguely sweet, but I don't know enough about alcohol to place any of the scents.

"Funky? *Merda*, you really don't trust me, do you?" he responds, sounding ever so slightly offended that I would suspect him at all.

"Well, I don't exactly know you. For all I know you could be a murderer or something."

"Yes, I'm a carpenter moonlighting as a murderer," Luca laughs. He takes another long sip of his drink. "I don't have time for a double life, Miss Serena. What you see is what you get."

Narrowing my eyes at him suspiciously, I finally taste the drink. It's actually rather delicious, and the liquor sends a warm wave right down through my body. Luca grins.

"What is this?" I ask.

"I like to call it a bastard Americano," he answers.

I snort. "A what what? I thought an Americano was a kind of coffee drink."

"Not this one," he says, shaking his head. "It's supposed to have vermouth, but I don't have that. It's Campari and soda water. An Americano for the pretty Americana," he adds, giving me a wink that makes me blush.

"So, if you've been drinking this stuff all day, does that mean you're drunkenly building my house?" I inquire, giving him a critical look. Luca scoffs.

"No, no. This is all for the end of the day. For me, at least. Some of the guys sip on beers throughout the day, but I like to keep a clear head while I'm handling heavy machinery, myself."

"Good, because if I fall through the floor because somebody was too drunk to properly assemble my back porch, there'll be hell to pay," I declare, trying not to sound too haughty.

"If you fall, I'll be there to catch you, *mia*

*passerotta,*" Luca says, and I catch onto the accent at last. It's Italian. Of course it is. I feel like an idiot for taking this long to figure it out. My mom's family has been in America long enough to have lost the accent decades ago, and my dad does his best to keep his accent under control, but most of his friends and colleagues sound a lot like Luca does. After all, this is New York.

"*Passerotta?*" I repeat, confused. My parents never spoke Italian with me growing up, so I unfortunately never learned it, even though everybody who hears my name assumes I speak it.

"Sparrow. Little bird," Luca defines, waving his hand.

"Never heard that one before."

"Good, then I'm the first," Luca says smoothly, downing the rest of his drink. "Your dad's not a cop or anything, is he?" he asks, half-jokingly.

I shake my head. "No, definitely not. But he would still be angry if he caught us doing… this. So we should probably get out of here."

"Get out of here?" Luca repeats, setting down his cup and climbing out of the van to stand in front of me. He's standing close. So close. I can feel the heat radiating off of his body, smell his masculine scent. He looks down at me with those green eyes and I almost feel my knees buckling.

"Where would you want to go with a guy like

me?" he asks softly. A shiver of something new, something dangerous, tingles down my spine.

"Serena! Time to go, pumpkin!" I heard my dad's voice carry from across the property and I freeze instantly. The last thing I need is for him to come around back and discover me standing here with one of the construction guys, drinking alcohol from a van.

I swallow hard and look up into Luca's face. He doesn't waver in the slightest, completely unafraid and unabashed. "Tomorrow night. S-six o'clock. The park around the corner from here," I tell him quietly. "I'll see you there. Okay?"

Luca smiles and lifts a hand to take the cup from me. He nods. "See you then, Serena."

I back away slowly, not wanting to leave. Then I force myself to turn and hurry back around to the front of the house to grab my stuff and head home with my dad. On the way home I dutifully answer my dad's inane questions about my day, listen to him talk excitedly about plans for the house, and complain about extended deadlines the foreman keeps missing.

And all I can think about is Luca. Those green eyes.

I'm going to see him tomorrow. Tomorrow. *Tomorrow...*

~

The alarm goes off and I sit up violently in bed, my heart racing as I search blindly in the dark to turn off the sound. It's time to get up and go to work. It's time to shake off my dreams, shake off those years of waiting, and get back to my life.

Without Luca.

My chest aches as I drag myself out of bed and into the shower. I wish I could climb back into bed and resume my dream where it left off, go back in time to relive those first early days, when Luca first appeared in my life like a mirage. We were just kids then, and so stupid. We had no idea that there was a big, scary world waiting to close its jaws around us. We thought the only thing that mattered was setting the next date, waiting for the day when we could sneak out to be together again. God, I wish I could go back in time and live those days over and over again. Things were so simple. Or at least we weren't yet aware of how complicated they could get.

It's been two years since they took my Luca away from me again, threw him behind metal bars, locking away my heart and soul. He's in prison, and even though I'm free to walk around outside and go about my life, I'm imprisoned, too. Because none of my freedom means anything without being able to share it with the man I love.

Everybody and everything conspires to keep us apart, and I don't know how to break through the chains and get to him. Every second we're apart, that bridge between us crumbles just a little bit more. I have his pictures everywhere and I stare at them every day. I refuse to forget a single detail of his face, even though I'm sure his time behind bars has changed his face, has changed his heart.

I can only hope that one thing won't change: his love for me.

wo years.

It's been two years today since I was put into this hell-hole, sentenced to ten full years at Sterling Correctional Facility. Two years since I breathed fresh air as a free man.

But my love for Serena, my one shining light, has only gotten stronger.

I feel my muscles burning as I push the heavy weights up. With each passing moment, I feel the cold metal grip against the palms of my hands. I feel the tension of the weights from my thick forearms to bulging biceps, all the way down to my shoulders and pecs. A thin sheen of sweat covers my bare chest as it slowly falls while I push the weights up. I let air out of my lungs while I push up, my body working in perfect sync to make the rep happen.

I reach the top of the rep, and I hold it there for a

second, and I can feel every muscle that works to hold it up. Since coming to prison, I've had nothing but time, and in that time, I've devoted myself to working out. I never realized how inexperienced I really was before I had endless time to hone my body.

Now, though, no muscle moves in my body without my knowing it. Each move is deliberate, measured. I'm not just holding a set of weights up. I know which muscles to tense and relax, exactly how to breathe. I even know how to feel my heart rate going up and down with my workout.

The natural rhythms of my body have become my only friends in here. And I know them better than I ever have in my life.

My arms slowly bend to lower the weights down, and I feel that sweet, familiar burn ripple through new places in my upper body as it comes down and I breathe in. I don't let this position last as long, and it's on to another rep immediately after.

My body stopped aching and complaining during these exercises long ago. Exercise has become the one thing I can rely on in here. Without something to hang onto, despair swallows you in this bleak place. I've seen it happen to other men. Prison drains you. It breaks you. It flushes out your whole world and makes you see nothing but empty grayness.

From the first day, I decided not to let that happen to me.

I started working out in my cell. I did push-ups to keep the feeling of aching arms with me as much as I could bear it. When I couldn't do any more, I did sit-ups. Every time the guards marched us out, I would hit the exercise equipment and do that until I couldn't handle any more.

My body became my focus. It never disappointed. Each day, I found new parts of me to refine and perfect. More muscles to work out, new parts within me to exercise. Every time I thought I'd perfected something, I'd find new ways to make the best use of it.

When I was a boy, Uncle Carlo taught me how to fight. He knew more than you would guess from his humble look. He had served in the Special Forces, and he passed that training on to me, as much as he was willing and as long as he could hold my attention. I learned from him, and I could fight well. But now that I really know what the human body is capable of, I know what those lessons were for. I remember things he taught me that my body wasn't capable of then.

When I've worked out so much that I can't push any part of me any further, I go over old fights in my mind. With each day that I grow stronger, I think of things I did wrong. Things I could have done better. I remember my fights with Lorenzo, and I laugh at how easily I could have killed him if I'd known the things I know now, if I was able to do the things this machine of a body can do now. When I lift the weights, I see a scar on my forearm that I got from that last fight in the Abruzzi compound. It's been a reminder of Serena, something that's always in sight when she can't be.

After twelve reps, I let my spotter take the weights from me, and I take a breath before sitting up and swinging my leg over the bench. My spotter gives me a clap on the back, and I nod to him. When I stand up, I notice other men in the exercise yard glance at me. My gaze passes over them as they look away. Nobody holds eye contact for long. When I stand up and take a step away from the bench, it's like a statement. My presence is bigger than theirs here, not just in the way I'm built, but how I carry myself.

Nobody fucks with me.

The other prisoners took notice when I started getting stronger. Every prison has a hierarchy, a pecking order of men who rule each other, gangs who keep to themselves. When I first showed up here, I knew I had to find my place in that pecking order, and it would happen sooner rather than later.

The first time I got jumped, I made my place clear, and the punk who tried to pick a fight with me has the scars to prove it from when I drove him into the hard concrete.

He wasn't the last, either. But after a few months, people knew not to send mooks to pick fights with me unless they wanted them to come back with bruises and a few less teeth.

Still, every now and then, some new kid sees my body's stature and how the other guys tend to stay out of my way, and they decide to do something stupid.

That's the feeling I'm getting from the blonde new guy eyeing me across the exercise yard. He's not a scrawny guy by any means, but he's got the look in his eye of someone reckless. You learn to spot that look fast in prison. Some asshole with a chip on his shoulder can be a real problem if you don't see him coming.

I pretend like I haven't noticed the guy eyeing me, though, and I carry on like I would any other day. I look to my spotter and jab a thumb to the bench, moving over to spot for him in turn. I might not get tangled up in prison politics, but I'm not an asshole.

"I'm good," the guy says. "Pushed something too far yesterday, don't want to risk tearing anything."

"Smart," I grunt, and we exchange a short nod before parting ways.

I head to the bathrooms, making my way past the clusters of my fellow prisoners getting what they can out of our short rec time. I've come to learn the different gangs around and how to keep myself out of trouble that doesn't come looking for me.

There are Russians from Brighton Beach who

keep to themselves for the most part, even more than the others. There are other Italians here from groups I don't tangle with. And of course, the Cleaners are here too.

Not directly, for the most part. A few of them have passed through in my time, but they're good at keeping their kind out. Makes me wonder just how many palms are greased in the NYPD by Don Abruzzi. But they make their presence known in other ways. Word gets in from the outside, and prison politics do what they do naturally.

And when I notice the blonde kid out of the corner of my eye following me, I have a feeling I'm about to see some of that in action.

It's a quiet walk to the bathrooms, which is never a good sign. Like the calm before the storm, except the calm means there's no witnesses. And sometimes worse, no guards.

But I step inside, do my business, and as I'm heading to the sink and wash my hands, I hear a series of slow footsteps entering the bathroom, coming to a stop near the door.

*He really wants to do this, doesn't he?* I frown. We prisoners would be better off having each other's backs instead of watching them, but some kids learn the hard way.

"You should think hard," I say as I face the blonde guy standing in the doorway with his arms crossed, jaw set, "about whether you really want to lose some of those teeth on your first week in here."

The man's face twists into a scowl, and he cracks his knuckles. "Tough talk for a marked man."

I raise an eyebrow at him. "Look, kid, you're new. I'm giving you a chance most of these guys wouldn't think twice about. Turn around and let me wash my fucking hands, and we'll forget this happened."

With that, I step toward the sink to wash my hands, but I see his knee move out of the corner of my eye.

*Well, can't say I didn't warn him.*

I reach up and catch the first punch he throws. He's stopped mid-lunge, and my arm doesn't budge a hair. He brings his other fist in for a shot to my gut, but I twist his wrist around and thrust him back against the wall. He hits it hard, and I hear his head hit the back of the tile wall. He gives his head and wrist a shake, and I turn to face him as he recovers.

"Don Abruzzi's got a price on your head, *Luca Lomaglio*," the guy says, rolling his shoulders back like he's getting ready for the fight of his life. "Didja know that? And man, the Cleaners are payin' good for anyone who can fuck you up."

This is news to me. My brow furrows, but when he comes in again, I can see his moves coming from a mile away. He tries to tackle me, and I move in with a quick shot to his gut, then another, and I hurl him to the ground, but he manages to keep his footing. He's a big guy who clearly works out, but he's got no finesse. Probably an enforcer.

He comes in swinging, and I put up my fists to parry and dodge the onslaught before I give him a quick jab to the nose that surprises him for a second. That's all I need. I seize his wrist and twist it around him, shoving him up against the wall and holding him there.

"Tell me some more," I order him.

"Get fucked!" he barks.

"Wrong answer," I say, twisting his arm a little more, and he grunts in pain and throws his free arm back, getting a hold of my ear.

He wants to fight dirty.

I don't give him the chance to do any damage. I spin him around and slam his face into the white ceramic sink, *hard,* and there's red on it after he cries out in pain and crumples to the ground.

He doesn't get back up. I hear him groaning in pain, but it's muffled. He's holding his mouth as blood trickles out, and when he moves it, I hear the clatter of a few teeth falling to the ground.

As he starts coughing, I move to a different sink and turn on the hot water, calmly washing my hands off with soap and drying them off on my clothes.

"Tell the guards you fell," I say as he writhes on the ground. "Ratting and getting thrown in the hole after a botched fight isn't a good look."

But I hear the sounds of boots running outside,

and I give the kid on the ground an almost pitying look. "Tough luck, kid," I say, moments before guards burst into the bathroom, and I don't resist as I'm wrestled to the ground by two guards while two more handle the blonde.

～

I'm marching back to my cell with the rest of the inmates, and it's a thoughtful walk. I narrowly avoided getting put in seg, though I have no idea how. These guards are the kind to throw anyone in there, if they have any excuse. I got lucky.

Though how lucky can I feel? I knew the Cleaners had it out for me, and I've been waiting for one of their soldiers to try something on me, but if he's spreading the word to random thugs, Don Abruzzi must just want to make my life a living hell.

I was careful in that fight. I held back more than I would have when I first got in here. Push your opponent too far, and you both get thrown in the hole, no matter who starts the fight.

At least I'm not entirely alone in here. As I walk past the cells, I glance into those occupied by my fellow Costa soldiers and enforcers. We trade knowing looks, sometimes nods, but we keep a low profile behind bars. I'm not dragging old grudges in here if I can help it.

They have a way of finding me easily enough.

But I know that the Costas in here with me are why I haven't had even more trouble from our enemies. I was arrested right after the assault on the Abruzzi compound, but word spread like wildfire, and I got word that I was a hero to the mob.

I gave the Cleaners a bloody nose they wouldn't forget anytime soon. Don Abruzzi vanished off the face of the earth for a while, probably hiding in some manor upstate.

Load of good that did me now. Stolen from my girl, from the only thing that mattered at all. I put it all on the line for her, and though the Costas might think I held my tongue to protect them, it was to protect her. I accepted my punishment to keep her safe. That was the deal.

*Nothing* can ever happen to Serena. And if I have to do time, then I'm still going to do everything I can to make sure that remains true. If I'd drawn out the court proceedings, turned the Costas on me...

Well, it wouldn't have been a wise decision, and I'd still have gotten my ass locked up.

When I get back to my cell, I notice two things. First, my cellmate isn't here. I don't know the guy very well, so I don't think much of it, because the second thing is a lot more interesting: I have mail. I smile at the sight of the handwriting on it, because I recognize it.

It's from Serena.

Serena and her letters have been a ray of hope

shining through to this bleak and dark place. The crushing isolation is something that nobody is ever prepared for. Writing letters to prisoners is something so many people on the outside never even think about, but reading the words of someone not in prison is like a breath of fresh air. They're reminders that we're still ourselves.

They remind us that the outside world hasn't forgotten us, and that we're still loved.

And Serena's love could keep me going for a lifetime.

Everything I've done in here to perfect my body, everything I've done to keep myself sane, to keep hope alive, to remember the outside world, it's all been for her. The sight of her face before getting thrown into the back of a police car is both my dearest memory and what haunts me.

But letters are one way we can stay in touch. She writes to me as much as she can, even though her schedule is so busy running the shop alone again. As I run my fingers along the paper that I know she's touched herself, as much hope as it gives me, I feel a pang of guilt in the back of my mind.

I stepped back into her life for a moment of joy, only to get snatched away, just when we thought we would be together. Just when things seemed to be going *right*.

Those are thoughts I have to keep down deep. They'll consume me if I'm not careful, and I've seen guilt and regret eat people alive in here, driving them truly mad. I can't blame myself for what's happened.

But I can blame someone.

Detective Price has been my shadow, even since being in here. He haunts me, dropping in from time to time to summon me to interrogation rooms, drilling me for more information about "my case." He uses it as an excuse to push my psychological limits.

Taking me down earned him a reputation, and since he's deep in Don Abruzzi's pocket, that means he's had more leeway to investigate mafia operations in the Bronx, which means putting pressure on us.

And since I'm both the highest-ranking Costa member behind bars and the living symbol of his success, he has a close eye on me. I have a feeling he's also the reason that most of my letters out to Serena get mysteriously lost in the mail.

All letters get screened by guards. If something is deemed worth censoring, the letter goes in the trash. End of story. A lot more of my letters get censored than Serena's, but I know not all of hers make it in, either.

I cherish the ones that do, though.

I unfold the paper and read her fine handwriting.

.   .   .

*ear Luca,*

*Things were great at the shop this week! I started a new promo based on an idea Rafaela had. I'm having people bring back a few old shampoo containers to recycle in exchange for a free hand-soap to advertise that new scent I told you I was working on. It's been a hit so far! Also, Rafaela says hi. She says Nico does too, but you still owe him a beer... or five.*

*So, I forgot to mention it in the last letter I sent, but we just passed the anniversary of that time we went down to the beach. I know, I know, it's dumb to keep date-anniversaries, shut up! But when I'm lonely in bed at night, sometimes I picture us back on those sands again. I feel you pulling my shirt up over my head and tossing my bra to the side. My heart starts racing, and I think of your strong hands feeling me up. God, your fingers are so thick, but they were gentle with my nipples... at least, as gentle as they should be. I remember the feeling of your teeth grazing them, and my whole body misses you even more. Do you remember how wet I was for you when you touched me that night? I could never forget how good you felt, and your thick shaft going into me made me feel more whole than I've ever felt.*

*I've treated myself a little since you've been gone—I'm writing this wearing a new... outfit. I spent a little extra on some lacey pink and black lingerie. I love it! I'm looking down at the way it hugs my thighs, so close to where my legs meet, and all I can think about is you running your rugged carpenter's hands along them, your stubble brushing up against it before you let that tongue of yours out.*

*I can't stop thinking about you, Luca. I tried to make this letter about the usual stuff that's going on from day to day, but just thinking about us has got me in a different headspace. As soon as I'm done writing this letter, I'm going to go take care of that, and I'm going to be thinking of you inside me. Then I'll try another letter and see how that goes! I keep thinking about how much stronger you've gotten since you've been working out in there, and I wish I could be with you so badly. I wish I could slip into your cell for just one night. I've thought about that, and I've thought about you doing everything you could ever dream of wanting to do with me. Think about me the next time you're feeling lonely in there, and remember that I'll be thinking of you.*

*Serena*

*S*he signs her name with a bunch of little hearts drawn next to it. I smile and read the letter over again, and I feel the beast between my legs stirring at the thought of her. Steamy letters do usually get through, and they're a blessing.

My mind is already swirling with the thoughts of the things I'd do with my Serena if I had her with me. We don't get the conjugal visits some married couples enjoy, so letters like these are the best we can do. I'm not much of a writer, at least not like Serena is, but I've been trying my hand at returning the favor as best as I can.

I read the letter over a third time before I stow the letter with the rest, under my bed. I've barely finished doing so when guards appear at my cell door, and I give them a puzzled look when they open the barred door.

"New cellmate," the guard says gruffly to me as I stand up, keeping my face stony. A new cellmate could mean any number of things, and after that new guy tried to jump me earlier, I don't think it bodes well.

"What happened to John?" I ask, but the guard just grunts.

"Transfer."

Arching an eyebrow, I look to the two guards behind him to see who they're leading into my cell, flexing my fist.

*J*check my phone incessantly throughout the day, taking every excuse to leave class and run to the bathroom or go out to the courtyard for a "breath of fresh air." I know it's becoming an annoying habit, and all of my friends roll their eyes at me when I take out my phone and click the screen open during a face-to-face conversation, just to see if I have any messages from Luca. They don't understand. It's rude of me, I know. But I can't help it. I just can't stand the thought of accidentally missing one of his rare, almost cryptic messages.

It's a different number every other time or so, because he uses those disposable, pre-loaded crappy little phones from the supermarket. I don't know if it's just because he can't afford a regular cell phone like mine, or if he prefers the air of mystery those burner phones give him.

I don't ask questions like that.

It's not important, really. All that matters is that he stays in contact sometimes. I wish he talked to me more often, but I know he's a busy guy. We couldn't be living more different lives. Class is back in for me and I've started my junior year of high school, and my thoughts are filled with the prospect of prom and passing my exams and turning in term papers. I think about making sure my stupid school uniform is cleaned and ironed every evening before bed, about how I'm going to do my hair and makeup in the morning. I think about whether I'm going to try out for our school's production of *A Midsummer Night's Dream* to bolster my college applications with some performing arts credits. I worry about which colleges I should apply to and whether I will qualify for scholarships, even though with my dad's money I probably won't need them.

Or at least I *used* to think about those things. I should still be worrying about that kind of stuff now, too, but instead I'm just checking my phone and zoning out in AP U.S. History class, my mind circling around Luca and wondering when I'm going to finally see him again. Since the day we first met a couple months ago at the construction site — which has been almost totally finished up by now — we've only seen each other in person a handful of times. Three times, to be exact. We did end up meeting at the park around the corner from my house in Riverdale, but we only had about an hour to spend.

I convinced my mom that I was just going to my friend Gemma's house for dinner and to watch a movie, and then I took a cab to the park. By the time I got there, Luca had already been waiting for a while. I was late, having been forced to endure my mom's interrogations. But he didn't seem to mind at all. His face lit up when he saw me, and my heart skipped a beat at the sight of him. I nearly floated down the pathway to the little pond where Luca was sitting on a bench. He had a small bouquet of flowers, as well as a half-full bottle of Campari.

It was a magical hour, just sitting there slowly getting tipsy with my mysterious new beau. Of course, we didn't *do* anything. Just talked for a while, comparing our favorite books and movies, talking about everything and nothing at the same time. I honestly couldn't even recall what all we discussed, because I was so blissfully caught up in just being in his presence. It was intoxicating, even more so than the Campari we took turns sipping straight from the bottle. Every time our shoulders brushed together, every time he looked directly into my eyes, I felt like I could simply melt into the bench. A puddle of goopy infatuation on the ground.

I hadn't wanted to leave, but I knew the longer I took, the more likely my mom would suspect something was up. Despite the fact that she's never been super involved in what I do with my time and I definitely consider myself closer to my dad, she does seem to have a weird sixth sense about my actions.

Dad always says it's because she and I are so similar, she can anticipate what I'm going to do. But I think that's crazy. We're nothing alike!

The next two times I saw Luca, it went about the same. I lied to my mom about where I was going, and then I took a cab to see him. Our second date was a movie. Some over-the-top horror movie that normally would have given me nightmares, but since I spent the whole time obsessing over whether or not Luca was going to try and put his arm around me, I hardly noticed the movie. Even with all the blood and guts and screaming. Luca is infinitely more interesting.

And he did, in fact, put his arm around me. It was enough to make me all tingly and loopy for the rest of the flick. Thank god for the darkness of the movie theater, because I must have looked absolutely crazy, grinning giddily while watching a horror movie.

The third date was a few weeks ago. We went to dinner in Harlem, some tiny Italian place where he spoke Italian to all the staff. It was a romantic candlelit meal, complete with accordion music and sparkling grape juice. Afterward, he walked me to my cab and just before I climbed inside, he kissed me.

I sigh to myself thinking about it as I slump

against my locker, closing my eyes for a moment. I can't believe how lucky I am. That kiss was amazing, like nothing I've ever experienced before. Yeah, I've been kissed in the past a couple times, but it was always sub-par. Just another boring teenage first to tick off the list. But this kiss with Luca… felt different. Like it was *truly* the first one. Like it meant more than I can even express.

But that was three weeks ago. I haven't seen him since then, and he's only sent me one text message in all that time, about a week after our date. It was short, just "I miss you. See you soon."

I replied, of course, with lightning speed. I've sent him message after message, asking when we can meet again, what's going on, where has he been all this time? But I haven't gotten a single reply. In fact, there's a little voice in the back of my head that has recently started speaking up, chiding me that maybe he doesn't want anything to do with me anymore. I've run through so many scenarios in my head. Maybe I was just a summer fling, and now that school has begun again, he's over me. He's a high school dropout, working full-time as a carpenter with his uncle. He's got his own life path and maybe it doesn't include me. Maybe I was such a bad kisser that he wants to just forget about me. Maybe he found someone else. Maybe he moved away.

All these thoughts plague me during my waking hours and make it very difficult to keep living my life. I've fallen behind on my assignments for the first time in my life, and I've been withdrawn from my friends, unable to really confide in them about what's going on. They're all obsessed with guys from our school— the football captain, the trust fund boy whose dad owns a yacht, the artsy guy whose band might just make it big. I know they wouldn't understand my feelings for Luca. They wouldn't understand the kind of life he lives. Money is everything to them, and they wouldn't get why I'm interested in someone who can't "provide" for me, which is code for "he's not the kind of guy who will make me his beautiful, spoiled trophy wife." If that's what my friends want, then all the power to them. Hell, I used to think that was what I wanted, too.

But not anymore. I know I'm young and we've only seen each other a few times, but I know this is something big. This is real. The way I feel about Luca is real, and it's more important than anything else.

I check my phone for the millionth time. Still nothing. My heart sinks even lower.

I jump at the sound of the school bell ringing to tell me it's time for my next class. I groan and roll my eyes, closing my locker as I start to make my way down the hall to calculus. But one of the ladies from the front office suddenly steps out in front of me and gives me a smile.

"Hi, Serena. We just got a call to say that you're

being checked out early today, so you can go ahead out to the parking lot to get picked up, okay? I already took care of the paperwork up front so don't worry about that. And, um, if you need anything just… just call us at the front desk, alright? We can get you a meeting with a counselor or get you an extension on your term papers— whatever you might need," she says, her voice sickly sweet as she pats me sympathetically on the arm. I give her a confused frown.

"What's going on?" I ask suspiciously. "I don't think I'm supposed to be getting checked out today. I don't have a doctor's appointment or anything…"

"Ah, well," she says, her eyes darting around nervously like she wants to do anything possible to avoid this conversation. "It's official. I don't have any details, but I'm sure everything is just fine. Okay? Have a good day, dear."

She hurries away, leaving me completely lost. My parents wouldn't just check me out of school without warning me first. In fact, they hardly ever pull me out of class for anything less than an emergency. They're really obsessed with my school attendance. And I don't have any messages on my phone. If something was wrong, surely they would text or call me.

Then it occurs to me: maybe this is one of Luca's tricks.

It sounds crazy, sure, but it wouldn't surprise me

in the least if Luca somehow found a way to make himself sound official on the phone and get me checked out of school. He told me that back when he was still enrolled, he used to find all kinds of ways to get out of class. Once or twice he even called the front office from a burner phone pretending to be his uncle to check himself out of class for an imaginary dentist's appointment! If he could pull it off then, surely he can still pull it off now. He does have a pretty deep, authoritative voice. I could absolutely believe that he could make himself sound really impressive on the phone with the front desk ladies. He probably had them swooning just from one phone call!

A grin spreads across my face and I hurry out to the parking lot, feeling light on my feet. If this is Luca's work then I will *totally* forgive him for ghosting me these past few weeks. Maybe that was the whole point, letting me stew in silence to build up the surprise! Once I'm outside, I look around, thinking I'll spot Luca skulking around.

But he's nowhere to be seen. In fact, the parking lot is pretty much empty except for a big black sedan slowly snaking its way out of a parking spot and over to the pickup lane in front of me. My stomach turns as I realize that this car is clearly here for me. I try to lift my spirits by telling myself there's a chance Luca somehow wrangled a car for a date with me. Maybe it's a rental. Or just a fancy cab. Who knows?

The car slows to a stop and the passenger side back seat window rolls down. I lean forward a little hesitantly, and to my dismay, Luca is nowhere in sight. A middle-aged man is in the car, and he says simply, "Get in."

I hesitate, my heartbeat picking up. "Um, I-I don't know. I think you might have the wrong person, sir," I reply quietly. But the guy simply stares at me, unblinking.

I try to reason with myself quickly. If this isn't Luca's work, then it must involve my parents. I can't imagine any other scenario. Maybe my parents did, in fact, check me out of class, but there's some reason they're tied up and can't come get me themselves. Besides, some of my dad's associates drive big black company cars like this one. This guy probably knows my dad.

"You're Serena De Laurentis, yes?" the man verifies, one eyebrow raised.

I nod. "Y-Yeah, that's me."

"Then you are exactly who we're here for. Get in."

I hesitate. Nothing about this feels right.

"Your father has been in an accident and we've been sent to collect you. Your mother is already at the hospital with him."

My world goes dark for a moment. I'm helped inside the vehicle by a middle-aged man who is wearing all black.

I try to regain my composure, my control, but I fail and lean back against the seat. I just have to focus on the here and now. I have to take in my surroundings. I look to the man next to me. He's big and burly, with facial features that make him look permanently stern, like he's constantly on the verge of giving someone a serious talking-to. He has thick black eyebrows, a contrast to the thinning dark hair on his head.

Going over the mundane details helps bring me back to earth.

"Wh-what? What happened? Oh my god, is he okay? Is he alive? Oh my god," I ramble, my eyes wide. The man beside me slips an arm around me, which only makes me stiffen up even more.

"He is in critical condition, but we expect he will pull through. Don't worry," the man says to me, giving my shoulders a squeeze that fails to be reassuring. "I'm Claudio, by the way, and our driver is Dino."

"I-I'm so scared," I murmur, staring down at my hands in my lap.

"We're associates of your father, and we're going to take care of everything. We will take you to him. Just remain calm," Dino tells me emphatically.

I nod, falling silent. I can't even think straight. The thought of something terrible happening to my father never crossed my mind. My big, strong, capable, powerful dad. I never imagined anything could ever bring him down. He's always been subtly immortal in my mind, impervious to the dangers of this world. He's a constant. A rock in my life, keeping me tethered to reality. What the hell could have possibly happened to him?

I stare down at my hands in complete numbness for what could have been minutes or hours, as time seems to stop entirely. The world has faded away entirely. Nothing matters. My mind runs in circles and my heart hammers away violently in my chest. I can't wrap my mind around this. I want to ask more questions, demand further details. I want to know what exactly happened, what kind of force of nature could possibly bring my father down. It seems impossible. I never could have predicted this. Why hasn't my mother texted me or called or anything? What kind of horrible chaotic situation would possibly keep her so busy and distracted that she wouldn't think to fill me in on what's going on?

Is my father going to survive? The man said he's in critical condition. That's bad, right? That's really bad. But he's supposed to pull through... I hope. God, I can't lose my dad. Not like this. Not now. I'm too young. I still need him in my life. And the house is only just now getting finished. If my father dies before he has a chance to see his project completed...

Suddenly there's a massive, violent jolt as the car runs over a pothole, and I am ripped out of my thoughts and into the present. I look up from my lap, blinking confusedly, and immediately my stomach flip-flops. Looking out the windows, I can see that we're nowhere near a hospital. We're on the other side of Central Park. I assumed they would have taken my dad to Mount Sinai. That's where several of his well-connected doctor friends work, and he's always said that's where we would go if anything were to happen to us. But we're not going in the direction of Mount Sinai, even though the surroundings do look familiar.

That's when I realize we're heading into my neighborhood, where our Manhattan apartment is located. Why are we going home instead of to the hospital?

"Where are we going? I-I thought we were going to the hospital to see my dad," I protest, panic clear in my wavering voice. The guy beside me, Claudio, gives me another squeeze. I want so badly to wiggle out of his grip. I hate having strangers touch me. My family has never been particularly affectionate, so it's extra weird to have this random guy with his arm around me.

"No worries, *signorina*," Claudio says coolly. "We are just going to swing by your place so you can grab some stuff for your dad. An overnight bag. He's going to be in the hospital for some time, and I'm sure he will deeply appreciate his daughter bringing him some comforts of home."

I relax a little, but *only* a little. This sudden change of plans seems very suspicious to me. Why didn't they tell me we were going to my apartment first? I'm impatient to get to the hospital and be at my father's side right now. The last thing I want to do is take a detour.

But something about the heavy silence hanging over this black company car tells me I should just keep my mouth shut. This is not the time for me to throw a tantrum. My dad is in trouble, and I need to just do as I'm told. Whatever he needs. In fact, I reassure myself, my mom is probably the one who suggested to Dino and Claudio that we go by the house first to get stuff for my dad. She *would* be the type to think of such a thing in a crisis. If these guys are associates of my father's, then I should trust them.

Right?

Still, I really, really hope this detour is a short one. I just want to see my dad.

We pull up to the curb outside my apartment and before Dino starts the laborious process of parallel parking on the street, Claudio opens the side door and lets me out.

"Go ahead up and get started on packing a bag so we can save time. We'll be up in just a moment. Be sure to grab some things for you and your mother, too. I have a feeling you're all going to be hanging around the hospital for a while," he instructs. I nod quickly and rush around to the front of the building, my heart racing as I bolt past the doorman and down the hall to the elevator. I mash the button for the seventeenth floor and pace back and forth in the elevator as it lifts, biting my lip as the tears threaten to spill from my eyes. Now that I have a moment alone, the full gravity of the situation is hitting me. My dad is hurt. Badly. I don't know what happened, but it's serious. My life as I've known it might be changing… forever.

There's a cheerful ding as the elevator reaches my floor. "Come on, come on, hurry up," I murmur impatiently as the doors slowly slide open. I race down the short hallway to our apartment, my hands shaking as I fumble to fit the keys into the lock. Once it's opened, I nearly trip over the threshold in my rush to get inside. I toss the keys onto the coffee table and bolt for my parents' suite to start rummaging through the closet and armoire. I've never put a lot of thought into what kind of clothing my dad wears, and it feels really strange to be going through his stuff, but I try to push the weirdness out of my mind. It doesn't matter right now. Nothing matters except going as fast as I can so we can get out of here and get to the hospital.

I snatch up a black duffel bag from the hallway closet and start throwing a few pressed white shirts and black trousers into it along with a few of my mom's pants and blouses. I rush into their bathroom to grab deodorant, a hair brush, toothpaste, toothbrushes— anything that looks like it might be useful and fit into the bag. Then I remember that I'm supposed to be taking some stuff for myself, too. With a groan I heave the duffel bag onto my shoulder and run across the apartment to my room, tearing the closet doors open. I hear the sound of the entryway door opening and closing, then the jingle of keys in the lock, as though someone is locking the door.

Weird. But I can't let myself be distracted right now. I'm on a mission.

I pull a few t-shirts and pairs of jeans from my wardrobe along with some panties and bras before making my way into my own ensuite bathroom to grab the necessary toiletries. All this time, I can hear the faint sound of Dino and Claudio walking around in the apartment, waiting on me to finish up so we can go. I realize upon looking at the contents of the bag, I probably haven't been the most efficient packer, especially in regards to what my dad might need. So I run back to my parents' room, passing Claudio on the way.

"How many days should I pack for?" I ask him desperately. "I-I have no idea what I'm doing here."

Claudio slowly saunters into the room, looking very much not in any hurry.

"I would suggest packing his best suit. Whichever one you think is most appropriate for a funeral viewing, since he is going to die any second now," he says calmly, fiddling with the cuffs of his sleeves. My heart stops.

"Wh-what? What are you talking about? Don't joke about that," I shoot back, totally dumbfounded by his callous demeanor. "You said he's in critical condition. That means he's not dead yet. He could still make it. How the hell do you know if he's going to die or not?"

He smiles and steps up to me, taking my chin between his fingers as he gazes down into my face. I freeze up at this intrusion of my personal space.

"Because the Costa boys don't make mistakes, *signorina.* We excel at clean, tidy executions. If we say a man is to die, you can be certain he will die," he says cruelly. I jerk away from him, shaking my head.

"No. No, no, no," I mumble, realizing that I've been tricked. I don't know exactly what's going on, but I know I'm in big trouble here. I throw the duffel bag to the ground and make a run for it, darting around Claudio and racing for the bedroom door. But Dino steps through the doorway and closes it behind him just as I approach the threshold, and in one swift movement he grabs my arms and pins them behind me tightly.

"No! Let me go! What did you do to my dad? Where is he? Who the hell are you people?" I shout tearfully, fighting Dino's grip with every ounce of my strength. But I'm deeply outmatched. He's a strong, powerful man, and I'm just a skinny sixteen-year-old girl who's never been in so much as a scuffle. Dino keeps me held in place with almost no effort. It's like trying to fight with a brick wall. Claudio walks around the room, picking up vases and peering at framed photographs of my family on the wall, wrinkling his nose in distaste.

"All of this money he's taken from his brothers and *this* is how he spends it? I should have guessed Armando De Laurentis would have such poor taste. After all, he did marry that spoiled little Gaspari *puttana*," he sneers, knocking a portrait of my mother off the wall. The glass front shatters on the hardwood floor and he gingerly steps over it, crossing back to stand in front of me.

I take a deep breath and let out the loudest scream I can manage, but I'm promptly cut off by Dino's huge hand clapping over my mouth, strangling the sound in my throat. Claudio glares at me with disgust.

"Of course you would be a screamer," he sighs, rolling his black eyes. "Just as petulant and worthless as your mother. *Tale madre, tale figlia.*"

"Where do you want her?" Dino asks. The question sends a prickle of primal fear rippling down my spine. Are they going to kill me?

"Bedroom. Hers," Claudio indicates. Dino nods and drags me, his hand still over my mouth, out of my parents' room and across the apartment to my own quarters. Claudio follows slowly, closing the doors behind us as we go. Once we're in my room, he snaps his fingers to get my attention. When I look over at him, my eyes widen. He's holding a small dagger.

"I'm going to have my associate here take his hand off of your mouth. I trust that you will be quiet. If you do scream, I will have no qualms about cutting out that pretty little tongue. You won't need it anyway," he threatens. "Are you going to be obedient?"

I reluctantly nod as much as I can manage under Dino's grip.

"*Bene*," Claudio says. He waves his hand and Dino takes his palm off my face.

I stay quiet for a moment, proving that I won't scream.

"*Brava ragazza*," he croons. "You see? Things work much more smoothly if you just behave, *signorina*. We don't want to have to lay hands on you... well, actually that is a lie. I would *love* to touch you. But I would be gentle. Probably." A sick smile spreads across his ugly face.

"What do you want with me?" I ask softly, my voice breaking. There's no stopping the tears now. There's no point. I know I've lost this battle before I even got a proper chance to fight back. I'm helpless here. I'm useless.

"Oh, it's a pity you even have to be involved. But

if you are looking for someone to blame, you would do best to blame the dead. This is all your father's doing," Claudio begins, obviously taking great delight in telling me that my father is dead. I don't want to believe him. I want to think he's lying to me, just trying to upset me. But something tells me he's telling the truth about this.

My father is dead. My father is dead.

"What do you mean?" I press on, gritting my teeth. The tears roll down my cheeks in hot lines. Claudio heaves a wistful sigh.

"Well, for many years we considered Armando a brother. A good man. He was loyal, trustworthy even. But something changed. He became too greedy. He married the Gaspari girl and had a daughter and suddenly his priorities shifted. He no longer worked for the good of the brotherhood. He put his own family above us, his original family. His *real* family. He earned good money for us in the beginning, and we all prospered. But then do you know what he did? He started to keep it for himself. Lying to the Costa family. Squirreling away money that was not rightfully his. He betrayed us. For years. We are not without compassion, *signorina*. We gave him many, many chances to redeem himself, to come clean and return to the fold. But he continued in his traitorous ways. He was foolish, complacent. He got too comfortable," Claudio spits angrily.

"He thought we would forgive him again and

again," Dino adds. "Your father was nothing but a snake! Running illicit business right under our noses, using our turf, our rules, our backing to build his fortune without cutting his brothers in on the spoils. We don't operate that way."

"No. No, we do not," Claudio cuts back in, shaking his head. "He was a liability and a thief and he had to be eliminated. How do you kill a snake in your garden, Dino?"

"You cut him with a rake," Dino answers, almost gleefully.

"All those years and no back-pay," Claudio swears, making a fist. "We aren't bad men, *signorina*. But we are debt collectors. And this kind of debt cannot be paid with purely money. We claim a life. This debt is payable with blood."

"So, if you've already taken my father," I start, nearly sobbing through the words, "what the hell do you want from *me*? Are you going to kill me, too? If so, just go ahead. You've already taken everything from me. I don't have any money for you. I can't... I can't fix this."

Claudio laughs derisively. "Oh, maybe not. But you can certainly suck some of the poison out of the wound your traitorous father left in our side."

Dino bursts out laughing. "Oh yes, *that* you can definitely do."

"You'll pay for your father's mistakes by whatever means necessary. You may not have any money to pay the debt, but you certainly have something else to offer."

"That is one jewel we can repossess. One thing your father cannot keep hidden from us."

My blood runs cold. Maybe they aren't going to kill me. But what they're hinting at... well, it almost seems worse.

No, it *is* worse.

I would sooner die.

Claudio walks over to the closet and slides the doors open, digging through my clothing.

"I've never been much of a clotheshorse. Dino, release the girl so she can help me pick out an ensemble that will best show off her assets," Claudio instructs. Then, glaring at me with a sickening grin on his face, he adds, "You've got a big night tonight."

*I* throw Giovanni to the ground and fall down after him, getting my arms through his as he thrashes and swears at me. The group around us cheers for me or urges Giovanni to get his shit together.

Giovanni's tough, though, and he works his way out of my grip in the dirt and tries to get the upper hand on me, and we grapple as dust gets kicked up. Our work shirts are already stained brown, and we've breathed as much sawdust as dirty air. This is nothing.

We're in the little yard-space behind Uncle Carlo's workshop, and by the way things look right now, you'd think it's a regular community picnic of Italians.

Some of the other guys around my age are

watching us wrestle, waiting for their turn to take on the winner. They're alright guys. I got into my share of serious fights with them the first few months I was in this big new country, but sometimes a bloody lip and a good fight are all you need to make a solid friend.

And the girls aren't far away. Most of them are Italians, but some of them are more local, come to see how we have a good time in the old country. We boys like showing off for them, and they sure as hell seem to like watching. A few of them are cheering us on, especially Giovanni's sweetheart.

I hate to make her man disappoint her, but I've got something to prove to these second-generation kids!

Giovanni has his knee in my stomach for a moment, and I almost think he's about to get the better of me. Just as he starts to try and pull us over and pin me down, though, I remember a trick my uncle taught me, and I move *just so* in his arms, making Giovanni lose his grip and giving me just enough advantage to turn him over on his stomach and wrench his arm behind his back.

"Fuck!" he groans, and he taps the ground to the cheers of some of the crowd around us as I stand up, holding my arms out and strutting around with a big, stupid grin on my face. It's a strut that's gotten me in more fights than I'd like to admit, but

Giovanni and I are on good terms, and he's a pretty easygoing guy when it's all said and done.

As I put my hands on my hips and let myself breathe, raising my eyebrows at some of the girls cheering and clapping for me, I see past them to the handful of tables, where some of the older adults are hanging out.

Teenagers aren't the only ones who spend afternoons behind Uncle Carlo's shop. With a few tables, some decks of cards, and some homemade limoncello, Uncle Carlo managed to turn this little yard into a regular community center.

It's not unlike back home. Back in Taranto, we're all just a bunch of workers and workers' kids, so it doesn't take much for us to figure out how to have a good time with what we've got. And days like this, I'm starting to see why Uncle Carlo likes this country as much as he does.

These wrestling matches happen pretty fast and loose. Anyone who wants a turn dives in, and every now and then we get some grudge matches going, but we're all pretty good-natured. If anything gets too heated, we laugh it off over a drinking match when the adults aren't around, or if they're nice enough to turn a blind eye.

My next opponent is a big guy named Ricky, but the fight with Giovanni hasn't come close to wearing me out.

The fight is a back-and-forth of him trying to get a hold of me and me being too quick to let him. Just when I think I've got a hold of him, he surprises me, and vice-versa. Even though I've been here a while, there's still some national pride that goes into these fights. We're all Italians, but I'm fresh off the boat, so to speak. I've got to show off how we do things in southern Italy, and they want to see if they measure up to a hot-blooded European like me.

Their parents all tell them stories about how tough people in the old country are, and I aim to prove them all right.

The fight ends with me getting up under Ricky and suplexing him into the dirt, and the crowd of teens loses their shit. Apparently wrestling is pretty popular on TV here, so theatrics like that are impressive.

Ricky groans on the ground, and I stand up with a confident smirk on my face. There's no way I'm not the clear winner after that.

"Jesus, Luca, glad I got outta the ring before you turned that shit up!" Giovanni laughs as I step to the side of our little circle of friends, and he claps me on the back.

"Your mug's already ugly enough, don't wanna mess it up more," I say with a grin, ribbing him in the side, and he punches me in the arm as our friends laugh.

"Fuck, you've gotta get your uncle to teach us

some of that ex-military shit!" Ricky says as he gets himself to his feet and dusts himself off. Ricky's big, but he's a softie deep down. He's already working in his parents' bakery, and he'll be happy to stay there. "You got an unfair advantage!"

"Hell, Ricky, if you wanna get your ass thrown down again, all you gotta do is ask," I say back as Ricky makes his way over to me, and in response, he grins and wraps a big arm around my neck and grinds his knuckles into my head. I jab my rib into his stomach, and we break apart, everyone laughing.

"I wouldn't mind seeing that!" calls one of the girls from the other side as the circle starts to break up, girlfriends reuniting with their boys and some of the boys passing out beers to us.

I pry off one of the caps with my hand while I shake my head laughing, but Giovanni calls back, "Oh no, our boy Luca's only got eyes for that hot thing from the nice part of town!"

I punch at Giovanni while some of the guys laugh, and the girl rolls her eyes.

Serena and I hardly ever see each other, but all it took was someone to get one glance at us talking before rumors started spreading like wildfire. If you asked half of them, they'd tell you I was planning to steal her daddy's car and run away with her upstate at a moment's notice.

And honestly? If that spoiled little rich girl asked me to, I don't know if I could say no.

Serena De Laurentis is the *definition* of off-limits. She comes from a totally different world, her family is miles above me in the social ranks of the Italian community, and best of all, I'm just a dirty worker getting paid under the table at her daddy's new house.

Maybe that's what makes it all the sweeter the few times we do get together.

I don't even know her that well, but I feel like there's something about her that I just can't stay away from. She's stuck in my mind, teasing me even when we're away from each other. Rich girls are trouble, everyone knows that... and maybe all that's what gets my blood going all the more.

"I gotta see this gal they keep talking about," Ricky says, crossing his arms. "An American girl who can get our native Italian's attention? Damn, she must be something."

"You gotta teach her some Italian and bring her to one of these things, man!" Giovanni says, and I roll my eyes.

"And let you sons-of-bitches get a load of her? I don't think so," I say jokingly. "But nah, her dad's an asshole, there's no way I could get her away from her... shit, what do rich people do for fun? Galas?"

"Opera," says another guy with a knowing nod. "My brother's a cook at that opera house they got, says all the girls there are decked out in dresses more expensive than his car."

"Think our boy Luca's a baritone, or...?" Giovanni starts, but I make like I'm about to punch him and he trails off, laughing.

While we talk, I've noticed a black sedan rolling up out front out of the corner of my eye. I glance over to Uncle Carlo and the other adults, and I see that he's noticed too.

There's a frown on Uncle Carlo's face.

A few of the guys notice where I'm looking, and we watch the doors open, and a few big guys step out. Two of them aren't dressed too differently from us, with simple jeans and white sleeveless shirts that show off some big-ass muscles and tattoos. The third guy, on the other hand, looks fancy. Nice shoes, black slacks, and a gray button-down shirt with the sleeves rolled up to his forearms. That guy has a sharp look in his eyes that I don't like, set under thick brown eyebrows and thinning hair.

I look back to the adults, and I notice the mood has died. Some of them look uncomfortable in their chairs, card games have ended, and Uncle Carlo is getting up with a grim look on his face to go meet the men.

I don't have to be told what that could mean.

*Mafia.*

My jaw is set tight as they make their way up the dirt driveway. If the mafia is bad here in America, it's way worse back home, especially in southern Italy. The mafia acts like their own government, running everyone's lives and dealing brutally with anyone who steps out of line. They're a cancer, and they're strangling the whole country. I was raised to hate them. I was raised to fear them, too, but I'm not afraid of anything.

Because these bastards live on fear.

"Must have missed my invitation to your little party," the man in the nice outfit says as he exchanges an awkward hug with Uncle Carlo. If he's involved, then it's my business too, I decide. I hand my beer to Giovanni, who gives me a concerned glance, but I shake my head and push past him to approach the group.

"Just winding down a little after work, boys," Uncle Carlo says with a weary smile to them. "I figured you bunch would be starting your busy days right about now, is all."

"Ain't that considerate," says the well-dressed man, who looks at me as I approach. He smiles, and Uncle Carlo follows his gaze, shooting me a look that says I should have stayed in the crowd.

"Well well, you're getting bigger every day, aren't you, Luca?" says the well-dressed man.

"There a problem here?" I say, and the two big guys with the well-dressed man crack smiles as he raises his eyebrows.

"Fuck me, Carlo, is that how you teach your nephew how to talk to guests?"

Uncle Carlo flexes his fist, then looks to me.

"Luca, this is Claudio," he says, nodding to the well-dressed man. "I don't think you've had the pleasure of meeting."

"No, but I know you," Claudio says, grinning at me. I don't return the look. "Look at you, you've got your uncle's courage."

"Is there something I can help you with?" Uncle Carlo says with a weary look at Claudio.

"Actually, all I came here for was a word in private with your Luca here," he says, and both me and Uncle Carlo's eyes widen in surprise.

"What?"

"What?" I say in tandem.

"It's family business," Claudio says to Uncle Carlo, "I'm sure you can appreciate that."

"If it's family business, then I should-" he starts, but I interrupt him.

"It's alright," I say, glaring daggers at Claudio, "we'll talk in the shop. No big deal. I'll come back when we're finished." I know there'll be trouble if we don't play ball with these fuckers, and there are too many vulnerable people around for me to be okay with that.

"Good man," Claudio says, patting me on the shoulder, and it takes a lot of energy for me not to whip around and bust this asshole's lip open.

The shop is pretty simple inside. Carpentry equipment and wood are laying all over the place, but it's pretty well organized. Uncle Carlo has always been tight about keeping things presentable. I know, because I spent my first week and a half here cleaning up the shop with him while he talked me out of running away.

I ran anyway, but I came back.

I walk with the three guys into the shop, and I lead them to a counter that I lean on, facing them with crossed arms and a set jaw. "So?"

Claudio is looking around the shop, though. He has an annoying, amused smile on his face. "Wow, your uncle really put together something respectable here, you know?"

I don't say anything.

"Bet he's teaching you all the ropes, too," Claudio says, finally making his way toward me, his goons flanking him obediently. "And just look at those hands of yours—you'll make a fine carpenter one day, kid."

"There a point to this?" I say curtly.

The kind expression fades from Claudio's face a little, and he puts his hands in his pockets, stepping a little further. "I see you've got your father's attitude, too. *That* might be something your uncle needs to work on a little harder, kid."

"How do you know dad?" I say, feeling my patience shorten by about half. I don't like where this is going already, and he's hardly said anything.

"Just through the family business," Claudio says,

that crocodile grin spreading back over his face. "Which is what I want to talk to you about today."

"The hell you are," calls a voice from the back of the shop, and Claudio turns his head to see Uncle Carlo storming in, red-faced. "For fuck's sake, Claudio, he's only sixteen!"

Despite Uncle Carlo's entrance, Claudio is unfazed, and he looks back to me. "Well I'll be damned, your body's outgrowing your age. That doesn't change things, though," he says dismissively as Uncle Carlo approaches, but the goons give him a look that says he's not going to come any further.

"Look, Claudio," he says, breathing heavily and regaining his composure. "I don't know what you're here for, but if it's got to do with his father, you can take it up with me."

"My orders are clear, actually," Claudio says, "and it runs a little thicker than blood." Claudio pulls up a stool and sits down, resting his arms on his legs, hands clasped as he looks up at me. "Luca, I'm sure your father was very happy to be able to send you here to America," he says, and I narrow my eyes at him as he smiles. "Land of opportunity, you know? You're better off here, getting everything you need from your uncle and his shop here. Can't blame a man for doing that, the old country's no place for a bright boy like you."

"Get to the point," I say, and Claudio gives a laugh.

"You're as impatient as your father, too. See, plane tickets aren't free, Luca, nor is a passport and all the other nice things that just happened to fall into place to let you get over here."

I can see Uncle Carlo's eyes widening, and I have a bad feeling in my gut. Claudio continues.

"Your dad borrowed a nice little chunk of money from my friends back in Italy. All out of the love of his heart, of course, but he's fallen on some hard times, and well, he's having trouble making his payments."

"I've got money," I say quickly, standing up with a furrowed brow, but Claudio and his goons laugh.

"You don't have the kind of money he owes," he says simply, "and even if you did, this is a matter of reputation, you see."

I feel my muscles tensing as I look at all three men. "If you plan on shooting me, you'd better not miss."

"Don't be stupid," Claudio says, standing up. "My boss here in America has spoken up for you, Luca. We take care of our own. He has a solution that my friends back in Italy have agreed to—something that will remind your father to be timely with his payments *and* help me out, all without spilling a drop of your family's blood."

I stare him down, and neither of us breaks eye contact.

"Now, I know you don't like the idea of working

for us, Luca," he says coolly, "but this offer isn't really negotiable. I have one job for you—just one. You'll do it, and I know you'll do it well, and then we can forget all about this little meeting and us big bad criminals," he says, making scare-quotes with his fingers.

I take a step forward so I can lean into Claudio's face when I pronounce slowly, "Fuck. You."

The smile leaves Claudio's face. He takes a deep breath, then gestures to one of his goons. In the blink of an eye, the goon whips out a gun and points it at Uncle Carlo, who freezes, eyes wide. "Claudio, don't do this," he warns, putting his hands up.

"Listen, Luca," Claudio says in a still tone to me, folding his hands behind his back. "I appreciate your spirit, I really do. But this is a done deal. And if I go back to my boss and let him know how rudely you've been treating us, he'll have to tell my friends in Italy that our deal's off. And that will be *very* embarrassing."

Every muscle in my body is tense, and I'm ready to fight. I'd throw myself at them all right now if there weren't a gun trained on Uncle Carlo.

"You have a lot to learn about patience, Luca," says Claudio, his dead gaze cold as ice. "So I'll put this in terms even a punk-ass teenager like you can understand. You're going to do a job for us, and if you don't, not only will you have to use this carpentry shop to make a coffin for your uncle here, but my associates in Italy will start mailing you your mom and dad's fingers."

His cold face splits into the most chilling grin I've ever seen. I exchange one tense look with Uncle Carlo before Claudio speaks again.

"So, what do you say?"

It's cold.

I can hear the rain hammering against the cracked window pane, smell the foul odor of damp trash down in the street. Sirens wail in the distance, but I don't dare allow myself to believe they might be coming to save me. Nobody is coming to save me. There's nobody left who even could. My father… my hero, my rock, he's gone. And he's never coming back from where those evil *Mafiosi* sent him. I grit my teeth and feel my whole body tense up as I curl my hands into tight fists. I need to stay calm. I need to accept that this—whatever this is—is my life now.

I can't save myself. And none of my friends know where I am or what I'm about to do. I haven't had any chance to talk to anyone, not with Claudio and Dino shadowing my every step and monitoring my every breath. They took my cell phone. I have no idea where it is now. For all I know they've used it to tell everybody in my contacts list to fuck off and never speak to me again. Anything to isolate me further. I wonder if they did. If so, maybe they sent a message to the last number Luca was using. Not that it matters. He's probably moved on to a new number by now, and besides, he hasn't shown any interest in me for weeks. I shouldn't count on him or anyone else. I'm all alone in this, and I better get used to that.

I'm standing in a dimly lit motel room, the blinking neon vacancy sign sending faint strobe lights through the thin curtains in shades of sickly pale green. Across the room is a rickety-looking bed with a lumpy mattress and threadbare brown sheets. The light bulb in the bedside lamp flickers ominously every few minutes like it's ready to burn out any second. There are stains on the carpet I don't even want to think about, pools of rust red and dark gold. Who the hell knows what all has gone on in this room? Or in any room of this shitty motel? I don't want to know, but I have a feeling I'm about to find out. I'm going to get a taste of something horrible soon. It's coming.

My mouth is so dry. I wish I could get a glass of water or something, but I don't have any cups here, and even if I wanted to try and collect tap water in my hands to drink, something tells me the water here probably isn't quite up to drinking standards.

So I just swallow hard and stare up at the ceiling tiles, trying to breathe slowly and calm my racing heart. The tears burn in my eyes but I can't let them fall. It won't help. And Claudio was very emphatic about keeping myself pretty. I need to prevent my eyeliner from running down my cheeks.

I blink rapidly to stem the tears and hurry into the creepy little ensuite bathroom, slamming my hand against the clicker light switch. One of the bulbs over the mirror pops, sending tiny shards of thin glass flying, and I let out a shriek as I fall backward into the tub, tearing the shower curtain down as I go. I sit there stunned for a moment, my bare legs sticking up out of the tub while my head pounds from the pain of knocking it against the porcelain. I heave a deep breath and reach back to make sure I'm not bleeding. Thankfully, I'm not.

"That's gonna bruise," I murmur to myself as I gingerly climb back out of the tub, trying not to step on any of the shattered glass. In this moment, I'm grateful for the ugly, oversized black platform heels Claudio forced me to wear. If I were barefoot right now, I'd probably have my feet all sliced up. I crunch across the glass to lean over the counter and survey my face in the filth-streaked mirror. My eyes are pink-rimmed from crying and even my designer mascara and eyeliner can't conceal how tired and broken I look. I use my pinkie finger to fix a slight smudge of the dark red Yves Saint Laurent coloring my lips. It feels so strange, wearing my expensive makeup and slinky La Perla lingerie under my little black Moschino dress in a disgusting, barely-functional roach motel like this. I bought these things to impress my classmates and fellow fledgling socialites, my high-end friends. Shopping on Fifth Avenue was just part of my persona, the reputation I built for myself. It was expected of me then. Just a given. The lingerie I bought a couple weeks ago in anticipation of the time I would inevitably find myself stripping down for Luca. It was a distant dream then, something I suspected would happen once we'd been together for a year or so. Once things smoothed out and we could see each other more regularly. I was already planning a life with him. Sixteen years old and in love and so, so stupid.

Now I just want to rip off the lacy bra and panties and toss them in the dumpster below the window of this horrible motel room. I can't believe how different I am now from the girl I was just a few days ago. I still had dreams then. I was so certain of how my life was going to play out. Even though it had been weeks since I last heard from Luca, I was still holding out hope that he would show up and sweep me off my feet. I was thinking about the future, not realizing that even my present was in jeopardy. Everything I had, everything I was, I took it for granted.

Not anymore. Maybe this is payback for how

wonderful my life was up until a few days ago. I was so fortunate, with my loving parents and my fancy apartment and my designer clothes. I never wanted for anything. I can admit it now easily: I was spoiled.

I guess it makes sense that now I'm being punished. Good luck or good karma or whatever you want to call it… can't last forever, can it?

It used to be that my job was just to get good grades, make myself appealing to colleges, maintain my looks, and stay out of any major trouble. I used to think all of that was so boring, so mundane. Now I would give anything to go back in time and slide back into that comfortable, dull life.

Tonight I have a different responsibility. Claudio drilled it into my head.

I am here to seduce a client. Well, not so much a client, as a victim of the mafia. A man who owes them money and has a penchant for underage girls. In other words, a complete and total scum bag in every imaginable way. I'm posing as a sex worker tonight, pretending to be something I absolutely am not. For god's sake, I'm a virgin. I mean, I've seen movies. I've read books and magazines. I haven't been living under a rock or in a convent for my whole life. I get the idea, the general setup I'm in right now. But I'm not prepared for it.

Of course, Claudio told me that I won't have to actually go through with it. I'm just supposed to act as bait, lure the guy into a false sense of security. I'm supposed to distract him and make him think he's in for a treat.

I shudder involuntarily. Ugh. *Gross* doesn't even begin to cover it.

And once the guy is totally vulnerable, caught up in the game, Claudio said that's when the Costa boys, his associates, will swoop in to "take care" of the guy. I honestly don't want to know what exactly that entails. I just hope my part in this will have ended by that point. It's bad enough I have to pretend to seduce the guy. I know I don't have what it takes to actually hurt him or anything. I just hope to god he doesn't touch me.

But that's too much to hope for, I think. And I doubt that tonight will be the end of my servitude to the Costa family. It's too easy. They've caught me, killed my father, distanced me from my mother—I have no idea what's happened to her—and they have so much rage toward my family. I know they won't be finished with me after tonight. Who knows how many more nights I'll have to do this very same thing?

Or worse?

Claudio and Dino didn't explicitly tell me I'm going to have to work for them more after tonight, but I can put two and two together. If my dad really did take that much money away from them, then surely one night isn't enough to repay his debts. They probably just think they can trick me into thinking this is the only thing I'll have to do for them. I know they think I'm stupid. And maybe I am. For believing that my father was a good, clean guy, that our good fortune was well-earned and deserved. For thinking that my amazing life could go on forever that way.

Nope. Tonight is just the beginning.

That thought makes me feel weak. Lost. Full of despair. My life as I knew it is over. This new, horrible chapter is on page one, and I dread reading the rest of the book. Sure, I could try to make a run for it. Climb out the window and shimmy down to the street. Beg somebody to let me in their car and drive me to the police station. But I know I wouldn't make it that far. I can't see where they are, but I know Claudio and Dino are close by, watching and waiting for the moment to strike. They'd stop me before my shoes even touched the pavement. There is no escape.

A bright light flashes through the window and I rush over to look outside. There's a beat-up truck pulling into a parking spot below. A dark green truck. The driver steps out and my heart sinks as I recognize that he fits the description of the mark for tonight. A tallish man with a potbelly. Balding. A graying mustache on his paunchy face.

That's the guy.

My pulse quickens and I start to panic. It's happening. It's really happening. I feel my knees buckle beneath me and I stagger backward, grabbing hold of the chipped counter of the kitchenette, trying to steady myself. I close my eyes and count slowly to ten. It's something I read online once, that when you're having a panic attack you're supposed to try and clear your mind and just focus on counting. Focus on the numbers. Slow your breathing down. Find your center and push away your surroundings.

But there's no pushing away this world around me. I glance out the window again. The man is gone, clearly on his way through the building to get to me. "Oh god," I mumble, nervously tucking the loose tendrils of hair back behind my ears. My hair is pulled back into a messy half-updo, which Claudio suggested. I wonder how I'm supposed to act when the guy gets here. I know he's going to knock five times and then I let him in. I'm supposed to smile. Be coy, but available. Vulnerable, but not easy. I'm supposed to be the innocent young girl, but still be sexy.

I'm not sure I know how to do any of that. But there's a knock at the door, followed by four more crisp knocks, and I know I have to try. It's time.

With my blood rushing in my ears I walk over and undo the three locks, opening the door to allow the man inside. I plaster a smile on my face and greet him.

"Good evening," I say, willing my voice to stay strong. I have to act natural.

The man steps inside and immediately looks me up and down, his eyes drinking in my tight little body, my breasts squished together in my fancy bra, the glittery lotion on my skin, the way the straps of my black dress slip ever so seductively off my shoulders when I shrug.

"You're much prettier than what I'm used to," the guy says lewdly. "The agency did really good this time. All along I thought they was sending me their best, but it looks like they've been holdin' out on me. You new or somethin'?"

For a moment my voice seems to have disappeared. The guy stares at me expectantly.

"Oh, uh, yes. I-I'm brand new. Just started," I reply. "You're—you're the first."

A huge grin splits his face and he crosses his arms over his broad chest. "Oh, I am, am I?"

I nod and smile, taking a few steps backward. "Yep. Yes. So if I'm a little nervous, that's why. I-I'm sorry if you were expecting someone more experienced."

"No, no. The greener the better," he says, a predatory flash in his beady eyes. "I've been hopin' for an opportunity to break a girl in. It's an honor."

"Oh. Well, I'll do my best not to disappoint," I respond, desperately looking for some way to stall. It occurs to me how little I know of the plan tonight.

How far am I supposed to let this go before Dino or Claudio or whoever is out there steps in to take over? I'm not prepared for this.

"Well? Let's get started then. I paid for an hour and I intend to make every second count," the guy remarks, rubbing his hands together. I freeze up, glancing around nervously. But I have to try to be calm. If this guy catches on and realizes something is up, who knows how badly this could turn out. If I let the mafia down… I hate to think what they'll do to me.

"Okay. Yeah, um, just m-make yourself comfortable," I suggest with a smile. I throw in a wink for good measure and gesture toward the bed. To my relief, he follows my instruction and walks over to sit down on the edge of the mattress, starting to take off his boots.

But when he begins to unzip his slacks, my stomach turns. I feel like I might vomit. This is all getting far too real now. I can't do this. I can't.

But I have to.

"Wait!" I interject, and the guy looks up at me with a confused, slightly put-off look on his ugly face. "Um, let me… let me dance for you first."

The guy sits up and fixes me with a suspicious look. Then he shrugs. "You're a little awkward. I can tell you're a beginner. But why not. Go on then."

With my heart racing, I take a deep breath and start to sway, shaking my hair down out of its updo to fall in loose waves around my shoulders. I turn around and move my hips slowly, shaking my ass for this complete stranger. I move this way for a minute or so, turning in circles, raising my arms up over my head, tousling my hair, blowing kisses. I feel incredibly stupid, like it's obvious how inexperienced I am. I know this isn't going to keep him entertained for long. After all, he didn't come here for an amateur burlesque show. He came here to fuck me.

I keep hoping that any second now, the Costa guys are going to burst through the door and end this charade before it goes much further. But the seconds tick by with no sign of the cavalry. I'm alone here with this guy, and I have to up the ante or he'll get suspicious. Or worse... angry.

So I bite the bullet and start sliding the straps of my Moschino dress down my shoulders, peering back at him coyly. I bite my lip and look down at the floor, trying to glance up at him through my eyelashes like a sexy girl in a movie. The guy is watching me with a hungry expression on his face, his jaw twitching slightly as though he's trying to rein himself in. I rotate back to face him, curling my fingertips over the bottom hem of my dress to slowly slide it up my thighs, exposing myself in tiny increments. I'm doing my best, even though I have no real idea what is supposed to happen here, but I can tell it's not enough.

He wants more. He's expecting *much* more than this.

"Take it off," the man says gruffly, waving his hand in a forbidding gesture.

"I-I, uh, I'm a little shy," I stammer quietly, feeling my face turning bright pink. His eyebrows furrow together and he narrows his eyes.

"Shy? In this business? You'll get over that fast," he comments. Then he stands up, a smile pulling at the corners of his mouth. "I can help you get over it."

As he takes a step toward me, I reflexively take a step back. A flash of anger flickers in his eyes and he walks toward me more aggressively. I fall back and shake my head, feeling my stomach turn with dread and anxiety.

"No. Please don't," I murmur helplessly. It's getting hard to breathe, my heart is pounding so fast and hard. "I-I'm a virgin."

The man stops in his tracks for a moment, staring at me blankly. Then he grins, a shark-like, ravenous smirk. "You know, I've had other girls feed me that line before, but I never believed any of 'em. But you… I believe you. I bet you really *are* a virgin, aren't you?"

Instantly I realize that was the wrong thing to say. It was a reflex, an instinct to plead for mercy. But it's had the opposite of the effect I hoped for. He doesn't pity me… he just wants me even more. He *wants* a virgin.

"I'm sorry. I can't do this," I whisper, my throat tightening so it's difficult to even get a word out. The guy shakes his head and quickly closes the space between us, his hands falling on my shoulders in a tight grip.

"I didn't pay for an hour of teasing and moping," he snarls, leaning in close to my face. "I paid to fuck a pretty girl for an hour. Do whatever I want with her. I don't give a shit if you're a virgin. I don't care who you are or what you want. For this hour, you belong to me."

He easily rips the straps of my dress and starts yanking it down my body as I whimper, tears springing to my eyes. This is it. I can't fight him. It occurs to me that maybe this was the plan all along. I'm not here as bait. Claudio and Dino brought me here to be punished, to be some gross, horrible man's sex toy. I bet they've got some candid camera set up somewhere in this shitty motel room so they can watch, get their sick, sadistic pleasure out of watching me suffer.

The john scoops me up and throws me over his shoulder, roughly carrying me across the room and tossing me onto the lumpy mattress. The tears fall heavily now, and I don't make any effort to stop them. It doesn't matter if I cry or not. This guy is going to fuck me anyway.

He starts to crawl over me, stripping off his jeans as he comes my way.

In this moment, I wish I were dead.

*Bang!*

I scream and scramble backward against the headboard in fear at the deafening sound from across the room. The man turns around, bewildered, and we both see it at the same time: someone has burst through the door, through the various dead-locks, and is barreling across the room toward the bed.

"What the hell," mutters my attacker, swiftly pulling his jeans back up and reaching down into one of the back pockets to pull out a small, shiny metal object. My heart does a somersault as I realize it's a gun. But before he can turn and aim, the dark figure quickly grabs the john by both arms and jerks him off the bed, wrestling him down onto the filthy carpet. The gun goes flying across the room, sliding across the linoleum of the kitchenette area. I flatten myself down on the bed, my instincts warning me that it might go off, like it does on television. Amazingly, it doesn't.

"What the fuck is this? Some kind of sting operation?" shouts the john. He protests furiously, flinging his legs and arms around in a vain attempt to throw off his assailant, changing his story every couple seconds. "I wasn't gonna do anythin' to her! That girl... she—she's my daughter. No harm, no foul. Okay, she's not my daughter, but we—we're on a date! It's all consensual, I met her at a bar. I ain't a pedophile, man! And she said she was eighteen!"

I'm so in shock that it takes me a full ten seconds to register what's happening. I went from being in fear of imminent sexual assault to complete and utter confusion. I don't know if this is following the script Claudio led me to expect. And the man who burst into the room isn't Claudio. It isn't Dino.

But he's not a stranger either.

I realize with a jolt that nearly knocks me backward.

It's Luca.

~

*L*uca has my disgusting john pinned to the floor, the guy's flabby arms twisted behind his back with his face pressed into the stained carpet. I quickly move closer to the end of the bed to see what's going on. Just in time to see Luca calmly, smoothly wrap his hands over each side of the guy's head and twist it violently, fatally to the left with a sickening crack.

"Oh my god!" I shriek, feeling bile rise in my throat as I clap a hand over my mouth. Luca looks up at me, his green eyes flashing aggressively. He doesn't look like the romantic, attentive guy I shared a candlelit dinner with weeks ago. He doesn't look like the sweet, smooth-talking boy who poured me an illegal drink in the back of a construction van over the summer. This Luca is a different one. A stranger. Someone I should never be involved with.

He looks... like a cold-blooded killer.

Who is this guy? Where is the Luca I fell for? Have I been wrong this whole time? Is he involved with all this... this crap? Is he a mobster, too?

But then, just as quickly as it arrived, the darkness in his eyes fades away and he blinks a few times, clearly confused. He cocks his head to one side, never looking away from my face.

"Serena...?" he murmurs, like he just can't seem to understand how he's seeing me in this context. Like he doesn't believe I'm really here. The feeling is mutual.

He stands up, brushing off his hands on his dark pants. He's wearing all black, with a hooded sweatshirt hugging his muscles. He slowly steps around the fresh corpse on the floor and walks over to the side of the bed, his eyes locked onto mine. But I'm still afraid. I just watched the boy I thought was my prince charming kill a man with his bare hands. Sure, the guy was a slimy scumbag and it's probably better that he's no longer a threat to the community, but... still. That's generally an issue for the justice system to handle, not some handsome teenaged vigilante.

"Serena, what are you doing here? How did you —? Is this—?" he asks, shaking his head in confusion but never able to finish a whole question. I can feel the tears wet and sticky on my cheeks as I scoot backward away from him.

"Is he—is he dead?" I whisper, my whole body shivering. It isn't cold. I'm just terrified.

Luca nods. "Yes. He's dead. Clean and easy. That fucker can't hurt you anymore. Did he—did he hurt you?"

"He tried to," I answer meekly.

"*Merda*, Serena. I wish I'd gotten here faster," he says bitterly. He reaches out to touch my face but I shy away. I can see the hurt in his eyes. "You're safe now. It's okay."

"I'm sorry, but you just described a murder as *clean and easy*," I snap, my voice muffled slightly by sobs. "I-I don't understand what is going on. How did you find me?" I question, feeling totally confused.

"Don't worry about that right now. You're shivering. Where are your clothes?"

I point wordlessly across the room to the ripped and torn Moschino dress crumpled up on the floor. Luca looks over at it and sighs, his jaw tightening with anger. "I'm so sorry he did that to you," he says softly. Turning back to me, he adds, "Take my hoodie."

He takes it off and gently hands it out for me to take, respecting my boundaries. I put it on and slide off the bed to stand up. The sweatshirt is huge on me, nearly falling to my knees. I zip it all the way up to my neck. Luca and I stare at each other for a long moment, him too afraid to frighten me further, and me trying to decide how I feel. I'm so confused and overwhelmed. Is he one of them? Everything is happening so quickly and I don't know who I can trust.

But right now, I know what I need.

I race around to the other side of the bed, flinging myself into Luca's arms. He holds me tightly as I sob, running his hands down my back, smoothing my hair. "It's okay. I'm never going to let those fuckers hurt you again. You're safe with me. I don't know how this happened, but I'm damn well going to fix it."

I push back to look up into his face. He's gazing down at me with immense pain in his green eyes. Those beautiful eyes. "I'm going to make this right," he says resolutely.

There's a soft patter of footsteps and I seize up with terror, leaning around to look toward the door. There are two men coming in, walking softly. They're also dressed in all black, but carrying duffel bags which they set down on the floor. They pull their sleeves back to reveal bright yellow gloves, like the kind our maid wears to clean the bathrooms.

"Luca," I murmur, frightened.

"It's okay. They're the sweepers. They're just here to clean up the scene, make all of this go away so nobody finds out what happened," he explains calmly.

I have so many questions. Why is he so calm? How does he know what's going on? Why is he involved with something this horrible? How many times has he done this before?

And most terrifyingly, what does this mean for us?

"Come on," Luca says, interrupting my dark train of thought. "Let's get you out of here."

He puts an arm around me protectively and leads me out of the room. As we walk out, one of the sweepers says, "You know what to do." Luca stops for a moment and nods, without looking back at the sweepers, who have already begun the unenviable task of cleaning up a murder scene. Luca and I walk out of the motel and into a big black company car not unlike the one that picked me up from school what seems like ages ago.

I slip into the passenger seat, pulling my knees up to my chest. Luca turns the heat on, noticing that I'm still trembling. "What did he mean by that?" I ask suddenly.

"What?"

"That guy—the sweeper—he said you know what to do. What is that? What are you supposed to do with me?" I press on, reluctantly looking over at him across the console. He heaves a deep breath. Then he looks back at me, with a weary look on his face.

"Serena, I never wanted to get into this shit. I mean it. I don't want you to have the wrong idea, okay? Let me explain," he begins. I wait patiently. When he realizes I have nothing to say, he goes on. "Things are not good back home. In Italy. My family is poor, very poor, and the mafia runs everything back home. All the guys my age are being sucked into some really dark shit. There's just no other way to go. There's no alternative. But my parents, they didn't want me to fall into all that, so they sent me here to America, to work for my uncle. To give me a chance at a clean life. Only, the problem is, it's expensive to come here. I needed a passport and a visa and a plane ticket. Those things cost so much money, Serena, and my parents didn't want me to know how much they were sacrificing for me to have this shot at a better life here in New York.

"I'm glad I came here. I have a job. There are so many opportunities. I met *you*. But as it turns out, my parents didn't have the money to send me here on their own, so they had to ask the mob for money. To save me from the mafia, they put themselves in debt to them, thinking they could just pay it off over time. If I had known what kind of risks they were taking to send me here I would never have agreed to leave Italy, but they kept it hidden from me. My parents didn't want me to worry, and besides, they expected they could take care of it without my ever needing to find out. But it didn't work out the way they planned. Things have gotten worse since I left, and now the mafia is calling in those debts all at once. My parents can't pay. My uncle can't pay. And the mafia came to me out of the blue, threatening to kill my uncle and my whole family back home if I don't pay them back myself," Luca says, gritting his teeth.

I reach over and set my hand on his arm. He takes my hand in his and squeezes it tight.

"Apparently, the Costa family sees something in me. They think they can turn me into some kind of mindless soldier or mercenary. I get it. They think I'm just some dumb kid who will do whatever they tell me to do. I'm the right age. I'm the right type. And they have leverage, Serena." He looks over at me meaningfully. "I can't let them hurt my family."

"Of course not," I murmur softly.

"So they came to me with a proposition, a way to clear my debts. I was told to come to this location. They gave me a room number and a time. They made me kill that guy tonight," he says.

"Well, then," I start slowly. "That means it's over. Right? You did it. You—you killed that guy. He's dead. It's all done now. Your debt is cleared. Maybe mine is, too."

The look on Luca's face breaks my heart. It clearly hasn't occurred to him until now that the mafia is the reason I was here tonight, too. I stare down at my lap, fighting back tears as I begin to explain. "Turns out I had a debt, as well. My father's debt. Apparently, all these years he's been stealing money from the mafia. All this time I thought my dad was just a great businessman, maybe with some sketchy associates, but still a businessman at the heart of it. But I was wrong, I guess. He's been keeping this from me my whole life. And now it's over. They killed him. My father. He's dead now. I never even got to say goodbye."

"Serena, I'm so sorry," Luca says, squeezing my hand. "I had no idea."

"Me neither," I reply bitterly. I take a deep breath and force myself to stop crying. I'm running out of tears at this point anyway. There's nothing else to be done about it. I have to be strong. "Anyway, I guess it's over now. I did what Claudio told me. I was... I was bait for that horrible guy. I was supposed to pretend to be a sex worker and make him think he was gonna get lucky, you know. And I did. I fulfilled my end of the bargain. Now both of us are free."

To my dismay, Luca shakes his head. "It's not over yet."

"What do you mean? We both followed orders. It's done."

"No, Serena. Killing that fucker was only half of my instructions. I was supposed to come here, kill the john, and take the... the girl to a drop point," he reveals.

I feel my skin go cold. "Wait. So, you're supposed to take me away… back to—"

"Back to the mafia. Yes," Luca says sorrowfully.

"They were never going to let me go, were they?" I ask quietly.

"I don't think so. You—what you represent—you're too valuable. I think they're planning to make you do this again and again. And the other times, you might not just be acting as bait. Serena. I think they want you to do what you were pretending to do tonight, but for real."

Suddenly I feel like I might vomit, and I grind my teeth hard until I regain my composure. I look over at Luca, resigning myself to whatever fate I have to embrace. It's out of my hands. It's out of Luca's hands, too. This is bigger than both of us.

"I understand. Do what you have to do," I tell him emphatically.

He blinks in confusion for a moment, narrowing his eyes. Then it dawns on him what I'm saying, and he shakes his head vigorously. "No. No, Serena. That's not how it's going to happen. I'm not going to just hand you back to the wolves like they want me to. Fuck that. I agreed to this before I knew… before I had any idea you were involved. I can't believe I accepted this fucking offer in the first place. They *used* me."

"They used both of us," I mutter sadly. "And I can't let you disobey them. They'll kill your family,

Luca. They already killed my father. Hell, for all I know, they killed my mother, too. But you still have a family. People who care about you. Don't sacrifice them to save me. I'm not worth it, Luca."

He glares out the window for a minute or so, not replying. Then, suddenly, he jams the keys into the ignition and fires up the engine. The car peels out of the motel parking lot and down the street. My heart sinks. He's doing what he has to do, I tell myself. I can't hold this against him.

The car rumbles down the highway back into the city, leaving the motel far behind us as I fall silent, trying to keep myself from crying. I already told him I'll accept whatever punishment is coming my way. I won't go back on that promise. But after some time, it occurs to me that Luca doesn't seem to be driving me to some mysterious location. We take a turn toward Manhattan and I realize we're going toward my apartment. Why would the drop point be anywhere near my house? Aren't the police looking for me at this point? It seems too risky. Suddenly, Luca's deep voice punctures the silence.

"I'll be damned if I let those fuckers turn me into a monster. I can't hurt you, Serena. I refuse to. They can threaten my life and my family's lives, but I won't let them turn me against the only girl I care about," Luca says angrily.

"What? But you said I'm too valuable. They're not just going to give me up that easily," I protest. A crazy, impossible idea pops into my head. "But what if we just run away? We—we can go somewhere far off, where they'll never find us. We'll leave all of this behind and start over."

"Serena, I wish we could do that. I would do it in a heartbeat if I thought it would work. But this is the mafia. They have people everywhere, in the least likely of places. We could run, but we could never hide from them. Even if we had all the money in the world, they would find us, and we're both broke now," he explains.

"Then what are we going to do?" I ask. Luca is silent again, thinking.

Finally, he answers. "They made me an offer I couldn't refuse, and now it's my turn to do the same. I think I know a way to make myself more valuable to them than you are. In fact, I have a feeling I might be the one they're after in the first place" he growls. He takes out one of his usual burner phones and dials a number quickly, putting the phone to his ear.

"Who are you calling?" I whisper, bewildered.

"I demand to speak to Claudio," Luca says into the receiver. "No, you don't need to ask who the fuck I am. Claudio will know. Let me speak to him. Now."

My heart races. Why the hell is he calling Claudio? What is he doing?

There's a pause and then I hear the faint crackle of a different male voice from the phone, even though I can't make out the words he's saying. Luca replies in Italian, "This is Luca Lomaglio, you fucking scab. You've been a big talker up until now, but this time it's your turn to shut the fuck up and let me talk. Listen to me! I know what game you're playing. I know what you really want, and it isn't Serena De Laurentis. I am an asset, and all of you Costa fuckers know that. So, I'm going to make you an offer. If you swear to leave Serena and her mother alone, you will get something so much better in return. Do you understand what I'm giving you? I will work for you. Full-time. I'll steal. I'll fight. I'll snap whatever neck you want snapped. I'll belong to you. I'm from the old country, and my actions tonight should be more than enough to prove how valuable I can be. You let Serena go, and you can have me instead. As if that wasn't exactly what the fuck you planned all along, you fucking snake."

The car slams to a stop at the curb outside of my apartment building, and I sit completely frozen in place, staring at Luca in shock. The voice on the other end of the line is speaking, but I can't make out the words. Luca closes his eyes and lets out a deep exhale. *"Si, bene. Per sempre. Lo giuro,"* he says resolutely.

I wish desperately I could understand what he said.

And then, he hangs up the call with a click. The phone slides out of his hand and down into the seat.

"Luca… what did you just do?" I ask breathlessly. He turns to slowly face me, giving me a faint smile. His eyes are shining.

"It's over. You never have to worry about any of this again," he says.

"What do you mean? You didn't answer my question. What did you do?" I repeat, beginning to panic. Luca reaches over and touches my face softly, lovingly.

"Your mother is upstairs in your apartment. She is unharmed. Go up and see her. I'm sure she is worried sick about you," he says, still avoiding the question.

I shake my head. "No. No, you didn't…"

"Serena," he interjects firmly, "please don't argue with me. I did what needed to be done. It's what they wanted, what they expected anyway. You were just a pawn. This was never about you, understand? They just used you to get to me. And it worked."

"Luca! You can't!" I burst out. "I won't let you!"

"It's already done. I told you, it's over. It was my choice, and I made it. I chose you."

Tears burn in my eyes and this time I just let them fall. "It's not fair. They can't do this— we'll just go to the police. We'll fix this. We—"

"No, Serena. No police. Don't even think about it. This arrangement is… delicate. The Costa family need to know that they can trust me. I'm brand new. I pulled a power play by making this call tonight, and I need to build back that trust before anything else can happen," Luca explains. "You're free now, *mia passerotta*. You're going to survive."

"Without you," I murmur, my voice cracking into a sob. "I will never be free, not without you. I can't. I won't."

Luca gives me a warm, pitying smile and smooths the hair back from my face.

"Serena, listen to me. I could never turn you over to them. And even if I did, they would never let me go. Don't you see? This was the whole point. To make me give in. To bring me to my knees. I was never going to get out of this. But I found a way to get *you* out, and that's what I need you to focus on. Please," he adds, tracing his finger down my cheek to land on my bottom lip. I gently kiss the tip of his finger, closing my eyes. I can feel my heart shattering into pieces, but I know he's right. There's nothing I can do to change this.

I open my eyes again and Luca pulls me close, pressing his lips against mine in a soft, passionate kiss. When he breaks away, he says softly, "The best thing you can do now is leave. Go. Live your life. Try to forget any of this ever happened. And if you can… forget me, too."

"I don't think I ever could," I reply, leaning my forehead against his.

"Serena, my world has been so bright since you came into it. You've given me exactly the kind of hope and happiness my parents wanted me to find here in America. But some things, dark things, have followed me all the way from across the ocean. I refuse to let those dark things overshadow your light like they have mine," Luca tells me.

"You can't do this," I protest weakly, shaking my head as the tears drip down onto the slick leather seats. Luca gets out of the car and comes around to open the passenger side door, pulling it open and holding out his hand for me. Reluctantly, I take it and let him pull me to my feet. The cool night air breezes around my legs and I shiver. The city feels so huge and dark, like a monster waiting to swallow me up as soon as Luca disappears.

"You escaped a terrible fate tonight, *mia passerotta*," he says. "But I would be an even worse fate for you than that."

"I don't want to forget you," I tell him tearfully. He kisses me on the forehead, then peers into my face with those green eyes nearly glowing in the dim light.

"Try," he says simply. And with that, he walks back to the driver's side, slides behind the wheel, and drives away, leaving me standing alone on the side-walk in the darkness.

I crave her touch more than anything.

The energy pent up in my body with need for Serena spurs me on when I'm in the exercise yard. Today, my legs work back and forth on the machine, and I listen to the rhythmic clanging of the metal weights behind me.

On most days, I focus my mind entirely on the burn in my body, the strain on my muscles. It's the only way to truly know your body's strengths and weaknesses.

But today, all I can think about is Serena. Sometimes, even my mind gives into the temptation to escape to a fantasy outside these horrible walls and iron bars.

I picture myself coming back to my home to find her there, jumping into my arms as I press my lips to hers and walk her back into the room, shutting the door behind me and pushing her onto the couch. I think of the feel of her soft, fresh clothing, fabric I haven't touched in so very long, before I rip it off her with so little effort. I can hear her gasp in my ear as I expose her before me—my lover and my victim.

I think to myself about how I'll descend on her like an animal, tearing off the lingerie she described so sweetly, revealing her soft skin to me, turning to show me everything I've missed in these long years away from her. My rough hands have grown stronger and tougher, but the one thing they crave more than anything is *her*. I'd run my hands over her breasts, feeling the hard buds of her nipples as I run over them with my thumbs and listen to the soft, desperate sighing of her voice. Her voice is sweeter than the notes of a symphony in my dreams.

I can nearly feel her legs when I pull her panties down along her thighs, her calves, over her ankles, and I toss them to the side to devour her exposed body with my eyes.

Prison food is awful, but the one taste I've missed more than anything in the world is the taste of Serena's sweet honey. It's one of the many things I use to keep myself stable, to remind myself of the pleasures of the outside world. When I'm free from here, I'll bury my face in her pussy, rest her on my jaw and devour her with all the passion she deserves. I'll satisfy all the needs that have been so painfully pent up inside me for so long.

There is no privacy in prison, except for the little bit of it that comes with solitary confinement. I got a taste of that my first few months in here. One of the old big-shots on my cell block decided to pick a fight with me, and I left him with broken bones. Solitary is hell, but the one thing that kept me going was the thought of Serena.

I saw myself sinking deep inside her to the hilt after I'd feast on her pussy. I remembered the feeling of my balls hitting her ass as I enter her. I picture my thick, pulsing cock grinding against every inch of her inner walls, every depth that I'm so familiar with, yet there is always something new to discover in being intimate with Serena. In my mind, I'm right there with her, groping her breasts, letting my hands rove down to her hips and angle her up as I buck deeper into her, filling her up with myself in every possible way, my cock harder and stronger than ever before with my new strength.

When I'm free, my girl will enjoy every bit of my newer, stronger body. My *principessa* deserves nothing but the very best.

As I work out, I feel my blood running hot with my thoughts, so I use that to fuel my body to work out even harder. Eventually, I'm able to re-focus myself and clear my head. Going for a jog sometimes helps too, but in the heat of things, I can't keep her out of my head.

From the time we were young, I never have.

I finish my workout and stand up slowly, rolling my shoulders back and feeling my heart's steady rhythm in my chest. A jog might not be a bad idea to cool down. The recreation yard hardly passes as a good space for that kind of thing, but we all make do with what we have. I jump up and down a few times to shake my body out, then head off.

Jogging gives me some of the most privacy I can carve out for myself. Even on the exercise equipment, someone's always hovering around, but I'm rarely messed with when I run.

But I hear the sounds of footsteps running up behind me, and I get the feeling today won't be one of those days.

The footsteps are gaining on me. There's a chance it's just some hotshot trying to look tough and pass me, but I've been around long enough to know better. It's no surprise to me when I see two men out of the corner of my eye.

Dark hair and swarthy. They're Italians. I've seen them before, but we don't talk. That means this won't be a pleasant time.

"Good workout, Lomaglio?" says one of them, and I shoot them a glare as I slow to a stop.

"Cut the shit," I say, in no mood to be taken out of my private thoughts. "What do you want?"

"Woah woah," says the other, furrowing his eyebrows. "Don't knock *my* teeth out, big guy. You don't want to spend more time in the hole, do you?"

I look between the two of them, making sure to control my body language carefully. If I look like I'm about to start shit, we'll draw the guards' eyes, and they're not afraid to act before anything even happens.

But these two don't look like they're about to start a fight. There are tells you come to recognize, tense postures that are like red flags. The look of these two tells me they're here to talk more than act, though. I want to leave them be and walk away, but you learn better than to turn your back on anyone in a place like this.

"Then don't give me a reason," I say evenly.

"Look, Lomaglio," says the first guy, talking to me as if I were at a job interview. My face is unmoved. "Everyone knows you're a fuckin' maniac. We just wanna be clear on where we stand. You can appreciate that, right?"

"I don't know who you are, and I don't care," I grunt, my face stony.

"We're people who look after our friends," he says, crossing his arms.

"So some new guy slips in the bathroom and knocks his own teeth out, and you want to come start a fight in the rec yard?" I scoff. I'm careful with my words, because I know there's a good chance one of them is wearing a wire in exchange for benefits from the guards. Every prison has rats, and I don't take chances. I won't incriminate myself.

"No, you beat the shit out of friends of our friends, and we take offense to that," the other guy says, just as careful as me not to start bowing up and posturing.

"You're Cleaners," I say, a grim smile on my face. "You think you're a real gang on the inside. How sweet."

"Tough talk from a guy who's got a sweet piece of ass on the outside, all alone by herself," says the first man.

Now he has my attention.

"What was that?" I say, my eyes turning to him with a spark of fire in them. "I must have heard that wrong."

"Nothing to worry about, big guy," he laughs, "We can keep an eye on her a lot better than you can."

In my mind, I'm already weighing the satisfaction of breaking this man's face versus spending a few months in the hole.

"Yeah," says the second man, "you really oughta think about that before you go busting up our friends in here. See, you've got all that muscle on you, but her? I hear she's pretty soft. And anything you do in here is gonna bounce back on her, and buddy, that's gonna hurt her a lot more than it can hurt you."

"Not if you're dead," I say, starting to see red as I approach the men. I've forgotten all care for my stance, and a few other men in the yard are starting to look toward us. I don't care. Nobody threatens my girl.

"Lorenzo crumpled like paper in my hands. I wonder if all you Cleaners are made of the same stuff."

But just as the men seem getting ready to fight, I hear the sounds of whistles around us as a handful of guards rush over to us. The two Cleaners put their hands up innocently as the guards wrestle us away from each other. I could throw the guards around like dolls, but I go with them as they pull me away, my eyes glaring daggers into the smug men.

As I'm led back to my cell, though, I'm seething, because I know they'll make good on their threat. I can protect myself just fine in a place like this. But Serena? She's tough, but nobody can take on an entire mob on their own.

The guards march me down the path to my cell, and I don't pay attention to their yammering on about me being on thin ice for the last incident. I enter my cell stoically and hear the familiar sound of it shutting behind me.

My new cellmate's tired eyes greet me.

"Tough workout?" he asks, not bothering to sit up from his bed.

"Bad spotters," I reply, and he cracks a smile as I move to my bed and sit down. There's a piece of mail addressed to me that I push to the side for the time being. I need to refocus my thoughts.

My quiet cellmate is Eduardo Trueba. He's an old man, and I can tell by the way he carries himself in here that he's been inside for a long time and doesn't plan to see the world as a free man again. Men who have nothing to lose can be very dangerous, but Trueba is the kind of man who's hard to read.

His hair is white, he's got some weight on him, and he doesn't leave his cell very much. He has a book that he often reads with a cover in Spanish, but I haven't spoken to him very much.

He hasn't shown himself to be trouble, and that's good enough for me.

"You're a big man," Trueba says, "so long as you look like you're the biggest fish around, you'll always have little ones nipping at you."

I glance at him. He looks peaceful, sitting there with his hands folded over his belly.

"Maybe I should spend some time in the library, take a lesson from you."

He gives a chuckling grin. "Been here ten years, just one shank-wound to show for it. It's not a bad gig, if you can keep your blood cool."

I crack a smile of my own at that. In my case, both of us can tell that that's never going to happen. I pick up the letter again and push myself back on my bed against the wall. The others aren't back from the rec yard yet, Trueba looks like he's in the mood for a conversation, and hell, I could use a distraction too. I figure there's no harm in indulging the old man.

"Ten years?" I say with raised eyebrows. "You don't strike me as the kind of man who'd do hard time."

"That's what everyone says," Trueba chuckles. "Maybe I should get a few prison tattoos on my face. What do you think about a snake with flames coming out its mouth?"

I grin and nod, giving his face an appraising look. "That could be good, or maybe a knife. You can say your mind's still sharp."

He laughs out loud at that, a hearty laugh from the gut. "I like that, good thinking." After he settles down a little, he looks thoughtful again before he speaks. "I don't think my crime was so bad, but the law didn't agree."

It's an unspoken law in prison that you don't ask what people are in for, so I just nod, but he goes on.

"It was a bank robbery," he says, looking up at the ceiling with a wistful look in his eye. "We were damn good at it, too. Heard of the Harrison Avenue job?"

I raise my eyebrows and give a nod. I have heard of that one, in fact. It's one of the most famous robberies in the city's history, nearly forty years ago. A small crew hit a bank where some billionaire had a fortune in jewels, and as soon as the robbers had it, they all just disappeared, melted away into the city, and the jewels vanished too. It was like they were never there.

"That was me," he says, but there's no pride in his voice, just the simple words. "I planned the whole thing, and I got a hold of those jewels with my own two hands." He looks at his gnarled fingers. "It's funny, the only thing I could think about in the heat of the moment was how crazy it was, some punk like me from Harlem holding more money than I'd seen over my whole life. Apartment, car, everything."

"Couldn't imagine," I say.

He gives a sad smile. "Well, you do what you have to when times get hard. And times were hard for me and my wife. I have a big family, and where I grew up, you don't just leave them when you get married. Everyone just gets closer together. My friends and I, we saw a chance, took the risk, and..." he shrugs, "got lucky, I guess."

"Takes a hell of a lot of luck to knock over a bank," I say, folding my arms over my chest.

"Takes a lot more to get away with it," he says with a wink. "Dunno if I'm proud of what I did, but nobody got hurt, and boy, my family didn't have no problems for a good thirty years. And man, those were a good thirty years," he says, looking up at the ceiling, and I can see true happiness in his eyes. "Didn't live in luxury or anything, that would have gotten too much attention. We just kind of... did our thing, you know? Made sure my kids got college taken care of, didn't worry about bills, health, nothing. It was... it was nice."

"What happened?" I ask, interested now.

He shrugs. "They got better at tracking down people like me. That DNA testing stuff got invented, and eventually someone dug up my case, tested some old evidence, and the next thing I know, I'm getting arrested at my granddaughter's *quinceanera*."

"Damn," I say, shaking my head.

"That's what I said," he says with a sad grin, but that soon fades. "They roasted me in court, too. Wanted to make a big show of locking me up. I'll die in here," he says, nodding to himself. "I wouldn't mind, if it were just me. I've had a good run. Nice, happy years. But I worry about my wife sometimes. Sure, she's got the rest of the family to take care of her, and they couldn't trace what's left of the money if they tried, but still."

"Leaving someone alone like that without being able to do anything hits you hard," I say, and he looks over at me. I see tears in the old man's eyes as he gives a short nod, then looks away.

"You get that," he points out.

"Yeah," I say, flexing my fist. "I get that." He looks back at me.

"You're young though. I don't need to know you that well to know you don't deserve a place like this. You oughta have your whole life ahead of you. You love her?" he asks, seeing right through me.

I look at the scar on my forearm and think of Serena. "I deserve everything I get in here, but I love her more than anything."

He nods sadly. "I'm too old to blame the law for anything, but when I was in that courthouse…" he tightens his fist, and I see some muscle flex in his arm. He's tougher than the impression he gives. "To them, criminals like me are just stepping stones. The lawyer who put me away is probably drinking wine on a yacht somewhere right now."

The look on Detective Price's face when he arrested me appears in my mind, and I clench my jaw, nodding. "Men like that are no men at all. I know that too well."

"Yeah?"

While we have something close to privacy, I tell him my story, from how I ended up working for the Costa family to how I ended up shoved into the back of a police car by Price. By the time I finish, prisoners are starting to file back into their cells down the halls, and our privacy vanishes with it.

And by that time, Trueba is watching and listening to me with interest, and I can see him sharing my anger. "*Sangre de dios*," he mutters. "You live a more exciting life than I'd ever care for, my friend."

"More than I care for anymore either," I say. "And now, I've got another eight years to look forward to. As long as that fucker is around, I won't see parole."

"Careful with that kind of thinking," he says, giving me a serious look. "It's easy to lose hope in a place like this, and that kind of thinking will do it. I've seen that stack of letters you keep under your bed," he says, nodding to my mattress. "Those things are going to save your life. Stick to them. Don't let them slip away. Keeps you tied to the world outside, and that's something that vultures like your detective can't touch."

I give a nod, but his words remind me of the letter in my hands. I'd half-forgotten about it, talking with Trueba. I look at the front, and my eyes widen. It's not from Serena.

It's got a fake return address on it, one that I know belongs to Nico, my comrade.

I tear the letter open and look at the words jotted down in his neat handwriting. Nico has been a point of contact for me for all things that have to do with business. He writes in code, of course. To the censors, it reads like a normal letter from a friend, but he uses phrases and specific wording that I understand perfectly.

And what I read is not good. My hands tighten around the edges of the page, and I feel the urge to drive my fist into the wall.

According to Nico, Serena's place is being watched by the police.

Trueba sees the anger in my face, but he doesn't

ask what the letter says. He's sharp enough to know better than that. "Everything okay, Luca?"

"No," I say through my teeth. My mind flashes back to what those two goons tried to threaten me with. *Anything I do in here will come back to hurt Serena. And now, the police are watching her, the same corrupt cops that helped the Cleaners get me thrown in this hell-hole in the first place, no doubt.*

There's nothing innocent about what those cops are doing. Corruption runs deep in our part of the Bronx, and I know that this means trouble. And if they're already going after Serena, that means they really aren't going to leave us alone.

Even if I try to stay out of trouble in here, they're not going to leave *Serena* alone. Trueba's words ring in my ears truer than ever. If it were only me, it would be one thing... but this is more than just me. This is more than just the mafia. This is the one I love, the one good thing through all this misery.

This is Serena. And there's nothing I can do from inside this place.

I read over the letter one more time, and I crumple it in my hand. My jaw is set, and my eyes are resolute. Trueba looks at me with a concerned face. "You alright, man? What's on your mind?"

I look back at him, but I don't answer, because I know exactly what I need to do. I have no other option.

I have to break out. Soon.

got one letter out to Nico. One letter encoded with brief but specific instructions. A little time later, I got one back confirming that he got my message. Nothing more. A prison break has to be organized, detailed, coordinated, and needs a lot of planning.

Those aren't luxuries I have. All I can do is make sure I can come through on my end and hope that everything else falls into place.

And today is the day. But I have one hurdle to get over before then.

I'm being led down the dreary halls of the prison to an interrogation room that I've been to many times before. My face is stony. If you show any emotion going into these types of meetings, the people around you start to suspect you of talking to the police.

Not that it will matter after today. My biggest worry in this meeting will be resisting the urge to tear the interrogator apart.

My hands are cuffed in front of me. Two guards march me forward, and as we approach the door at the end of the hall, another guard opens it and lets us in. They sit me down at a simple table in the gray, depressing room with nothing but a light hanging from the ceiling and a one-way mirror on the wall in front of me. Once I'm seated, the guards leave, and I'm left alone.

Time passes. He's keeping me waiting, trying to let my thoughts eat at me before he takes his shots. It's never worked with me before, and it won't work with me now. I don't talk to police.

Least of all Will Price.

After what feels like an hour, the door swings open, and he strides in, hawkish eyes watching me with smug satisfaction.

"Good morning, Luca," he says candidly, as if we were good buddies meeting up for a beer. I glare at him.

He pulls a chair out and takes a seat, beaming at me, showing off lively energy. Price has seen a lot of me over the past couple of years. I haven't given him a word, but that doesn't stop him.

The worst thing about seeing this pig all this time, though, is that I've seen him doing better for himself, watched him grow happier, more confident, and more wealthy. When you're a child, you're told that the worst people in the world always get what they deserve.

I always knew that was a lie, but Price is living proof.

"It's been a bit since I saw you last," he says, opening a folder in front of him and thumbing through a few pages idly. "Sounds like you've had a busy week." His eyes flit up to me, watching me for a reaction. "Two fights for a guy who says he just wants to keep to himself tells me something's up."

My stony stare doesn't shift. I might as well be a statue. Anything I say would just be fuel for him. He lives for shit like this.

After a moment of silence, he gives a thin smile and says, "You don't need me to tell you this is one of the most violent prisons in the country, Lomaglio. And so I hope I don't have to tell you that when the inmates cooperate with us in getting that violence under control, we're a lot more willing to help them out in turn."

He's lying. The last prisoner Price got to start ratting to him got hauled off to solitary and locked away in there when the other prisoners caught on and stopped talking to him. Price is cold. He doesn't keep friends.

When I don't reply, Price leans forward, dropping some of the pretense of being polite. "Are you worried about them, Luca?" he asks. "This report says the men you attacked have gang connections outside the prison. You know this is my ballpark, Luca, I can help you out here. I just need you to help me first."

Prisoners get desperate, and this kind of talk sways many of them. But I can smell the threat through his words. I say nothing.

"You're kind of a puzzle, Luca," he says, sitting back in his seat and looking through his files again. "You do more for the Costa crime family than just about anyone I've seen in, god, ten years. But if what the warden's telling me is right, you're practically a ghost in here. What happened? Costa's been busy since you've been in here—why aren't you on speaking terms anymore?"

That much is true. Nico has been my only point of contact with my old comrades, save for the other Costas in here with me, and we hardly talk. When we do, it's never about business. I'm not in here to be a pawn for anyone. Price glares back into my eyes before he crosses the line he's been dying to cross this whole time.

"Is this about Serena?"

Just hearing him say her name makes me furious. He doesn't deserve to speak it.

"That's understandable," he says, leaning forward in his seat, "a lot of inmates worry about their loved ones while they're inside." He smiles an empty smile.

"Well, I can promise you, she's fine. I saw her just the other day, in fact."

I can't control myself, not in the face of such a blatant threat.

"This is between us, you coward," I growl, even as his smile splits into a grin. "Keep it that way, if you can call yourself a man."

"I'm sorry, what exactly am I keeping between us?" he asks, a mocking tone to his voice. Speaking at all was a mistake. I clench my fist and sit back in my chair, narrowing my eyes at him. "I'm just doing my job, Luca, you need to understand that. You're a high-profile offender, and you obviously have some enemies around here," he says, taking out photos of the men I've fought over the past few days and setting them on the table.

"Then why don't you tell the cameras why you're stalking some woman?" I say, nodding up to the camera in the corner of the room, hanging from the ceiling. These meetings are always recorded, and I'm sure he has a recorder on him to capture our conversation in case I say anything incriminating.

"I'm not stalking anyone," he says, half-laughing. "Luca, I don't have to remind you that Miss De Laurentis has mafia connections of her own. Quite a complicated past, in fact," he says, crossing his legs and folding his hands. "That's all in the past, of course, but as you know better than anyone, the past can come back to bite you."

My fists are tight, but I say nothing.

"It's in the interests of her safety that I keep an eye on her," he says, dropping his tone to a still, chilling one. "Just like it's in your interests to help me. Look, Luca, if I'm flying blind here for too long…"

He takes back the photos and closes his folder, standing up from his chair. "… then I can't guarantee that the people who want to hurt you won't make life hard for her on the outside."

"Don't threaten me, Price," I say in a low tone. He smiles back at me, but my eyes bore into him, memorizing every detail of his face, as if it isn't already seared into my memory. I'm going to make him pay for this. And I'll make him remember me.

"I don't make threats, Luca," he says as he turns his back on me to leave the room, his voice dripping with smug satisfaction "I'm just doing my job."

～

Back in my cell later that night, I'm reading over the letters Serena sent me one more time.

Trueba is over on his bed, hands folded on his stomach. His eyes are on me, but he knows to give me space right now. My hands go over some of the words that Serena scribbled out on her letters, places where she tested her pen with little squiggles of ink.

It's the imperfections that remind me most of all that she's still out there, the same Serena, the same face, the same person I fell in love with. And it's all for her that I'm doing this.

I might not make it out of this alive. And if I don't, I want her words to be the last things in my mind.

"You're sure you're willing to do this?" I ask Trueba once I've finished reading and I tuck all the letters back under the bed. I'm speaking quietly enough that nobody can hear us outside our cell, and I don't look over at him when I do speak.

We have a plan, and we can't look suspicious on camera for this to have any hope of working.

"I'm an old man, Luca," he says, and I can hear how tired his voice is. "I hardly leave my cell as it is. Some time in solitary will give me room to think. Maybe pray, I don't know yet."

"It has to look real," I say. We've gone over the plan before, but I'm not taking any chances.

"It'll *be* real," he says.

Sterling Correctional Facility is on a small island just off the coast, one long bridge connecting it to the mainland. There's some woodland on the island, then nothing but icy waters and a couple other smaller islands not far off, all of them uninhabited and off-limits to the public. This prison feels as remote as it can, despite being so close to the city.

Nobody could make it through those woods on

the island without getting picked up by the patrols, and they sure as hell couldn't hide out there. That means there is only one way off the island: the bridge.

And the only way a prisoner can get taken over that bridge is in the back of a police car... or in an ambulance.

The prison has its own medical wing, but they can't handle anything more than basic injuries. The news has been criticizing the prison for years, but they haven't lifted a finger. Even the guy I fought in the bathroom had to be driven to Emerson Hospital on the mainland, just a block away from the other side of the bridge.

The matter of me getting a serious injury is where Trueba comes in.

"Alright," I say, flexing my fists as Trueba swings his legs over to stand up. "Showtime."

"You wanna say that again, you Italian son of a bitch?" Trueba says loudly, strutting in the cell in the way the young men do when they're about to start a fight.

"I said you East Harlem fuckers are a dime a dozen," I snap back, standing up myself. Despite his age, Trueba is a tall guy, and he's got muscle under that fat. It doesn't look too out of character for a guy like him to square up with me. "I've fought punching bags with more fight than you chickenshits—no wonder the Cleaners moved into our turf!"

"You wanna see a punching bag, my friend?" he snarls, and he starts forward at me, pushing me in the chest with a firm hand. I barely budge, swatting his arm away, but then he reaches behind his shirt.

He pulls out a shank.

For an old guy, he moves fast. He brings the shiv around, and I brace myself. The pointed tip cuts through my hardened muscles and sinks into me, deep.

We've both been around violence long enough to know what wounds will cause some damage without killing a man, but that doesn't make it any less tricky to pull off and make it look real. The pain is the least of my worries.

I act like I've been taken off-guard and let out a grunt of pain. When he pulls the shank out and stabs it in again, I can already hear the boots of guards on the ground. We don't have much time.

I move as if trying to defend myself, but Trueba pops me in the nose with a quick, solid jab before he grabs hold of my shirt and drives the shank in again, and again, and again. I lose track of the stab wounds I'm getting, but the pain is incredible.

The last thing I see before falling to the ground are the prisoners across from us staring wide-eyed while guards appear at the door, getting it open and shouting to each other to call an ambulance.

Trueba gets one last good stab into me before three guards wrestle him off, pepper-spraying him in the eyes as he cries out in pain and gets tackled to the ground.

I've let myself take more of a stabbing than I got in some of the real fights with the Cleaners. My torso is on fire, and as I cover my wounds with my hands, I feel warm blood pouring from them.

In the confusion, I can hardly tell what's happening around me through the pain of the stab wounds. More guards come in. I think Trueba gets taken out, and when paramedics arrive, I hear bits of them shouting to one another: multiple stab wounds. Losing blood fast. Needs attention, stat.

Then come the golden words: "Get him to Emerson, *now!*"

I feel a twinge of pain in my side, and I have to fight to stay conscious as I'm loaded onto a stretcher.

What happens over the next few minutes is a blur. I feel myself getting rushed down some hallways in the prison. I try to move my arm, and I feel a clink of resistance. I manage to turn my eyes down to my hand, and I see it both covered in blood and handcuffed to the stretcher. There's some first-aid bandaging applied to my torso for the trip.

Fuck, I have to stay awake.

For a moment, I feel fresh air on my skin, the cool night breeze on the hot blood staining my clothes when they roll me across asphalt. I see the top of the ambulance above me as I'm loaded up into it.

I feel my body contracting, pain almost unbearable. It's like fire in my stomach. Just as much as Trueba was taking a risk in doing something like this for me, I knew I was taking a risk. There's no really safe way to get stabbed in the gut.

But this is my one shot. No matter how much pain I go through, no matter how much blood I lose, it's worth it for Serena. The words of her letters are in my thoughts when I hear the ambulance doors close, and the engine starts.

I can make out the paramedics above me, saying things I can't quite make out to each other before hooking me up to machines. I feel a needle go into my wrist, and a few moments later, I feel warmth rushing up my arm and into my whole body.

It's morphine. The pain starts to subside, and I let out a deep breath in relief as it gets into every part of me. I hate drugs, but if Nico pulls through for me, that morphine is going to be the only thing that keeps me going for what comes next.

And with the way things are going, I can only hope that Nico *can* pull through for me.

I can't tell where we are or how close we are to the end of the bridge. Now that I have something keeping the pain at bay, though, I don't feel like I'm about to drift into blackness anymore. I look down at my wounds, or try to. I can't see my bare flesh, so I can't see whether any of the shanks missed their mark and hit something vital.

If they did, I'm in trouble. No time to worry now, though.

"Jesus, who'd this guy piss off?" one of the paramedics mutters to the other.

"Wouldn't wanna meet the guy who'd pick a fight with this beast," he muses, checking something on a machine before turning to me. "How you doin', buddy? Try to stay awake, you should be feeling the good stuff right about now."

I give him a weary smile and lift my thumb.

The next moment, the whole ambulance lurches forward, then to the side as the vehicle comes screeching to a halt.

"What the fuck?" one of the medics cries, turning to the window to the driver. "Hey, what's going on?!"

"Fucking Christ, they've got guns," the driver says, and I see him raising his hands over his head. There's shouting outside.

One of the voices is Nico's.

"Hey," I say to the medics, who look from the road to me, wide-eyed. "You two seem alright. Keep your heads down and do what they say."

"You've gotta be kidding me," one of them says, but the back of the ambulance opens, and I look up to see Nico flanked by two other Costa boys with guns raised.

"Alright!" he shouts, stepping forward as the medics put their hands up. "I want his cuffs off *now*!

Make this easy on us, we'll make it easy on you, let's go!"

The medics comply, and in a matter of seconds, Nico is unhooking me from the machines and helping me down from the ambulance while the other men hold guns on them, moving up to get them to their knees and handcuff them there. The paramedics in prisons are trained to deal with violence, but they know when they're outgunned.

And none of them were expecting to be held up at the prison's doorstep by four cars full of mob enforcers armed to the teeth. Hell, I wasn't even expecting Nico to bring that kind of firepower.

"You good, man? Holy shit, what happened?" Nico says as we step onto the street. I can't describe the feeling the moment my feet touch the ground.

Free ground.

I breathe the night air in, and I smile at him. "Ran into a friend's knife... a few times. I'll be alright."

"Not if you don't get help," Nico says, "you look fucked up, man! Come on, forget the next part of the plan—let's get you into the car and go see one of our docs."

"No," I say firmly. "Someone will find me."

"But-"

"Nico, we've got about a minute before this block is crawling with feds. You need to move, and fast. We're going through with the plan, the whole way."

"There's no way, Luca," Nico says, looking at me

like I'm insane. And maybe I am. I haven't tasted freedom in two years, and it's almost as strong a drug as the morphine in my veins. "You'll die out there."

"Nico," I say, clasping his hand and giving a cocky smile. "I owe you more for this than I've ever owed anyone in my life. But now's not the time. Remember what we planned, and get your ass out of here, got it?"

Nico frowns, then shakes his head with a laugh. "Shit, man, you beefed up, but you haven't changed at all, have you?"

"I had something good to keep my mind on," I say as I part from him, walking away.

I'm walking toward the coast.

Back toward Sterling.

I cast one last look back at Nico, and the scene of what's going to be in the news tomorrow as the most daring prison break in the history of Sterling. "Tell her it'll be okay!"

I see Nico start to get the men back to their cars and peel out before I look away from them.

And the next moment, still bloody and bandaged, I get a running start and dive into the icy waters.

In the years since those cops dragged Luca away from me and threw him in prison, I have turned into a major workaholic. Sure, for the first few weeks after he was sentenced, it was all I could do to pull my ass out of bed. I shut down completely, refusing to speak to anyone for a while. Rafaela, Nico, and my mom all did their best to accommodate my wallowing in self-pity, at least for a week or so. They brought me meals in bed: chicken soup, poppy seed bagels with my favorite veggie cream cheese, tubs of low-fat ice cream. Rafaela sat in bed with me and watched soap operas, both of us silent except for the crunch of popcorn or sips of wine. But I don't think any of them expected me to be that heartbroken for so long. My life was on hold, and it felt wrong for me to try and keep living as though nothing had changed.

Because *everything* had changed.

How was I supposed to focus on work when the love of my life was wasting away behind bars, probably getting beat to hell by other inmates and probably even the prison guards. God knows the cops have an axe to grind against him, and I'm sure they took every opportunity to knock him down a peg, legally or illegally. So for those first few weeks, I was useless. I stopped living. I had to be coerced into the shower, encouraged to eat, persuaded to change out of my bathrobe. If a psychiatrist had come to see me, she would have definitely ticked off all the boxes under "depression" and probably given me some pill meant to perk me up and give me a false sense of purpose again. In fact, at one point late in my wallowing period, I overheard my mother in the hallway talking on the phone with someone in a hushed tone.

The tone of her voice made me curious enough to creep out of bed and press my ear against the bedroom door to listen. It sounded something like this:

"Yes. Oh, no, I'm not the patient. I'm calling on behalf of my daughter. No, she's not a minor. She's twenty-three. Yes, I am aware that she's an adult, but this is very serious and I know she isn't going to help herself. She's... she's too far gone, you see. I-I'm very worried about her. She's not herself anymore and I don't know what else to do. Yes. Thank you. Okay. I understand. I'll hold for the psychiatrist."

There was a long pause, and I could feel my heart sinking down to the floor. It didn't take a rocket scientist to figure out what was going on. My mom was trying to get me help the only way she knew how. And it may not seem like a big deal to most people, but my mother has always been staunchly anti-psychiatry. She's old-fashioned and stubborn and she thinks it's all a bunch of witch doctor stuff. I, of course, disagree. I think someone's mind can be sick just as much as someone's stomach can be sick. It's all the same. But for my mother to overcome her ridiculous prejudice and actually call a mental health clinic on my behalf... well, that was more than enough to convince me that I was truly frightening everyone around me. I had allowed myself to slip so deeply into my own darkness that I forgot about all the people around me who still cared, who had to keep on going even though they were worried about me.

Besides, I knew deep down it wasn't my mind that was sick, it was my heart.

So that day, I slipped out of my room and walked up to my mom with an apologetic look on my face. She looked shocked to see me out of bed by my own choice, and I mouthed at her, "You don't have to do that," pointing at the phone. She nodded and hung up before the psychiatrist could even get there and take her off hold.

"Serena, we're worried about you," my mother said softly. I could see tears shining in her eyes, which was a rare sight. My mom may have grown up a spoiled mafia princess, but when my father died she became even colder and tougher than anyone could have predicted. So when she cried, it was really serious. I gave her a hug.

"I know. I'm sorry. I'm going to try and be better from now on, okay?" I assured her.

"You don't have to go through this alone," she told me. I nodded and forced a smile.

"Yeah. I know," I replied quietly. Then I perked up, which took great effort, and added, "Okay, well, I'm sure I smell terrible. I'm going to take a shower and grab some lunch, then head down to the shop to do some damage control."

I arrived at Bathing Beauty to find my accounts in disarray, the floor and shelves needing to be cleaned, expired products needing to be moved out and replaced with fresher ones. I set to work imme-diately, throwing all the energy I'd been spending on sorrow into a new project: cleaning up my life. And I've been working nonstop ever since. In fact, I have to admit that focusing all my frustration into work has kind of become my new addiction, but at least it's a productive one. At least I'm no longer lying in bed, drowning in despair. It could be worse.

So I spend as much time as possible at Bathing Beauty during the weekdays, clocking in at dawn and staying overtime whenever possible. The shop is so clean it sparkles, and I've reorganized the books and logs a million times. With my newly-attuned attention to detail and superhuman work ethic, the shop is flourishing. I think my customers have all told everyone they know about my shop or something, because things are going great. The bestsellers are flying off the shelves as always, but now even the less-popular products are in high demand. I've even hired a second worker to help me out, a high school student named Naomi who works at the shop after school. By all accounts, I should be proud of myself. I've taken a failing business and turned it into a success.

People are buzzing about Bathing Beauty, and I'm finally doing way more than just breaking even.

But I can't be happy. Not really. Bathing Beauty is just the receptacle for my pent-up energy, where I go to dump all my sadness and frustration and loneliness. I spend hours in the back kitchen testing out new scents, new textures and colors. I'm bouncy and charismatic in the shop front, chatting with customers, making connections. But it's all a show. It keeps me from losing my mind during the week, but we're not quite at the point where we can handle being open all week long, so I still have Sunday and Monday every week left open to mope and fixate on the dire darkness of my situation. Of Luca's situation.

Today is Sunday, and I'm sitting at the vintage desk in my bedroom, my pen hovering over a letter I'm writing to Luca. I write him every day. Every single day, whether I've just worked a thirteen-hour shift or not, I come home and sit here to hammer out another letter to my long-lost love. I have no idea if he's even getting any of these. I never get a response. For all I know, the guards or cops have confiscated every one of my letters to him. They could be locked away in some filing cabinet, in a manila folder marked *EVIDENCE*. I've tried to visit him, but they won't let me see him. I have no idea what he looks like these days. Hell, in my darkest moments it occurs to me that he could be dead, and I would have no idea.

But something tells me I would know. I would feel it. Something in the air would smell different, feel different. The sun wouldn't shine as brightly. The birds wouldn't sing as sweetly. My heart would be even heavier than it already is.

I would know.

And so, despite the lack of a response, I keep dutifully writing letters. Sometimes it almost reminds me of how I felt years and years ago, when I first met Luca as a teenager. When I used to send him text messages to his burner phone, hoping against hope I would get an answer that never, ever came. I wonder how much of my life will be spent waiting on Luca, sending messages that get no response. It's a depressing fate, I know, but something keeps me from giving up. I can't give up. Luca may be far away, and there may be a gigantic brick wall between us, but I know in my heart he's still there, and as long as he's on this planet I will never give up.

A teardrop falls from my eye and dampens the page, swelling the inky words into an unreadable blob. I groan and push the letter away, swiping at my eye angrily. I'll have to start over.

But first I need to take a break. This is really starting to get to me. "God, I hate weekends," I whisper to myself. I should take a walk. That might clear my mind.

I get up and walk across the room to my closet, pulling a sweater out and slipping it over my head. It's been getting a little chilly in the afternoons lately, and I don't have time to catch a cold. Bathing Beauty needs me. And I need the work to keep me sane. On the way down the hallway I stop by my mother's room and knock on the door. She looks up from her iPad and gives me a smile. It's still so weird sometimes to see her trying to be more affectionate, but I think after watching me fall into that depression two years ago, she's realized it might be beneficial for both of us to be a little softer. After all, she has some idea what I'm feeling. She lost a husband when I lost my father.

"Going somewhere?" she asks, cocking her head to one side.

I nod. "Yeah, just out for a short walk to clear my head. What do you want for dinner tonight? We could get takeout. I've been craving orange chicken lately. What do you think?"

"Sounds fine to me, sweetheart," she replies. "Be careful out there, it's getting dark soon."

"Okay mom."

"Remember, text me X if you're in trouble."

"I will," I answer. "Bye."

"See you later," she says, going back to whatever she's doing on that iPad.

I jog down the stairs and out the front door, locking it behind me. The late afternoon air is crisp and cool, and I can feel autumn blowing in. It's the time of year that makes me feel sentimental. Nostalgic. I think about the jitters of classes starting back up, the anticipation of holidays like Halloween, Thanksgiving, and Christmas. But these days, it's an empty feeling. Those expectations of a warm, love-filled holiday season fall flat when I remember everything I've lost. My father. Luca. It's just my mom and me now. Sure, there's Rafaela and Nico, too, but they're a couple. They have their own hectic lives to deal with. And sometimes seeing them together, how happy they are, how much they love each other, it just makes me sadder.

I wish I still had all of that. Hope. Love. A future I could look forward to.

But my life is on hold for eight more long, lonely years.

I sigh and shove my hands into my pockets to stay warm as I walk down the long driveway and turn onto the street. The trees are in full bloom, all jade green and white flowers. It's beautiful here in Riverdale, and I'm grateful that I've been able to save the house. My father's legacy. Well, what's left of it, at least. I can rest assured that my dad would be proud of me for holding it all together here, for taking care of mom. When I walk around this neighborhood, I remember how badly he wanted to move us here, give me a more comfortable, safe place to live. It's easy to feel close to him again when I think about it.

But I have no way of feeling close to Luca. Sure, I met him for the first time in what is now my back-yard, but our relationship has fallen apart and come back together so many times that it feels fractured now. And besides, it's too painful to relive our memories together even now. It's been two years since they took him away, and it still breaks my heart every day. He shouldn't be in there. It isn't right.

Just then, I hear the squeal of tires and smell

burning rubber. I swivel around in surprise. This is such a quiet neighborhood that anything out of the ordinary sticks out like a sore thumb. I scarcely have a chance to react before a big black car jerks to a stop right next to me. My stomach flip-flops as I realize I'm in danger. I turn to run, but two broad-bodied people grab me by the arms and wrangle me into the car, slipping some kind of bag over my head.

I start to struggle, trying to scream, but no sound will come out. I can hear the engine roaring back to life as the car takes off from my abduction spot, moving quickly away from my home and safety. I finally manage to squeak out, "What is this? Who are you? Let me go!"

"This is for your own good," says a male voice to my left. He has some kind of accent, but it's so faint I can't recognize it.

"Yeah, fucking right," I swear, lifting my hands to try and remove the bag from over my head. But my arms get pinned back down by powerful hands, then bound behind my back.

"Please. Calm down," says a second deep voice, this one on my right.

"Calm down? I'm being kidnapped! I'm not going to be calm! Who are you working for? Who sent you? Where the hell are you taking me?" I shout.

The first voice speaks again: "You're going somewhere safe. Nobody knows you've been taken. And it's better that you don't see where we're headed."

"I guess I don't have any other choice, do I?" I snarl, settling back against the seat.

"No. You don't," says the second voice calmly.

I decide it's better to save my energy. There's not a damn thing I can do about this right now, and the more I struggle, the more likely my captors will do something worse to me. I've been under duress enough times by now to know the importance of picking my battles wisely. Besides, there isn't much fight left in me these days anyway. Without Luca, nothing seems to matter all that much.

We ride in silence for a long time, possibly hours. With the bag over my head, I can't even tell if it's light or dark, but I assume it's dark. Finally, the car rolls to a stop and my heart starts to race. I can smell something… water. Salty, briny water. The doors open and someone grabs me, dragging me out of the car and forcing me to walk beside them. I can hear water sloshing, the distant cry of seabirds. Where the fuck are we? Is this some kind of sick execution?

Am I about to be pushed into the water to drown? Is this some *sleeping with the fishes* cliché?

I start to turn and try and run away, but the arms holding me are strong, and I can't go anywhere. I cry out as loud as I can, but the bag muffles my voice, and something tells me there is nobody around to hear me scream anyway. We walk for a while, the cold, humid air sending shivers down my body. Then, someone scoops me up in their arms out of nowhere, and lowers me down into what feels like... a boat. A small boat of some kind.

"What the hell is this?" I murmur. There's no answer. "Tell me what is going on!" I scream.

Quickly, someone wraps an arm around my head, covering my mouth. Someone holds me still while another person jabs an arm up inside the bag, stuffing a wadded-up cloth into my mouth. I cough and gag, flailing as much as I can, but it doesn't change anything. These guys are stronger than me, and I don't know how many there are, but I am definitely outnumbered.

"Sorry about the gag. It's for your own good," the first voice says.

My shoulders sag as I just give up. I can't move. I can't scream. I might as well just wait for whatever cruel fate these guys have in store for me. There is the distinct sensation of the boat being pushed into deeper water, then the sound of oars chopping the waves. Are we rowing out to sea? What the hell is going on?

I sit there, freezing and stiff in the boat for god knows how long. The rocking of the boat makes me feel a little nauseous, and I focus all my energy on not throwing up, because I have a gag in my mouth. I don't know if that would kill me, but if so, it seems like a horrible way to die. So I just force myself to think about other things. Accounts at work.

Whether or not to hire a third worker. New products I would like to try out in the test kitchen.

And I think about this for... a long time. Until finally there is the nudge of the boat breaching the sand of another shore. Or at least I assume it's a different shore. For all I know, we could have been rowing in circles for hours, only to return to where we started. The men force me to get up, then they carefully lift me out of the boat and onto dry land. They walk me several steps forward, away from the water, and then to my immense shock they pull the bag off my head and take out the gag. I blink in the darkness, my eyes slowly adjusting. A dense forest begins to materialize in front of me and I stare into it in confusion. Then I look around to see the men who brought me here. Tall, broad-shouldered guys. They all look fairly young, around my age, and they have slightly apologetic looks on their faces.

"We've got a bit of a walk," one of them tells me, and I recognize his voice as the second one who spoke in the car. "Let's get started."

Wordlessly, I follow them through the woods, carefully climbing through scratchy underbrush and hoping I don't run into any spider webs in the dark. Finally, after several minutes of trekking, we come to a building— what seems to be an old, slightly dilapidated house. It looks abandoned, with nature beginning to reclaim it as vines grow over it.

"Come on," says another man, the owner of the

first voice who spoke to me earlier. We walk around back to a cellar door in the ground. He flings it open to reveal a rickety staircase. I swallow hard. This looks very much like I'm walking into a horror movie or something. I have no idea what awaits me down there, but I have a strong feeling it isn't anything good.

The men prod me forward and I reluctantly sigh and start to climb down the stairs, deep down into this basement in the middle of nowhere. To my surprise, when I reach the bottom, I'm standing in a big room full of expensive-looking vintage furnishings, all lit by a bright standing floor lamp across the room. "What the hell..." I murmur, trying to take it all in.

Then I see him. A tall, dark figure walking out of the shadows to stand in the center of the basement. He looks a little haggard and rugged, with his muscles even bigger than before, his hair longer and scraggly. But it's him. I would know his face anywhere.

"Luca," I breathe, my heart pounding a million miles an hour.

"*Mia passerotta,*" he replies, a slow smile warming his face.

"Is it really you?" I ask, scarcely able to breathe. I take a step forward, my thoughts spinning out in every direction. "This is impossible."

Luca smiles. "It's me. I swear, I'm real."

"No. I have got to be dreaming or something. I mean, how…? I don't understand. You—you were in prison. You *are* in prison. I-I watched them take you away. Luca, I sent you so many letters. Every single day I sent you one and I never got one back," I ramble, shaking my head in confusion.

A flicker of pain crosses his handsome face. I can see the exhaustion, the hidden agony tucked away somewhere behind his smile. I can see how hard he's had to work all this time to stay strong, to hold it together. He seems so real, so lifelike, but changed. There's no way it can really be him, though. There's no way. This is some kind of elaborate trick. But who would do that?

"The prison security must have intercepted most of your letters. And I figured they'd never let me send one out of those fucking walls. Serena, you have to understand... these people were doing every-thing they could to isolate me from everything. Especially you," he says grimly.

I run my fingers back through my hair, closing my eyes for a second as I try to put words to my confusion. I don't understand how this is happening. How it could be true that Luca is right here in front of me. Yesterday I was alone in the world, running in circles trying to stay busy to keep my mind from wandering back to him, to keep my heart from breaking. And now he's here.

But how in the world did he get out? And why was I brought here in such a harsh manner?

"You don't have to think so hard about it," Luca says gently. "I can see the cogs turning in your head right now, Serena. Trying to make sense of this. How it could be possible. Don't question it. Not now. There will be plenty of time to explain later."

"Later...?" I ask, my voice trailing off. "You mean, you're not going back? You're going to stay with me?"

Luca takes a few broad steps toward me, opening his arms wide. "Serena, I'm never going to leave you again, if I can help it."

Tears burn in my eyes and I can barely breathe as my feet carry me, almost floating, across the room to all but collapse in Luca's arms. I press my face into his chest, inhaling that familiar, woodsy scent I would recognize anywhere. This is him. He *is* real and he's right here. With me.

"I can't believe this," I murmur, just letting the tears stream down my face.

"Believe it," Luca says, kissing the top of my head and embracing me tightly.

"But Luca, I don't get it. Why all the secrecy? Why did those guys have to kidnap me and drag me across the water in a rickety little boat if you're free? Don't get me wrong, I'm a sucker for a romantic reunion, too, but couldn't you have just showed up at my house? Why all this drama?" I question, laughing a little. Luca holds me back to look into my face, those green eyes pulsing over me, reading into my heart the way he's always been able to do.

"It's more complicated than that, *dolcezza*," he answers gravely. "But for now, I just want to be with you. God, I've missed you more than words can even explain. I thought about you every single waking moment, and every time I managed to fall asleep in that fucking cell, I dreamed of you."

"I never stopped thinking about you. I never stopped loving you, just waiting for when we could be together again. Sometimes it was really hard to imagine a world where we would be in the same room again, Luca. I thought I would never get to touch you again. Kiss you," I explain, choking back a sob.

"You don't have to just imagine it anymore," Luca says, holding my face gently in his huge hands. He pulls me close and presses his lips against mine, his arms folding around me as I melt into his touch. There's the click of a door shutting somewhere behind me, and I realize that the men who brought me here have climbed back out of the basement, leaving me alone with Luca to give us privacy.

And thank god that they did, because I can't wait another fucking second.

Luca kisses me hard, his fingers tangling in my hair as he pulls me in close. I sigh into the kiss, feeling my body loosen up, probably for the first time in two years. My shoulders relax, the tension in my jaw slackens, and a smile tugs at my lips even as we kiss. This, all of this right here, is my happy place. My safe place. I've spent these two years rigidly going through the motions of a regular life, moving robotically from one place to the next. I've been all knotted up inside, waiting fearfully for the next shoe to drop. But now I can breathe again. Luca has brought back the light, the oxygen, the hope that once glimmered overhead.

I don't know what the future will hold, but I am so glad to be here with him.

Luca's other arm slides around me to hold me

close, his fingertips pressing into the arch of my back. There's a kind of desperation to the way he grabs onto me, like he's afraid I could evaporate at any second. He's holding me like I'm a life preserver floating out to him in the middle of the deep, dark sea as the sharks circle in on him. Like he never wants to let go. I hope he never does. I want to be that for him, the lifesaving breath of free air.

"I never want to lose you again," Luca says gruffly as we break apart for a moment. He rests his forehead against mine and cups my face, his thumbs tracing over my lips. He closes his eyes tightly as he touches my face, almost like he's trying to commit my features to memory.

"I'm not going anywhere," I murmur in response. "You said that to me once, years ago, when we met up and went for drinks at the Room With a View. Remember?"

Luca sighs, his eyes opening up again as he smooths the hair back from my face. He looks at me intently, that glowing green gaze boring into my soul. "I remember everything. Every moment. Those memories have been my only allies these two years. On the outside, I made sure I looked hard. Intimidating. I kept a scowl on my face and wiped away any trace of joy or love so that nobody could find a weak spot in me. If anybody had known about you, how I feel about you, they would have used it against me. So I had to hide it away. But every single second

I was in there, standing in line in the cafeteria, walking in the yard just daring anyone to even brush shoulders with me, sitting alone in solitary confinement… I was thinking of you. Reliving those little moments. Being on the inside fucks you up, Serena. You start second-guessing everything you thought you knew. Your life before prison seems like a dream or a TV show plot that happened to someone else. But it was different with you. I never second-guessed my feelings for you, the reality of what we have, even for a second. I didn't let myself forget a single thing."

I can feel the tears burning in my eyes again and I'm starting to wonder how much one person can cry before they physically run out of tears. I've got to be hovering somewhere around that limit by now. I reach up and gently take Luca's hands in mine, lowering them down away from my face and onto my hips, staring up at him wordlessly. He gazes back with equal seriousness, neither of us daring break eye contact. I can tell we're both just as desperate as the other, each of us terrified that this reunion will suddenly shatter apart, that we'll wake up from a shared dream in our respective solitary worlds. It's so hard to believe that he's here for real.

"Luca, I love you," I tell him emphatically. It's the only thing I can think to say right now. Words are so useless in times like this. Our love is too big to fit in a sequence of letters and syllables. It's more than that, and I'm going to show him the best way I know how.

I stand up on my tiptoes to kiss him, reaching up to pull him down to meet me. He leans into the kiss, his hands sliding down backward from my hips to grab my ass. He groans appreciatively when I press up against him, my breasts pushing into his chest while I can feel his cock stiffening against my hip. Just the sensation of that hardness pushing into me is enough to send a tingle down through my core, and I feel a warmth spreading between my thighs. It's been so long. I've only touched myself a handful of times since they took Luca away, and every time was painful, almost impossible. It felt like a trespass, a betrayal, and besides, nothing could ever, ever feel anywhere near as blissfully good as fucking Luca anyway. Everything I did, all my alone time could never come close to comparing. It's been a long time since I felt this good.

God knows I've had a long, long time to wait.

"Do you know how many times I've imagined you in my head? Fantasized about running my hands over your beautiful body?" Luca growls, squeezing my ass with one hand while his other wraps around my hair. He gently pulls it back and to the side, tilting my head backward slightly to expose my neck. He leans in slowly, his hot breath tickling my skin and making goosebumps prickle up on my arms and legs.

"I've been dreaming of this moment for so long, Serena," he continues. Every syllable is like a ticklish, delicious puff of warmth dancing down the slope of my neck. Then he bends to press a soft kiss into the skin there and I gasp involuntarily. I can feel him smiling against my skin. "Fuck, I never forgot how good it felt to make you gasp, make you sigh and scream. But my memories are never as good as the real thing, are they?"

His kisses become harder, less teasing as he nips and sucks at the soft flesh of my neck, and I shiver with the anticipation of seeing those blushing red marks on my skin, reminders of who I belong to and how good he makes me feel. That dull ache combined with the ticklishness is enough to make me wet. "Don't stop," I murmur.

"Don't worry, I have so many plans for you," Luca whispers. He lets go of my hair and uses both arms to hoist me up, my legs instinctively wrapping around his waist as he holds me up effortlessly. I run my fingers down his upper arms, feeling the swell of muscles which have definitely gotten bigger in the two years since we were last together.

"You've beefed up a little since you went away," I remark, biting my lip playfully.

Luca grins. "Not much else to do in prison. Besides, the stronger I am, the easier I can move you around. Do whatever I want with you."

He kisses me deeply, spinning around as he holds

me easily in his arms. He carries me across the room to a vintage-looking, luxurious chaise lounge chair, sitting down with me still perched on his lap, straddling him. His hands rove up and down my back, sliding down to grab my ass, then back up to tangle in my hair. I can feel the hard heat of his cock beneath me, straining to burst free of his pants, and I can't help but start to rock against it as we kiss. Luca groans, his hands slipping around to grope my breasts through my shirt. I've only got a thin sports bra on underneath the shirt, and I can feel every pass of his fingers over my stiffening nipples. I let out a moan, my head tipping backward as my eyes roll shut. It's been so long that every single miniscule touch feels like an electric jolt right down to my pussy.

"God, you feel even better than I remember," Luca says, his voice gravelly and rough with need. I know he's been craving this just as much as I have, and I can't wait for him to finally unleash the ravenous desire he's holding back. I want him to let go completely, give in to the wave of irresistible heat growing between us. I want him to fuck me mercilessly, use my body the way he needs to, fill me up and make me his own. He squeezes my breasts gently, his thumbs slipping over my erect nipples, making me whimper.

He reaches down and grabs the hem of my shirt, yanking it upward. I lift my arms and let him tear the shirt up over my head, tossing it across the room. My chest is heaving, my breasts plump and restrained by the tight sports bra. "I missed these," Luca says, a hint of a smirk on his lips. He massages my breasts through the thin material, my nipples clearly visible as he pushes my tits together. I can't stand it anymore, so I push his hands away just for a moment while I peel off the sports bra and throw it down to the floor, letting my breasts spill free.

Luca lets out a sigh of approval, his hands immediately going back to my tits as he gropes me, pinching my bare nipples between his fingers.

"Yes," I hiss, closing my eyes and giving in to the sensation. I nearly cry out loud when he tilts me backward, then pulls one of my nipples into his warm mouth. His tongue flicks over the stiffened peak while his lips gently suck and bite. Every movement sends a spiral of pleasure through my body. I can hardly stand it, my hips bucking involuntarily as I rock against his stiff cock beneath me. Luca moves to suck at my other nipple, kissing and biting my breasts until I'm whimpering and slack in his arms.

Luca stops for a moment to tear his own shirt off before cradling me onto my back on the chaise chair. He takes off his shoes and mine, then stands up and unzips his pants, letting them crumple in a pile on the floor before bending over me. He tugs at the waistband of my sporty leggings and I lift up my legs so he can pull them off. He lets out a guttural moan as he realizes I'm not wearing any panties— the leggings are so tight and form-fitting that it's just more comfortable without them when I go for a walk or jog. I'm bare-naked in front of him, vulnerable and exposed.

"You're so beautiful," he murmurs, shaking his head.

"You can look at me some more later. Get back down here," I reply, smiling. It doesn't take any more than that for him to comply. He bends down over me, kissing my lips as his hands explore my body. His fingers drag down from my breasts to my stomach and hips, then slide along my trembling thighs. He parts them with one swift movement, then begins kissing a slow path down my body. I watch him closely, holding my breath as his lips approach the warm, wet mound between my legs. He looks up at me hungrily before gently kissing my clit. I whine a little, feeling my whole body tense up in anticipation.

He pauses for a long, painful moment, just letting his hands rub up and down my inner thighs while my pussy waits for his touch. I'm nearly aching by this point, desperate for him to touch me there. "Please," I beg softly. "I need you so badly."

With that, Luca leans down and runs his tongue up and down the length of my slit, sending shock-waves of pleasure over me. I groan and instinctively reach down, my hands clasping around the back of his head, pushing his face into my cunt. He plunges his tongue inside my aching hole, then slips back up to softly toy with my clit, rubbing that tight little bud with his tongue. It feels so fucking good I can hardly bear it, but before I can catch my breath, Luca closes his lips over my clit, sucking and flicking his tongue over the bundle of nerves.

"Oh, fuck," I murmur, getting lost to the sensation. To my surprise, he then slips two fingers deep inside my dripping pussy, curling them ever so perfectly to stroke my g-spot deep inside while he sucks at my clit. The overwhelming combined sensations makes me scream out and roll my hips against him, grinding my pussy into his face. He doesn't relent, even for a second, his fingers slamming into me fast and hard. It doesn't take more than a few seconds of this for me to cry out as my first orgasm shatters over me, my honey gushing over his hand. Luca withdraws his fingers and licks hungrily at my cunt, soaking up my juices as my toes curl and my body twitches.

"That's my good girl," he growls from between my thighs. "I've wanted to do that for a long, long time. But I'm not done with you yet. Nowhere near."

He straightens back up and I scramble to sit up, getting to my knees in front of him even as I can feel my cunt still pulsing with the aftershocks of climax. Before he even gets a chance to, I grab the waistband of his boxers and pull it down, letting his cock spring free. He steps out of the boxers and I look up at him, licking lips. I've wanted this for so many months. I've dreamed of tasting his beautiful, massive cock again. I wrap my fingers around his thick shaft, feeling that warmth and hardness I've missed so much, and begin to slowly slide my hands up and down. His cock twitches and Luca closes his eyes, his lips falling open. His fingers press faintly at the back of my head and I feel a thrill of pleasure at how badly he wants this. He needs me to suck his cock just as badly as I want to do it.

I lean forward and softly lick the head of his shaft while my hands continue to pump him, letting my hot breath wash over. "*Si, bambina,*" he groans, rocking forward just a bit so that the head of his cock bumps against my lips. I look up at him and he opens his eyes at just that moment to watch me pull his cock into my mouth, taking him in as deeply as I can manage in one smooth movement. He groans and clutches the hair at the back of my head, pressing my face down on his cock so that I'm almost gagging. I flick my tongue along the under-side of his shaft while I pump him with both hands.

"Oh, that's so good, Serena," Luca says roughly. I begin to suck him harder, sliding his shaft in and out of my mouth faster and faster. One of my hands slips down to caress his sac while I suck his cock and his entire body shudders. I bob up and down on his shaft, devouring him with abandon.

"Fuck, yes," he groans through gritted teeth.

"Mmm," I moan, sending vibrations through his body. I'm sucking him hard now, sliding my hands up and down his flesh. I can feel him tightening up, like he's almost ready to explode. I'm so caught up in the moment, in the rush of making him feel good, that I don't want to stop. But just before I can make him come, he gently nudges me back, his cock sliding out of my mouth with a wet pop.

"Not yet, *mia passerotta*," he murmurs, grabbing me by the shoulders and spinning me around so that I'm on my hands and knees on the chaise lounge, my ass up in the air. "I need to feel that sweet cunt," he says, and I shiver at the sensation of his engorged shaft tantalizing my slick hole from behind. He's toying with me, rubbing the tip of his cock around my pussy. I'm aching with the need to be filled up, stuffed and fucked hard.

"Give it to me," I whimper. "Please. Fuck me, Luca."

Instead, I feel his fingers push inside of me while his cock rubs against my ass, teasing me, pushing me closer and closer to another breaking point. His fingers stroke at my g-spot again while he groans at the friction of his stiffness against my taut ass cheek. The sensation builds and builds until I'm bucking backwards against his hand, whimpering and clutching at the edge of the chair.

"Oh my god, oh my god," I gasp, and just before I

come again, Luca pulls his fingers back out and slides his massive cock inside of my pussy, filling me up and stretching my wet hole until it almost hurts. "Yes! Yes!" I burst out, slamming my ass back against him, letting him fill me to the hilt as he grabs hold of my hips.

"You like that, *dolcezza?*" Luca grunts. "You want me to fuck your tight little pussy harder? Tell me how it feels, baby."

"It feels... so... fucking... good," I choke out between thrusts, feeling my whole body tensing up as he fucks me harder and faster. He picks up the tempo, slamming into me again and again. He reaches around underneath me to stroke at my clit with his fingers while he fucks me and I cry out, my second orgasm exploding inside of me. "Luca!" I scream.

He doesn't stop, even for a second, fucking me hard even as my body shudders with waves of pleasure, totally overstimulated. "You're gonna make me come again," I mumble, clinging to the chaise for dear life.

But he grabs me and lifts me up, spinning me around and leaning back against the chair with his cock still inside of me so that I'm now straddling him again. His legs are hooked over each side of the chaise with me speared on his cock on top of him. He holds me up by the strength of his arms alone, holding me in air, in place, while he thrusts upward with his hips, his cock pounding into me harder and harder. It's all I can do to even remember to breathe while he's fucking me, his swollen head striking that deep, delicious spot inside of me again and again and again.

"I want you to come for me, Serena," he growls imperatively. "I want that sweet little pussy to gush all over my cock. I want to hear you scream, *mia bambina.*"

He fucks me so fast and hard that my cunt aches, burns with the ferocity of it. That arching knot of pleasure tightens and tightens until I'm gasping, climaxing with a shriek. "Fuck! I'm coming!" I cry out, bouncing up and down on his cock.

"Good girl, good girl," Luca murmurs, but I can tell he's starting to lose control, too. His thrusts are getting more erratic, more violent as he fucks me. He sits up straighter, pulling my legs around his waist so that we're face to face while I bounce on his shaft. I'm so wet that we're both slick, sliding against each other fast and hard. Luca grabs my ass with one hand, and my left breast in the other, squeezing and pinching my nipple while his cock hits my g-spot. He moves faster and faster until I'm almost slack, my body exhausted and giving in to the overpowering sensations of pleasure.

"Fuck me," I whisper, my eyes rolling back in my head. "Fill me up, Luca. I want... I want to feel you come inside me. Please. Give it to me."

"I'm gonna come for you, *dolcezza*. Gonna pump you full of my seed, baby. Gonna make you mine forever and ever," he groans, leaning forward to kiss me hard, his tongue pushing into my mouth while I feel his cock tightening up inside of me.

Even though I'm barely able to think coherently, I use what little strength I have left to squeeze my pussy tight around Luca's shaft, kissing him back as he groans into my mouth. With a few rapid thrusts, he lets out a roar and shoots his sweet, thick seed deep inside of me, his hands groping me, clutching me close to his chest. He thrusts a few more times and I can feel his come starting to leak out of me as we sit there, entwined around each other and breathing raggedly. Luca kisses my forehead and lifts me up, setting me down beside him. He stands up and starts to get dressed again, and I quickly follow suit, realizing that it's actually rather cold in the basement and my naked skin is getting goosebumps.

"I can't believe this is happening," I murmur, looking up at him as I tug my leggings back on. Luca walks across the room to retrieve my shirt and bra, returning them to me. "I can't believe you're really here. After two years."

"It's been too long," he replies. "I never want to be apart from you for so long again."

"Luca… all this time has been hard. Worse than I even predicted," I begin, biting my lip. I don't want to ruin the beauty of the moment, but I can't pretend like nothing happened. I want to pick up right where we left off but I can't deny that things have changed, at least a little.

"I know," he says, pain etched across his face. "I wish I could have come back to you sooner. Every day on the inside was a fight for survival. For sanity. At first, when they threw me in solitary confinement, it was almost a welcome break from constantly defending myself and watching my back. But after a while, that emptiness, that silence, it all starts to close in on you and you start wishing you could be back out with the other inmates. As it turns out, the only thing worse than being surrounded by dangerous men is being alone with your thoughts."

"I'm so sorry you had to go through that," I tell him, reaching up to touch his face. He leans into my palm, pressing his cheek into my hand before turning to kiss my fingers.

"All of that was bearable, though. The thing that nearly killed me was being away from the woman I love," he adds, pulling me into an embrace. "Not knowing where you were or if you were okay. That's the thing that kept me awake at night."

I give him a weak smile. "I was okay. Well, at first I had some trouble. When they took you away, I kind of fell apart. It was so hard to convince myself life was still worth living. I would just lie in bed and think about how badly you were being treated in there, how unfair it all was. I didn't want to get out of bed or do anything. Nothing felt right. Nothing seemed to matter. It was like, why should I try to go back to the life I had before you?"

"But you did. I can see it. I could tell as soon as you came down that ladder, you've been surviving. You have that look about you. Like you've taken on the whole world and you're winning," Luca comments, a hint of pride in his voice.

"I'm glad you see that in me," I reply. "For a long time I didn't see it myself. It was a struggle, picking myself back up and getting back into the grind. But I figured it out eventually: working hard kept my mind off of more terrible things. So I worked my ass off."

"How is the shop doing?" he asks.

"Good. Great, actually," I correct myself. "I've hired this girl to help out and sales are up."

"I'm proud of you," Luca says, beaming at me. I can feel my face heating up. It's crazy. I just had mind-blowing sex with the guy, he knows every inch of my body intimately, but he can still make me blush with just a few words of praise.

"Thank you," I mumble, looking away. Changing the subject, I pipe up, "So, what is this place? I know the prison guards didn't arrange this whole shebang just so we could have a conjugal visit. What's going on?"

Luca sighs. "This is an old bootleggers' nest, a place where they used to hide out from the authorities, lay low in between big operations. Italian, of course."

"That explains the classed-up decor," I joke, raising an eyebrow. Luca chuckles.

"Yeah, we can never resist beautiful things," he answers, looking at me meaningfully.

"How did you find out about this place?"

"A friend of mine, a cellmate called Trueba, he told me about it. This place is a well-guarded secret, one the NYPD doesn't know about even after all this time. I'm sure you noticed what a pain it is to get here. Not too hard to believe that those cops wouldn't want to drag their asses all the way out here anyway," he laughs.

"Trueba? So, this cellmate of yours... did he help you get here or something? How did you arrange it? Luca, did you… did you break out of prison?" I ask, my throat going dry suddenly.

He takes both my hands in his. "Serena, I did exactly what I had to do to get out of there and come back to you."

"So, what now?" I ask quietly. "I'm sure they're looking for you."

Luca raises my hands to his lips, kissing them sweetly. "What happens now is we go back to where we were before all this happened. We go to dinner. We go to the park. We wake up in the morning together and we fall asleep at night side by side. We go back to being *us* again."

I can feel that annoying, all-too-familiar prickle of tears in my eyes, but whether they're happy or frightened tears I'm not sure.

"I want that more than anything in the whole world. But Luca, how are we—"

There's a resounding thump-thump-thump from behind us and we both turn around quickly to see one of the men who brought me here climbing down the ladder, looking sweaty and distressed. He looks at Luca and says, "Sorry to interrupt, but we've got trouble."

"No... no, you've got to be kidding me," Serena breathes as we pull up to Bathing Beauty and see the big yellow sign posted on the front door. We don't even need to get out to see the big bold word *CLOSED* written at the top of it.

Coming here in the first place was a risk, but it was a calculated risk. I had some men scout around the area before us to make sure there were no police watching the area. But just to be cautious, I also had them draw the attention of any beat cops a couple blocks down.

There's still no word of my escape in the news. They likely don't want to draw attention to the fact that one of Detective Prince's prized inmates escaped and are keeping it hush-hush. Still, it's been eerily quiet, and I know it won't last. But I have to take it day by day.

When the guard had intruded on us back on the island, he said there had been sightings of police investigating Serena's shop. Looks like the reports were right.

As we come to a stop around the back of the building and Serena hops out of the car to run up to the sign, I pull my hood over my head and don my old aviators. It doesn't help make me look less suspicious, but it does make me a little harder to spot as anyone but just another shady figure.

There's no shortage of those, this time of night.

I step up next to Serena and put a big hand on her shoulder as she stares at the notice with a gaping mouth, and I can see anger rising in her cheeks.

It's a police notice. The sign is a bunch of jargon, but in short, it says the business is temporarily closed because of an ongoing police investigation, and that removing the sign is a punishable offense.

"How could they do this?" Serena stammers, looking up to me with panic in her eyes. "This place is-is my livelihood! They don't have anything tying me to... anything!"

"It's a threat," I say in a grave tone, reading the thing over again and glancing over my shoulder. My hand slides from her shoulder to her smaller hand, and I give her a tug to follow me around the back of the building. "Come on, we should get out of sight."

"Where?" she asks, following me.

"Inside," I say. "Looks like nobody's doing any

investigating right now, it'll be better than hanging out on the street."

We go to the back door, and Serena unlocks it to allow us to step inside. We enter, and I can immediately tell things are off.

Serena flicks on a light, and there are signs of tampering everywhere. As I step through the shop with her, I can tell that inventory has been moved around roughly, the office has been nearly torn apart from someone searching through any files Serena happened to have around, and even the front of the store has been looked through.

"They even took some of my chemicals," Serena says in disbelief, looking around at the damage, and as she turns on the office light, I can see the tears shining in her eyes. "How did they get a warrant so fast?"

I move to the front of the shop and find an envelope that was pushed through the mail slot. It looks official, and it has the police department's return address on it. "Looks like this is their notice," I say, turning it over in my hands and handing it to her when she approaches. She tosses it to the counter, shaking her head.

"I can't read that thing right now. I... I feel sick, Luca."

I wrap my arms around her, and she buries her face into my chest, where I feel her tears staining my shirt.

"This is my fault," I whisper, holding her snugly in my embrace, making her feel secure. God, I've missed that feeling, but I can already see the damage my return is causing. "They don't care about you. Not really. They know we're together, and this is a threat to let us know they're still watching. Hounding us."

"No," says Serena, looking up at me. Tear-marks are still streaming down her face, but she looks resolute. "No, this is about both of us. You've been strong for so long, Luca, but we're in this together," she says, managing a smile, and I move my hands down to her hips and give her a squeeze.

"You don't want to get dragged into this any more than you already are," I say.

"Are you kidding? This is my business, and whether they're after you or not, they're fucking with *me* now, too. That's why you're here again. I'm already in," she says, tightening a fist full of my shirt in her hand. "I'll be damned if I let everything I worked for go to hell because some... some crooked cop with a stick up his ass has a chip on his shoulder!"

I grin, and I scoop her up in my arms suddenly. She yelps, kicking her legs as she instinctively wraps her arms around my neck. "That's my girl," I say proudly, and she blushes in my arms. "I've missed that fire in you more than anything."

She smiles, and I bend down to kiss her on the

lips, then I pepper her whole face with kisses, and her teary face is soon blushing and giggling instead. I walk her back to the office and set her on the desk. My hands wrap around her waist, and we just look at each other for a moment, smiling.

In spite of all the hardship, being able to just have some privacy with Serena is worth more than anything in the world.

"I know this is a lot," I say, giving her a gentle squeeze to reassure her. "There's no easy way to live with the police breathing down your neck, I can tell you that. But I can tell you one more thing." I put my hands around her face, gently bringing her forehead forward to touch mine to hers. "I've tasted freedom, Serena, freedom with you. And nothing is going to tear me away from you again as long as my heart is beating."

I see her smile, and she slips her hands around my sides, feeling the muscles rippling under my shirt. "It was so hard without you, Luca. I mean, I could handle my business fine, I wasn't exaggerating that much in my letters. But just... going to bed alone every night, waking up and forgetting that you weren't going to be there beside me, thinking I wouldn't feel you holding me up for another eight years..."

She pulls her head back and looks at me with those warm, shining eyes that move me like nothing else on this earth. "If I can survive that," she says, "and you can hold up in prison for so long, then together, we can do anything." She puts her hand in mind and interlaces our fingers together.

"You've grown so much stronger since I saw you last," I whisper in a low tone.

"You're one to talk," she says with a grin, running her free hand up and down my muscular side, then sliding her fingers to my front. She lets out a contented sigh at what she feels, and I put a hand under her chin to make her look up to me.

We look at each other like we're meeting for the first time all over again. Every moment with Serena feels like that; the first skipping heartbeat that makes my hardened heart go soft for just a second. Just long enough to get a taste of her and lose all control.

I bring my lips to hers, and as soon as they touch, we're lost in each other.

I let my tongue explore her mouth, and she welcomes it, giving a soft moan into the kiss as her tongue plays with mine in turn. We share warmth as I come in closer, reveling in the feel of her mouth on mine. Her lips are softer than I remember, her blush redder, her voice sweeter.

We move slower than the furious waterfall of energy we felt when we were first reunited. We're even more private now. God, how I've missed having privacy. Really *feeling* alone with Serena, feeling like my time with her can't be intruded on by anyone. Like she can take her time enjoying my body.

Everything I've worked for and waited for is in Serena, and her satisfaction makes me happier and more fulfilled than even my first breath as a free man did.

She puts both hands on my pecs, and I lower my arms to squeeze her hips to let her explore my body. Her fingertips trace the muscles on my upper torso, then go down to my abs. They linger on each and every one while we kiss, then slide to my sides and travel down to my waist.

I rock my hips forward slowly, inviting her to feel more of me. She goes to my thighs and feel the hardness, my muscles so tight they don't have any give. It's pure power under there, just like the rest of me. Her left hand moves up my thigh to where my legs meet, and when she touches the equally hard outline of my stiff cock through my jeans, I feel her draw in a sharp breath.

"We fucked in the safe house," I say in a husky tone, breaking our kiss, "now I want to make love to you. In the place it all began again."

She nods softly, and I move back just enough to pull my shirt up over my head and toss it aside, letting her get a full look at my body. She feasts her eyes, her mouth falling open. Even with my wounds bandaged, so much of my carefully sculpted form is on display, my swarthy skin looking as healthy as ever over hard muscle.

I reach forward, and she lets me pull her shirt

over her head too, and I take off her bra to really look at her.

Her form has always been beautiful, but it's all the more irresistible to me after so long away from her. Her olive skin sets off the dark blonde hair spilling down her shoulders like the sun against bronze. I put my warm, rough hands to her breasts and feel them softly, my strong grip gentle. It teases a gasp out of her. I'm like a towering bear pawing at her as she sits there on the desk, exposed to me.

The way her breasts feel is incredible to me. I move my hands under them, feeling their weight in my palms before I bring my thumbs to the brown buds and run them over them, feeling them hardening, getting stiffer and more needy for me. They're begging me to devour them, and I will, soon. I want to take my time with Serena and learn more about this gorgeous new body I'm rediscovering.

I push everything off the desk to give us a clear space, and I gently lower her down onto her back on it and look at her. She's so beautiful that I almost feel like I shouldn't see her, like this is a holy ground that my sinner's heart shouldn't defile.

But I'm going to defile her, whether it's holy or not.

I run my hands down her sides this time, so soft and giving compared to mine. Every inch of her is velvety and pure, from her breasts to her hips to her belly button.

I bend over and breathe on her navel, then rove up her torso to her breasts, letting my five o'clock shadow brush against the soft flesh.

"I've dreamed about this," she confesses, and I'm close enough to watch her chest rising and falling gently yet excitedly, desperate for my touch.

"Have you?" I say, a teasing edge to my voice. I put my hands on her hips and stick my fingers under her pants. "And where did this dream take you?"

"I can't remember," she says, but I can tell she's lying, and I grin. "It all kind of got fuzzy, but I remember waking up and feeling all warm, like you were really there with me."

"Why don't we fill in the blanks, then?" I say, and I pull her pants down. She gasps as I expose her, and it's my turn to feast her eyes on her bare hips, thighs, and best of all, that beautiful place where her thighs meet.

I put my hands to the sides of her ass and bring my face down to her sensitive inner thighs, listening to her gasp as my stubble brushes that most sensitive area. Her breathy voice is like the note of a harp in the air.

Turning my face in, I let my teeth graze her inner thigh, from almost to the knee all the way up to her outer lips. There, I let my breath wash over her, and she shudders. Her fingers grip the edge of the desk, and she pushes her hips up just a little, just enough to let me know just how desperate she is for my touch.

My hands move up and down her legs, groping them greedily and feeling their warmth. I let my breath wash over her pussy once more before I give her what she wants. A taste I've missed for so long and couldn't possibly get enough of now.

I let my tongue out, and it dips just far enough into her lips to make her tense up and gasp, and I drag it up the length of her slit, all the way to the top. I've had a long, long time to think about how to kiss the most sensitive parts of her body just so, and so it's with the utmost precision that I let the tip of my tongue just barely flick the swelling nub of her clit.

Warmth radiates from her, and everything just feels *right* as I taste her. I can't contain a deep, gravelly groan from my chest as the taste awakens my tongue. Like a great engine roaring to life, my body feels energized with power. My grip tightens as I grope her ass, and my gentleness gives way to passion as I open my mouth and revel in the feel of her pussy.

My tongue goes out again, this time going deeper into her. The deeper I go, the hotter it gets, and each time my tongue darts out, I taste more of her, more of that sweet well that I've been thirsty for after all this time. I start to get more generous with my tongue, letting it widen to play with the sensitive outermost parts of her pussy while the tip dives deeper into her.

I let her feel me just like I'm tasting her. I arch my neck with the next stroke, letting my stubble brush against her warm lips that are getting wetter and wetter each time I go down to draw more of her honey out of her.

Serena overflows with feeling for me, and my cock swells stiffer and stiffer with each passing second. As my tongue darts in and out, I let my hands revel in the feeling of her ass and her hips. The way her flesh gives way to my strong hands is something I can't get enough of. I love that I can squeeze her and feel no hardness, just her soft, giving skin that I can't wait to sink my shaft into soon.

I feel her thighs squeezing around my head, and the grip I have around her hips gives me total control to keep Serena wrapped around my face. I have to tame my passion as I feast on her pussy, savoring every moment that I can feel her heartbeat against my tongue.

Her sensitive nub is so swollen, so needy for me, and each time I let my tongue roll over it, I can hear Serena letting out gasps of need. Her knuckles start to get white on the table as I get more rhythmic and relentless with each stroke of my tongue, never slowing down for a moment. My strokes are careful yet strong, dipping down into her lips and coming up to the clit. Each time, I let the tip of my tongue stay there at the clit for just a little longer, tormenting it, letting it kiss the honey from her depths

Soon, I feel Serena's hips starting to twist, and she writhes against me. She needs release, and her body is going to reach it soon.

I keep letting my tongue dart in and out, and her legs wrap around me as she pushes her hips up into me. She isn't looking at what I'm doing, her head back and her golden hair spread out over the desk so carelessly, but she wants more of whatever I'm giving her.

She needs it. Her body needs it. Her heels dig into my sides as best they can as I hear the tiny squeak of her voice as she draws in a pained breath. My hot breath washes over her soaking pussy as my tongue drives her over the edge.

She lets out a beautifully long, high-pitched gasp that fills the whole room while my face gets soaked, and I grip her hips tighter, arching her up into me, and when her tension finally starts to relax, I let my stroking get slower again, nursing her through the end of her orgasm.

I can feel her pleasure pulsing all around me. I can smell her in the air. It's a sensory overload for both of us, but I've been denied it all too long to stop now. I lift my head up and look down at her gorgeous form on the desk. She glows, a smile on her face as her eyes flutter open to look at me.

"Can you sit up?" I ask, and she pushes herself up on her elbow to tilt her head at me.

"Yeah," she says between breaths, "why?"

Instead of answering, I just smile, backing up and pulling her shoes off, then pulling her pants the rest of the way off, leaving her completely naked on the desk.

I hoist her up by the hips and move her aside to give me space while I lay down on my back beside her, and her eyes flutter in confusion before I seize her by the hips again and lift her up over me.

"Luca, what are you-" she laughs, squirming in my grasp as I hold her up with thick arms and strong hands, and I grin up at her as I sit her down on my chest.

"I'm not done with you yet," I growl, and before she can reply, I bring her forward and let her rest on my jaw. Before she realizes what's happening, I let my tongue out and swipe it up her slit

She shudders, nearly losing her balance up on top of me, but I'm in complete control of her. I slide my rough hand up to the small of her back to let her know I've got her, and I start lapping up her pleasure all over again.

She's wet and hot, and looking up at the landscape of her body just makes me love being able to hold onto someone so beautiful all the more. I have such a sure grip on her that she could go limp and I'd still be able to hold her up.

And the way she looks up there, that might well be what I have to do.

She keeps trying to make little thrusts forward into me, but I control her, making her entirely at the mercy of my hands. She is like a doll to me, and I can move her any which way I please. But I only want the angle that will let me play with her swollen, needy clit best.

The more my tongue strokes, the wetter my face gets, until the scent of her lust fills my every breath. With each move of my jaw, my stubble brushes against her and sends tingles up her body.

But I had already gotten her going, so it isn't long before I start to feel her getting tense again. I feel her thighs clenching around my head, and her pitiful thrusts forward get more desperate, more needy. I lose track of how long it takes her to tense up, but the second time feels even more tightly-wound than the first before it all comes spilling out.

She gives a shuddering gasp, and I dig my fingers into her hips and pull her closer to me to let one long, deep stroke of my tongue run the length of her slit while I feel her pussy tremble around me, the orgasm wracking her body in my iron grip.

"Oh god, Luca," she gasps, her face blushing furiously as I help her slide back onto my chest, resting her on me as I look up at her and lick my lips. "I... I think I need a second," she says, and I help her down while I stand up and bend over her, looking her in the eyes. I cradle her head in my hand as she pants, looking up at me lovingly.

"How does it feel, *dolcezza*?" I ask in a husky voice.

"Everything I've been missing," she manages to say through desperate breaths, and she puts a hand on my chest to feel my deep breathing before I bring my lips to her. My whole face is wet with her, and she moans into my mouth at the taste of her own passion. Our tongues play with one another again as I curl my fingers in and take a fistful of her hair.

We break our kiss so that she can breathe again, and her eyes look dizzy with ecstasy. "I want to keep going," she says, words that fill me with pride. I bring my lips to hers again, putting one hand on her thigh and one on her breast to grope her, squeeze her, feel her like I've wanted to feel her nonstop for so long.

"Every night I fell asleep in that cold place thinking of you," I say, my voice deep and rough in her ear, and she sighs contentedly. "It was the only thing that could keep me warm. Thinking of you, of each time we fell asleep in each other's arms."

"When I wrote that letter about the lingerie," she says, a playful smile coming across her lips, "I... wasn't exaggerating when I said I'd be thinking of you. I thought of you every time, Luca. Even during the day, I-I couldn't think about life without you."

"Those letters kept me going, Serena," I say, our eyes fixed on each other. I loved Serena dearly before I was put away, but you never know how thirsty you are for someone until you're taken away from them. Now, I'll let my eyes take in as much as I want of her. "I couldn't have kept going without them."

Our lips touch again, slowly, intimately. I can feel her heartbeat through her lips, and the heat of her body warms me. When our lips part, I stand up and run my hands over her legs. She can see the outline of my cock hard under my pant, and her eyes are locked on it.

"Ready for more?" I ask, my thumbs making small circles on her inner thighs. She shivers and nods, biting her lip in anticipation.

I reach forward and take her by the hips, then lift one of her legs up and drape it over my shoulder, holding her up with my other hand.

I unbutton my pants and let my cock spring free, and I see Serena watching it with hungry eyes. It makes me happy to see her take such pleasure in my body. She reaches forward, and I tilt my hips in just enough to let her touch my cock. She lets her fingers dance up and down the shaft, her palm brushing up against it before she gives it a gentle squeeze. Her thumb brushes over the crown, and I feel warmth up my body at her touch.

I can see that being able to get such a response from me excites her. She runs her hands up and down a little more, from the base to the tip.

"I missed this," she says through a smile, and I laugh quietly, rubbing the leg on my shoulder.

"Let me show you how much it missed you," I growl.

I take her hips, and she has a second to remove her hand before I put the swollen, needy, dark crown of my cock to her lips and enter her.

I only put the tip in, and I rock back and forth to move it in slowly, because her mouth is already hanging open. She must be tingling all over just from the feeling of my tongue, so I'll be careful... but my passion can only be slowed so much.

Bit by bit, inch by inch, I slide myself into her, and she's so slick and ready that it feels like I'm gliding into her.

Biting her lip and clenching her eyes, I feel her tightening around me with every bit that I put into her, feeling her pulse around me. When I'm about halfway in, I give her thigh a loving squeeze before I start bucking.

My rhythm picks up fast. I rock back and forth, my balls heavy and full of virile seed that aches to be released. Serena is the only release worth having, and she's worth every moment of wait.

I drive myself into her, then back out, leaving almost nothing but my crown inside her before I go back in again. Each time, I feel her shake. Each time, she gasps, a loving, ecstatic moan in the air that's getting hot with our fucking. I go a little further in each time, and soon, I'm feeling my heavy balls hitting her ass.

I feel every inch of her insides as I get faster and faster, and my rhythm becomes more machine-like with every thrust. I feel her squirming, and I move with her to get closer and closer to those places inside her that drive her wild. I know so many of them, but rediscovering Serena is endlessly rewarding.

She gets more tense the more I go, and before long, I'm down to the hilt inside her, pumping in and out over and over again like a piston, nothing but love and raw power between us, charging the room. It's like electricity, and I feel it coiling up within me with all the passion and energy of our very first time.

With each thrust, I'm holding onto her hips and keeping her steady, watching her body laid out on her side, her mouth frozen open and her eyes looking up at me.

"Oh... oh... oh fuck, Luca," she gasps.

"This is for you, *dolcezza*," I growl, "I love you."

No sooner have the words left my mouth than I twist her hips just enough to start grinding up against her g-spot, and she arches her back as I feel her tense and start to shake, barreling closer and closer to the edge of ultimate pleasure. At the same time, I feel my balls start to tighten as fire fills my cock, running up into my torso and spreading to every limb.

At the same time, we both come, my fingers digging into her thighs while her nails claw at the desk. My seed shoots out in a hot, long, filling burst that floods her pussy and mixes with her honey. It's messy, hot, and our groans fill the room with noise, but it's our private love, something more intimate and wonderful than I could dream of in my wildest fantasies.

Pulse after pulse, I pour myself into her. My every muscle tenses and relaxes with that unmatched feeling of release. Her body goes limp, and I'm the only thing holding her up after a few moments. She's like a ragdoll in my hands, our fluids spilling out through the great shaft of my cock inside her.

When our orgasms relax, I'm still hard, and I grind inside her gently for a few wonderful, blissful moments. My cock twitches a few more times as the last pulses of my love for her empty out into Serena.

Finally, slowly, I carefully start to work myself out of her. I have to be careful with so much stimulation. Her pussy is on fire, I know, but I'm gentle with my girl. She whimpers as I take myself out of her, watching some of my seed run down her olive skin. One last bit of pearly fluid comes out of my cock's head, landing on her pussy's lips like a jewel.

I want to stand back and admire our work, but I can't bring myself to tear away from Serena just yet. I stroke her body, watching her bare chest rising and falling, and her eyes finally flutter open just enough to look at me. Her tired lips crack a smile, and I wink at her.

"Good practice for later," I say, my voice still husky, and her eyes widen.

"Practice? For what?"

"A proper bedroom tonight," I say, and I give her ass a slap that rings through the room, making her squeak. With a grin, I add, "we've got a long time to make up for, baby."

"It's been a long time since I was last out here," Luca says, looking around through the windshield, his hands gripping the steering wheel. There's a hint of nostalgia in his voice, a smile tugging at his lips. He reaches over the console to take my hand, giving it a squeeze. "Not since our one night here."

He glances over at me with a wink, which immediately makes me smile.

"I suppose the mafia isn't usually so concerned with suburbia. That makes sense. I definitely remember thinking Riverdale was a kind of stepdown for my family, even though my dad was convinced it was the right choice. I just thought it would be so boring living so far away from the action in the middle of the city. I mean, after living in Manhattan I think any place would feel pretty dull by comparison. I remember being so scared that I would fall out of touch with my best friends who all still lived in the city."

"Did you?" Luca asks.

I chuckle, rolling my eyes.

"Yep. I mean, it's not like they cut me out intentionally or anything, but we definitely drifted apart. Turns out, nobody was particularly excited about the idea of driving all the way out here to hang out. And besides, after what happened with my dad and… you know… I kind of shut down for a while. My mom and I had lost everything — my dad, our money, our reputation — it was just a lot to deal with all at once. I found out really quickly that most of my so-called best friends were more like fair-weather friends. They didn't want to come all the way to Riverdale just to pat me on the back while I cried. And, you know, they were all rich kids. They couldn't relate to me anymore after my family lost our fortune."

"I don't know how you did it," Luca says, shaking his head.

"Well, at first I didn't do anything except cry. We both did. My mom is a tough lady, and the only time I have ever seen her cry was during those first few weeks after Dad died. It was scary, seeing her like that. Dad and I had always joked that she was like a fortress or something, that nothing could get to her. Tear-jerker movies, sad songs; nothing could break her. But during that time, she *was* broken. We both were. Broken *and* broke."

"I wish I had been around to help you," Luca tells me sadly. I lift his hand to my lips and kiss it gently.

"You did help. You saved me from... from having to *repay* my father's debt. You paid it for me," I assure him. "After I laid in bed crying and feeling hopeless for a while, I managed to scrape myself out of bed and get back to work. Thankfully, my dad had paid all my private school tuition ahead of time, so I didn't have to worry about being kicked out of school. So I jumped back into the flow of going to class and doing homework, preparing for college applications. All that normal stuff. Because of you, Luca. Everything I have, after my dad died... it's because you cared. Because you sacrificed every-thing to make sure I could keep... so I could keep living."

My fingers run over the back of his hand and I smile at him gently. He was the reason I was able to pull myself out of my self-pitying slump. I knew he didn't save me because he wanted me to be lost in grief. I lost my dad and him in the span of a week, and it broke my heart in pieces. But neither of them would have wanted me to throw away my future.

"And my mom finally got out of the house and went back to work. I use the word 'work' loosely because, truth be told, she didn't really know what she was doing. Bathing Beauty was more like a hobby for her back in the day. We employed real workers to keep the place running, and my mom would occasionally drop in to micromanage or just check to make sure things were still going okay. After Dad died, we didn't have the money to pay them anymore, so we had to let them go. That was hard. Hell, one of the ladies who worked there was an old babysitter of mine from when I was little. But they all understood the situation, you know. So my mom took over all the business of running Bathing Beauty. My mom, who was a mafia princess, who had never had to hold down a real job in her life."

"Sounds like a recipe for disaster," Luca comments.

"Oh, it was," I agree. "She really struggled to even manage the store front properly, much less balance the accounts or deal with shipments. Back then, the shop was just stocking artisanal soaps and stuff from other people who actually made them. The kitchen was just kind of sitting there, unused. My mom didn't know how to cook a meal at home, much less cook up all-natural bath oils and stuff. It was definitely disastrous, because we didn't have the funds to keep stocking other people's work, but we didn't know how to make that stuff on our own. The summer after junior year, I started working at Bathing Beauty with my mom to help out, because things were getting pretty desperate between trying to keep the business afloat and keep paying for the house."

"What a nightmare," he says, squeezing my hand. I love how he looks at me. How he listens to me. I feel like I'm talking so much, but he's just engrossed, fascinated by what he missed, all those years ago. All the things we never got to talk about when we got our second chance together.

"It felt like one, for sure. Trying to work with my mother, who was both an uptight micromanager and totally incompetent at the same time. It drove a wedge between us for a bit, because tensions were just so high at the shop and at home. We spent way too much time together, especially considering the fact that before all that, we were never super close. I was always more of a daddy's girl. Finally, though, she started letting me take more control over the shop. As it turned out, I kind of had a knack for business. I was a good salesperson, more approach-able than my ice-queen mother. When she no longer had to focus on the storefront, she was actually fairly good at the bookkeeping aspect of the job. When I asked her about it, guess what she said?"

"What?"

"That she was actually a mathlete in high school," I answer, laughing. "Which was so weird to picture. My mom as a student in the eighties, rich and popular but secretly on the mathletes team. I never would've guessed."

"Well, the apple doesn't fall too far from the tree. Seems like every woman in your family probably has some secret strengths nobody knows about," Luca says pointedly, smiling.

"I discovered one of my own when I started working at the shop. One day, my mom got in a really nasty phone argument with one of our suppliers and he pulled out, refusing to work with her again. On a whim, and a little bit out of desperation, I decided to try my hand at making soaps and oils myself. We tricked out the kitchen with some extra tools and appliances and I got to work, reading dumb how-to articles on the internet to teach myself as I went. The first batch wasn't pretty, but it did smell nice. The second batch, though... it was pretty much perfect. So we started selling our own stuff that I made myself in the kitchen. That was a great feeling," I reminisce.

"And you were so young then, too," Luca remarks.

"Yeah, I was seventeen at that point. And I fell in love with the business. My mom and I, we were still hurting from what happened, both of us trying to recover. And Bathing Beauty was there for us, something we had to pour our hearts and souls into. Something to distract us from how scary the world had gotten. For a while we were a pretty good business partnership, and there were even times when we got along, laughing and joking around in the shop in between sales. I remember one weekend, I decided to take on making a huge batch of products, so my mom brought an old TV we had in my dad's study into the shop kitchen. We put on a classic movie marathon; you know, *Arsenic and Old Lace*, *Bringing Up Baby*, all that stuff. We worked side by side to get it all done."

"Never underestimate the power of two women in a desperate situation," Luca says, his words filled with pride. The car turns a corner and we start our way down my street.

"It was great. I mean, we were still struggling to get by, but we were finally treading water instead of just drowning. Things were really turning around," I explain. "Senior year started back up and I had to go to class during the day, but I worked at the shop after school and on weekends. My mom was starting to get a better handle on running the shop while I wasn't there, so after graduation I started college, thankfully on several scholarships."

"Smart cookie," Luca comments, grinning.

"College was awesome. I finally had a little more freedom, and for a while I even moved out of the house and got a roommate in the city."

"Rafaela."

"Yep," I answer. "Rafaela. Finally, I had a friend who was in the same boat as me. She wasn't a rich kid or even a former rich kid; she was working her ass off to get by the same as I was. It was refreshing to not have to hide how hard my life was. She was so understanding. She still is. I'm really glad I met her."

"She and Nico are good people. Certainly the kind of people you want on your side," Luca agrees. He pulls the car into the long driveway of my house, headed toward the garage.

"When my mom got hurt on the job — she burned her arm pretty badly mixing chemicals in the kitchen — I moved home to help look after her and the shop. I have no idea how I managed to run the shop and still graduate from college with my degree. Rafaela wanted me to stay, but I just knew in my heart I had to go home. It was probably an overreaction on my part, but I had already lost one parent, and I was terrified of losing my mom, too. I kept imagining her falling down in the shop one evening after closing and nobody being there to help her. I know it sounds crazy, but her little injury scared me to hell," I admit.

"It doesn't sound crazy at all," Luca says. "She's family."

"Wow, I'm sorry for talking your ear off," I laugh, a little embarrassed.

Luca parks the car and turns to look at me, an earnest look on his handsome face as his hand cups my jaw, staring into my eyes.

"Don't ever apologize for talking about yourself. For sharing your excitement with me. I love hearing about your history. Just proves to me again how tough and determined and capable you are."

He leans in, his mouth gently pressing into mine, and I feel my shoulders soften into the tender kiss. I've never met someone like him before. When we were young, he was so hot and cold. Of course, now I know what he was involved in to make him so distant.

I'm determined to make sure we never have that distance between us again. My dad and Luca protecting me from the Mafia has never saved me from heartache for long.

"I know it seems ridiculous to keep paying for this house even when my dad died. It would have been easier to try and sell it, just keep living in that apartment in Manhattan. But I just couldn't do it. This house, huge and unnecessary though it is, meant so much to Dad. He poured his heart and soul into this place, and I just can't bear to part with it. Not yet anyway."

"I understand," Luca says, getting out of the driver's seat and coming around to open the passenger side door for me. He gives me a hand, helping me out of the car. "People do crazy things for family. For the ones they love."

"Ain't that the truth," I agree, smiling at him. "Wow, it's crazy to be back here. With you."

Luca nods, looking around with a look of mild surprise on his face.

"Yeah, I never expected that I would get a chance to see the house in its finished state. It was still kind of a mess when I was last here."

"Can I ask you something?" I start suddenly, biting my lip.

"Of course. Anything."

"Why didn't you come back? I mean, after the first day we met when you were working on the construction crew, I never saw you here again. We had to sneak around to other places, remember?" I ask, cocking my head to one side.

Luca smirks.

"Well, the contractor gave me some other assignments, other houses to work on at the time instead of your house. He claimed that my particular carpentry skill set would be better suited for other projects. But the short answer he never outright admitted to was that he saw you and me together and didn't want to run the risk of getting in trouble with your father."

My face flushes hot.

"Oh no. I'm so sorry. You mean I cost you a job?"

"No, no, it was fine. I had plenty of assignments on hand to keep me busy," Luca assures me, taking me by the hand as we walk up to the garage entrance to the house. "That was one thing my uncle was always adamant about: keeping me busy. I think he was worried that if I had too much free time, I'd end up going down the wrong path like so many other guys my age in the same position. He wanted to protect me, I guess."

"Okay. Good. I'll take your word for it. I could never forgive myself if that was all my fault," I tell him honestly.

He waves his hand dismissively as I fish out my keys and open the door to let us into the house.

"It's not like you forced yourself on me. I was pretty assertive with you, if I recall correctly."

I can't help but grin, remembering how suave and flirtatious Luca was then as a cocky teenager who knew exactly how good-looking he was, how impossible it would be for even a straight-laced good girl like me to resist his charms.

"You certainly weren't lacking in confidence, that's for sure," I laugh.

"I was a little arrogant back then," he agrees, smiling.

"You had every reason to be. You still do," I tease, strolling into the kitchen. "Do you want something to drink? My mom thinks beer is gross so we don't have any of that but we do have wine."

"Sounds just like the Luisa Gaspari I remember hearing about from the guys back in the day. Classy woman."

"It's okay. You can say 'uptight.' I live with her, I know what she's like," I joke, taking out a pair of wine glasses and a bottle of Shiraz. I pour us each a glass as Luca chuckles.

"Your words, not mine. So, where is Mama De Laurentis today?" he asks. "I hope she wasn't too worried about your sudden disappearance."

I shrug, turning to hand him his wine. "She was definitely concerned. I had a bunch of missed calls and voicemails, of course, but she believed my story about going into the shop to do late-night paperwork. At least, I think she did. I mean, I'm an adult, so she can't exactly call the police just because I'm gone a little longer than expected. Either way, she's out of town today, visiting one of her cousins down in Newport."

"So we've got this giant house all to ourselves, then?" Luca inquires, raising an eyebrow. I nod, taking a sip of my wine to hide my smile.

"Yep. I don't think she's coming back until tomorrow."

"Well, I'm sorry to miss out on meeting your mother but… I'm not *that* sorry," he says.

"I guess now we just have to figure out what to do with all this free time and space we have to fill today," I tell him innocently, sipping my wine as I bat my eyelashes at him. He grins.

"Yes, whatever will we do to pass the time? I can't think of a single thing I want to do with you right now," he says, his voice low and deep. "Any ideas?"

"We could… play chess. Or watch daytime soap operas. Oh! I know: we could dig that Monopoly box out of the attic. So many fun options," I remark.

Luca downs his wine in one long draught and sets the glass down behind him on the counter, sauntering over to me. I can feel my heartbeat quickening instantly, my body warming in anticipation of his touch.

He backs me against the kitchen island, putting both hands on the counter on either side of me. He takes the wine glass out of my hands and places it on the counter behind me, leaning in close to my face. I can see the deep ivy green of his eyes, the tiny flecks of gold scattered around his irises. I can see now that there are a few tiny freckles across the bridge of his nose, and that his lips are so full and soft-looking. I can't help but lick my own lips.

"Huh. I just thought of something we could do together today," Luca growls softly.

"Oh?" I murmur, my breath catching in my throat. "And what is that?"

"What are your feelings on getting bound, blindfolded, bent over, and fucked from behind?" Luca suggests, his lips mere centimeters from mine.

I can scarcely remember to breathe. "Positive. I-I have positive feelings about that."

"Good," he murmurs, and captures my mouth in a deep kiss. His hands come up to cup my face, sliding back through my hair as he presses into me. I can feel his cock hard against my hip and it's all I can do to keep from reaching down to touch it. The space between my thighs feels so warm, tingling with desire already.

His tongue pushes into my mouth and I let out a groan, feeling my body go limp in his arms. He has the magic touch— the ability to make all my tension melt away, turn me into a lovesick ragdoll. He can do whatever he wants to me. Anything.

I instinctively reach up to touch his face, but he quickly moves my hands behind my back, holding my wrists there with one huge hand. For a split second a thrill of true fear shocks through me, as though my body is remembering the times I've had my hands behind my back before... the *bad* times.

But I quickly remember that this isn't a bad time. I'm safe. I'm with Luca. And even if things get a little rough — and god, I hope they do — he will never actually hurt me or push too far. The trust between us, the knowledge that he will always listen to and respect my wants instantly calms us.

And I know that if I ever say our safe word — Crimson — that he would instantly stop. Knowing that allows me to relax and feel the thrill of arousal run through me.

He wedges his leg between my thighs, rubbing against the tingling heat of my crotch. I shiver at the rolling wave of pleasure even this small movement gives me. Luca chuckles, a low, guttural sound. Almost sinister, but not.

"You're so hot for me, *dolcezza*," he murmurs,

gently biting my bottom lip. "Maybe I should help you cool down."

With that, he spins me around, pinning my arms behind my back again as he deftly slips off his leather belt. I hold my breath, glancing over my shoulder to watch as he binds the belt around my wrists. The sight of my hands tied with his own belt, still warm from his body heat, turns me on more than I could have ever predicted.

He spanks my ass with a resounding slap, then moves my hair over one shoulder and bends to kiss my neck. The combination of delicious stinging and ticklish kisses makes me tremble, and I back into him slightly, rubbing my ass against the hard cock straining in his pants.

"What a dirty girl," he hisses in my ear.

It occurs to me suddenly that I might actually be literally dirty at the moment. After all, I did go straight from jogging in my neighborhood to being rowed across a body of water, through the woods, and down into a dusty basement. And we fucked there. It's been a very hectic 24 hours.

"Well, maybe I should clean up a little bit, then," I remark suggestively, trying to make my plea for a shower sound somewhat sexy. Luca chuckles, kissing the side of my face as he frees my wrists from his leather belt. I'm a little disappointed at this, but I hope to god it's just a rain check and not a cancellation.

"That's not a bad idea, as long as I can come, too," he replies. My heart flutters.

"Oh, I hope you will," I answer mischievously. My plan is working!

He breaks away for a second and goes over to the refrigerator. He opens up the freezer drawer for some reason, looking for something.

"What are you looking for?" I ask.

He takes out an ice tray. "A-ha. You know, I'm a little surprised. I thought a fancy kitchen like this would certainly have an icemaker built into the fridge."

"Yeah, after Dad died and I took over the finishing touches on construction I decided to cut corners with some cheaper appliances. But why do we need ice?" I press on, totally lost.

Luca grins as he walks over and sets down the ice tray for a moment, then scoops me up in his arms easily, holding me with my legs around his waist while he picks the ice tray back up. I'm amazed again at his strength and control, although by this point I shouldn't be shocked by anything he does anymore. And besides, I'm sure two years with nothing better to do than lift weights and work out has definitely increased his physical abilities.

"Just wait and see," he answers simply. And with that, he carries me out of the kitchen and, more impressively, all the way up the staircase, and down the hallway. He carries me to my room, crossing my bedroom and setting me down in the bathroom.

"You know I *can* walk, right?" I joke.

"You work too hard already," he replies, shrugging. "The least I can do is get you off your feet every now and then." He turns on the shower, eyeing the detachable shower head as he adjusts the heat and closes the bathroom door. I start peeling off my clothes, thankful to be out of them since I've been wearing them for way longer than I would like to. Luca follows suit, revealing his powerful chest and arms, the rippling muscles of his stomach, his strong legs. Even though we've already fucked twice in the past 24 hours, I can't help but feel that same overwhelming wave of desire for him again. I wonder if it will ever wear off. I hope not. I doubt it.

"After you," he says, gesturing to the shower. There's a rather naughty glint in his eye, but I don't question it. I climb into the shower, sighing with relief as the hot water cascades over me, warming me up and washing away the grime and stress of the past day and night. Luca comes in after me and squeezes body wash into his palm to start washing first himself, then me. I inhale sharply as his huge hands slide up and down my body, sudsy and slippery. His fingers toy with my nipples, slipping over them and cupping my breasts as I close my eyes and lean into him. My hair falls in soaked tendrils down my back as I tilt my head back slightly, giving in to the combined sensations of soothing hot water and Luca's hands caressing me.

Suddenly, a new sensation explodes into my attention: icy-cold burning across my nipples. I open my eyes and look down to see Luca sliding a quickly-melting ice cube around the stiffened peaks of my breasts. The sensation is confusing at first: both slightly painful and uncomfortable as well as strangely arousing. My body responds with a warm dampening between my thighs, my heartbeat quickening. Just as my nipples start to go a little numb, Luca dives in and captures them in his hot mouth. I let out a little whimper at how amazing it feels. I never considered ice-play before; it just never seemed to make any sense to me.

But it *certainly* makes sense to me now.

"How's that feel, *mia passerotta?*" Luca asks as he moves from one nipple to the other.

"Fantastic," I sigh, closing my eyes again.

Luca lowers down to kneel in front of me, sliding another ice cube down the length of my body as he goes, making me shiver. He gently pushes my legs open further before slowly circling the ice cube around my pussy, getting close but never actually touching my clit. I tremble, my mouth falling open as I look down at him. Luca locks eyes with me, watching my face as he moves the ice over my clit. I cry out, almost recoiling from the strange burning on my most sensitive part. But he leaves it there only for a second before grabbing my leg and holding me steady as he hoists my thigh onto his shoulder and leans in to run his tongue along the length of my slick vulva, circling around my clit and finally closing his mouth over it.

"Oh fuck," I breathe, my arm reaching out to balance myself against the shower wall. Luca licks and sucks at my pussy ravenously, his tongue plunging in and out of my hole while his hands slide up my thighs and around to grab my ass. Without even turning away from my pussy to look, he reaches back suddenly and grabs another ice cube, then rubs it against my opening while he gently nibbles and sucks my clit. By now my legs are trembling, struggling to hold myself up in the throes of pleasure.

"Luca, oh my god, I-I'm gonna fall," I whisper, afraid of my legs giving out but not wanting the amazing sensations to end.

"I won't let you fall," he says gruffly, releasing me so he can put my leg back down and prod me to turn around so I'm facing away from him, into the spray of water. There's a metal safety bar in front of me that I bend and reach down for. Quick as a flash, Luca opens the shower curtain and steps out dripping wet to grab his belt, then walks over to fasten it around my wrists and the safety bar, binding me there.

He gets back into the shower behind me, grabbing my ass and sliding an ice cube down to my slit. "You look so beautiful tied up here for me," he growls, giving my ass a hard smack.

My pussy tingles and aches from the cold and wanting.

"Fuck me, please," I moan.

"Is that what you want, baby? My cock inside your tight little pussy?" he teases.

"Oh god yes, please," I beg, shaking my ass against him. I look back over my shoulder and he smiles widely, a devilish look on his impossibly handsome face. He slides his cock against my ass, rubbing into me as I feel my pussy aching for him. I need it.

Finally, he shoves his cock deep inside me and I cry out with pleasure as the head of his thick shaft bumps into that sensitive little spot. He holds still for a moment, just letting my pussy clench around him. I can't stand it... I need him to move. I need him to fuck me.

"Can't believe I never tied you up like this before," he comments, his voice thick and low.

I rock my hips, sliding back against him, my body begging for him to thrust.

"Greedy little girl, aren't you?" Luca groans, and I can tell it's taking all his willpower not to just give in and fuck me.

"I need you so bad," I manage to mumble.

At last, he rears back, his cock nearly sliding all the way out of me before slamming back into my pussy hard, again and again. I have to bite my lip to keep from screaming out, my wrists aching from being bound while my body trembles at the overwhelming pleasure of his cock spearing into me.

"You feel so fucking good, *dolcezza*," Luca moans, slapping my ass. His hands fall to my hips, gripping me tight as he thrusts into me faster and harder, animalistic needs overcoming his willpower as he loses himself to how good it feels. I'm already gone, my thoughts totally scattered to the wind and replaced with nothing but blinding hot pleasure.

"Harder," I murmur, and Luca obliges eagerly, picking up the rhythm and striking deeper inside me. My orgasm appears out of nowhere, and I can feel my cunt pulsating around him, shuddering with wave after wave of bliss as I whimper incoherently.

"You just love being bent over and fucked, don't you, Serena?" he grunts through gritted teeth. "Dirty little angel."

"God, I love your cock," I pant, my words slurring as I close my eyes, riding the waves of pleasure. "Feels so... fucking... good."

"I've missed this so much, your filthy mouth, your perfect body, your tight little cunt," Luca groans, his fingers digging into my hips as he fucks me. His tempo is getting erratic and wild and I can tell he's getting close to the edge, so I start moving my hips a little bit to bounce against him, adding a little more tension to each powerful thrust.

"Show me how much you missed me," I demand between thrusts.

Luca fucks me faster, leaning over slightly and reaching around underneath me to toy with my clit, rolling that sensitive little bud between his fingertips as I let out a shriek.

"Fuck! *Just* like that, Luca, yes!" I whine, feeling my second climax fast approaching.

He doesn't slow down for even a second, even when I cry out, coming again as my pussy shudders around his thickening cock. I can feel him tightening up behind me, his fingers rubbing at my clit almost too hard.

"Yes! Yes!" he grunts, and with a few more quick snaps of his hips I feel him explode his hot seed inside my pussy. He thrusts several more times, pumping me full of every last drop before withdrawing. I feel my legs trembling, my knees threatening to give out, but then Luca reaches around to undo the belt and free my hands. He tosses the belt back out of the shower and helps me stand up and turn around to kiss him passionately under the hot spray of the water. He takes the detachable shower head and sprays me down thoroughly, then to my surprise, he turns me back around and begins washing my hair with gentle hands. I can't help but sigh appreciatively at the soothing gesture.

"Ever since I was a little girl I loved having my

hair played with," I mumble as he massages green apple-scented shampoo into my scalp.

"I love you," he says suddenly. "I dreamed of doing this the whole time I was in prison."

"What? Washing my hair?" I ask, half-joking.

Luca laughs. "No. Fucking you. Holding you. Just being with you."

"I never want to be without you again," I tell him earnestly as he uses the shower head to start rinsing my hair. After that, he rubs conditioner into my hair, paying close attention to every strand. Hell, he's doing a better job of it than I do.

"I don't plan on being apart from you ever again, Serena," he says seriously.

He rinses the conditioner out of my hair, combing his fingers gently through the tangles and snarls before setting the shower head back in its dock. I turn around to face him again, planting a kiss on his soft, perfect lips. "What are we gonna do?" I ask him quietly. "We can't stay here."

"I know," he agrees.

"My mom isn't here now, but she'll be back tomorrow, and Luca… you're still a fugitive. If she sees you, I don't know what will happen. I mean, she'll ask questions. She's never met you, but I know her. She's been waiting for me to find a guy and settle down for years now," I explain.

"I know," Luca repeats. "I will have to find somewhere to hide out, at least for now."

My heart sinks. "You mean 'we' will have to find somewhere to hide out."

Luca kisses my forehead. "You have a life here, Serena. I won't disappear on you, but I also can't let you just throw away everything you have for me. I refuse to derail your life yet again. It wouldn't be fair."

"Fair? How about I let you know when something isn't fair to me, huh?" I reply adamantly.

Luca smiles fondly. "You're a spitfire, you know that?"

I shrug. "Takes one to know one. Besides, if you think I could possibly live my life the way it was without you in it… well, you don't know me half as well as you think you do. Wherever you're going, I'm going with you."

"But what about Bathing Beauty?" he asks.

Sighing, I shake my head. "Well, it's shut down for now anyway, right? Not a whole lot I can do about that. Luckily, things were going really well for a year or so there and I've got money saved up. Enough to last me a good while. To last *us* a good while."

"I can't let you do that," Luca protests, gazing into my eyes meaningfully.

"Luca," I begin, raising an eyebrow, "no offense, but I'm a grown adult. I make my own decisions. I'll spend my money and my time however I see fit. And I want to be with you. Whatever that might mean."

A smile splits his face, pride shining in his green eyes.

"You never stop amazing me, Serena De Laurentis. But I don't know where I'm going to be. My contacts are still distant at the moment, and I don't have a blueprint for the next stage of my plan yet. Things will probably get a little hairy before they get better. Who knows where I'll end up until then."

Suddenly, an idea slides into the forefront of my mind. "Wait. Let me think for a second."

"What is it?" he asks, his thick brows furrowed.

I can't help but grin as a plan hatches in my head. "I know a place. Upstate, there's this cabin my parents rented for us a couple summers when I was a kid. We went up there for some 'peace and quiet' so my dad could fish and sit in a hot tub while my mom mostly just complained about the lack of restaurants and shopping. I used to play in the woods and go swimming in the pond. Build bonfires with my dad. Grill hotdogs and hamburgers. You know, all that stereotypical family time summer stuff."

"Wow. Talk about the American dream," Luca remarks. "But I don't know if that's a great idea, Serena. Any place your parents rented must be high-profile. Fancy. The opposite of a good hiding place."

I shake my head, turning off the shower faucet and reaching for a couple of dry towels from a shelf, handing one off to Luca. "No, no. It's perfect. I'm serious. It's out in the middle of nowhere. I mean, it's probably about an hour from Ithaca, but I promise it's remote and private as hell. We didn't even have cell service the whole time we were there. Nothing. It's a dead zone."

Luca's expression changes from skeptical to considerate. "Well, I suppose we could look into it. But what about your mother? Won't she worry?"

"Pfft," I snort. "I'll just tell her I'm taking a little sabbatical. And the dead zone is a great excuse to not be in touch. It's perfect."

"And what about paying for the cabin? Don't those kinds of places usually require ID for checking in? I can't exactly show my face in public places at the moment," Luca says.

"Nah. From what I recall, the guy who runs the property isn't even there most of the time. I think he lives in a town far out of the woods. And he seems like a very laissez-faire type of guy. I don't think my dad even paid with a card. I remember him just handing over a wad of cash and getting a set of keys in exchange. Easy-peasy," I say, shrugging.

Luca nods, tying the towel around his waist. He's silent for a moment, clearly deliberating on my suggestion. Then he says, "Okay. We can try it. But I can't leave town yet. Not without taking a parting gift."

*I*'m still a wanted man. Every second I spend in this city is a risk, every night a threat of getting thrown back into that hell-hole I escaped.

I should disappear, smuggle myself back to Italy and vanish from the face of the earth for the rest of my life. But that would mean leaving Serena behind, in danger. That is no life I want to live.

My old friend Trueba comes to mind often. I worry for him, knowing he's spending time in isolation on the inside. But there was no hesitation in him when he agreed to do what he did. Old men want to live through the young, sometimes. The best thing I can do for his memory is not make the same mistakes as he did.

I won't get caught.

But I've given it more thought than that. When I realized I'd have to do something big to get the money I need to keep me and Serena safe, I couldn't help but think of Trueba's story. One big heist was all it took to make sure they were set.

But it caught up to him eventually.

Jewels are hard to trace. His mistake wasn't the heist.

It was who he stole from.

"Are you sure your man will come through for us?" I ask Nico, who sits in the passenger's seat of the car next to me. We're parked in the lot behind an old convenience store, waiting for a word from one of Nico's friends.

"I'll skin his ass if he doesn't," Nico mutters, watching his phone.

There's a jewel handoff going down tonight. While the Cleaners moving into our territory was harsh on the Costas' business, seeing which of our old contacts started working for the enemy told us who we could trust. When the Cleaners moved into the south side of the borough, a small ring of jewel smugglers we knew went silent.

That means they're working with the Cleaners now, who probably need the money, badly. Nico did some investigating and got a tip that a handoff is happening tonight. Before the sun rises, tens of thousands of dollars' worth of jewels smuggled into the country will be handed over to the Cleaners... but we have other plans.

All we're waiting on is Nico's informant to give us a location. Smugglers like this don't stick to the same sites.

I hate the jewel trade. It's a bloody business, and if there were any other way, I'd have nothing to do with it. But I'd rather the money not fall into the hands of the Cleaners, and I can use it to secure a better life for me and Serena.

As for Nico, my accomplice tonight, he's planning to use the cash to buy Rafaela a wedding ring. Since he'll be fencing the goods and putting the money in my account, I promised him I wouldn't tell.

I take a drink from the thermos of coffee in my hand when I see Nico's screen light up, and he smiles.

"Got it."

"Then it's show time," I say, and I pull out of the parking lot to start heading toward the coordinates Nico's man gave us. By the looks of things, it's just outside the city.

I drive down the highway, following the directions Nico gives me. I have to be careful out on the road. If I get pulled over, it's all over. Besides the fact that I'm a wanted fugitive, I'm carrying a lot of guns, and I don't exactly look like a harmless sportsman.

It's late at night, though, and the police are watching for drunk drivers, not men on their way to a heist.

"You know this is insane, right?" Nico asks after taking a swig of the coffee and checking his guns. "We haven't cased wherever we're going, we don't know what kind of manpower we're up against, we can't call for backup since the rest of the boys don't know we're doing this tonight."

I open my mouth to answer, but Nico interrupts me, "You're gonna say 'love makes you do crazy things, my friend,' aren't you? Don't fuckin' do it, I swear to god I'll push you out of this moving car.

Words stolen from my mouth, I just smile smugly while Nico scoffs.

❧

"He can't be serious," I say as we pull up to the wire fence near the coordinates. "Nico, I mean it, is he joking?"

Nico is biting his lip with his eyebrows raised as he looks up at the site the handoff is supposedly going down at. "This guy doesn't joke much."

We're looking up at an old, broken-down Ferris wheel, long since rusted and out of use. Not far from it is a booth advertising cotton candy and funnel cake, but the glass windows are long-since smashed in, and some of the lettering is missing. I see a rat scurry across the counter of a shooting booth that's had all the toy guns ripped out of it.

An abandoned fairground.

"Not a bad cover," I admit under my breath before I pull my ski-mask over my head. Nico does the same. We're outfitted in all black, and we have our guns strapped to us. I think about the way I looked last time I went out on a job like this, and it makes me feel like I was just a kid back then. Maybe what was left of the young buck in me died in prison. I still have the energy, but I know how to handle myself now.

Time to see if it was a change for the better.

Communicating through signs, Nico and I find an opening in the old fence and make our way inside, moving silently.

The shadows of the fairgrounds all around us seem to move out of the corner of my eye. Every now and then, I think I can hear the sound of something skittering. I know it's a rat or a bird, but I can't shake the feeling that old ghosts hang around this place.

I've never liked fairs.

Soon, I stop Nico as a more human sound reaches my ears: footsteps. I gesture for him to follow me, sticking to the shadows, and we creep closer after the sounds of several men and hushed voices up ahead.

We come around the corner of what looks like an

old haunted house-type ride, complete with a badly painted giant bat looming over the entrance. We get low and stay put, because at the open space up ahead in front of it, I see our targets.

There are five men total. It's hard to tell who is who at first, but their body language gives them away. Two of them are Cleaners: one of them is receiving a large black bag from the others, and the other man stands close to him, tall and as imposing as I might be at a meeting like this. The other three look a little more nervous as they hand off the bags. They are right to be. The Cleaners aren't to be trusted. It must have been hard for them to set this meeting up in the first place.

I smile under my mask. Icing on the cake.

Hand on my silenced pistol, I wait until nobody's gaze is turned toward us, and I raise the weapon to take aim. My sights set on the big Cleaner, but when I get a better look at the other man handing off a bag full of jewels, my heart skips a beat.

That face. I know that face.

I lower my weapon as my eyes widen, and Nico looks at me, puzzled. Any other time, I would swear my eyes are playing tricks on me, but I'd recognize that face anywhere.

One of the smugglers is a cop who was at my arrest two years ago.

Nico looks confused, but I give his arm a warning squeeze and shake my head ever so slightly, so I don't draw attention. Things just got a lot more dangerous. We can't risk killing a cop. My head is buzzing with questions, most of all, why is he here?

I'll have to worry about that later, though. For now, I have to figure out how we leave here without a cop's blood on our hands, because I'm not leaving without the jewels.

I hold Nico's arm until the men finish their transaction. Nods are exchanged, and the groups part ways. Thankfully, the smugglers are in a hurry. They'll be out of the way soon enough. We're still as shadows as each one stalks off, and the moment it's safe, I nod for Nico to follow me.

We're going to have to take down the Cleaners separately.

Nico is giving me a "what the fuck are you doing" look, but I press on. We move as quietly as we can around the building to head off the Cleaners. I'm moving faster than I should, and I have to catch myself to slow down. My thoughts are all over the place, but I have to stay focused. I can figure the rest out later.

We round the corner, and we both freeze in our tracks.

At the far end of the haunted house's side stands a third Cleaner we hadn't noticed. A lookout. And he's looking straight at us.

I have no time to think. I raise my gun, aim, and fire, all in the span of less than a second. The man jolts and staggers back, a bleeding hole in his forehead, and he falls to the ground. We'd be in the clear... if the two men with the jewels weren't just about to pass by him, each of them carrying bags.

"Fuck!" one of them shouts, and they take off in opposite directions.

There's no hesitation in me. "You take the fast one, I've got the big guy," I say, and I take off sprinting. Nico takes off the next moment, and we're on our targets like bloodhounds.

My man goes back the way they came, toward the haunted house. I round the corner just as he rounds the one further down, bringing him around to the front of the house. I curse silently as I go after him, and when I reach the corner, he's gone. There are no hiding spots nearby that I can spot, except…

My eyes fall on the haunted house, and I grit my teeth. It's a tight space with many shadows, places to hide, and a service exit somewhere inside. He chose a smart place to hide. That's not going to stop me, though.

I take my weapon out and move in after him.

It's hard to stay quiet inside the creaky old building. Each step I take risks making the rusty metal floors groan, and I can hardly see anything. The only upside is that he's at the same disadvantage. But I don't underestimate him. He had the luxury of casing this joint. He might know it better than I expect, so I can't let my guard down.

Every other thought leaves my head. I don't worry about Nico, or about what might happen outside. I'm focused on my sole task.

Keeping low, I move past the ticket stand inside. If there's a service exit, it's probably toward the back of the ride. I have no idea whether the entry or exit tunnel is the fastest to take, so I check the doorways of both before darting down the entryway.

Then I hear the sound of a shuffling footstep some ways ahead, and I know I made the right choice. If he moves too fast, he'll alert me to where he is. My eyes slowly begin to adjust to the dark, and I look in the direction of the sounds.

As if on cue, though, I hear the sounds of running footsteps down the winding hallway, and I take off after him. To my sides, I see the old deactivated skeletons and rusty monsters used to pop out at people on the ride. They're more unnerving when still and lifeless.

There's the sound of a gunshot, and I come to a halt and dive into cover, pressed up against an animatronic werewolf in a nook as I raise my weapon, ready to fire back. But there are no more shots. I peek out just long enough to look into the darkness. If he can't see me, I can't see him, but if he's blind-firing back at me, he's starting to panic. I have to use this to my advantage.

Moving as silently as I can, I hold my gun out and

start to feel my way along the wall toward the source of the gunshot.

As my hand runs along a wall, I feel it brush against something cold and metallic. I feel it more and realize that it's a switch. An emergency power switch? Brakes? Security? I hesitate a moment, but I know I need some kind of distraction, anything, so I pull the lever.

The whole building seems to shudder as the last sparks of energy course through the place. Down the hallway ahead of me, loose wiring overhead pops loudly and rains sparks down, and it lights up the room enough to show me my man, white-faced at the end of the hall.

We raise our guns at the same time and fire off, and I feel the sting of the bullet grazing my shoulder. I sprint forward and start zig-zagging my way down, but when the wires spark again, the man is gone.

The sounds of his footsteps are muffled by the mechanical whirring I hear all around now. Some generator somewhere must have a little juice left in it. I curse my luck. The half-working haunted house is a lot creepier than a dead one.

I get to the end of the hallway and halt at the corner. Behind me, I hear a rolling sound, and I turn to see one of the empty ride cars clunking its way down on the metal tracks. I let it roll around the corner, cobwebs hanging overhead, and as soon as it appears in the next hallway, I hear two gunshots ricochet off the empty car, followed by a curse.

He's waiting for me. I have to think of something.

My eye catches something across the deadly hallway that's frankly, horrifying. The ride has sparked to life, which means the animatronic monsters within are trying to move like they did when the fair was running normally. Across from me is a robotic mummy, and every few seconds, it starts to jolt around awkwardly as if trying to pop forward and scare a guest, but a big loose cable running across its chest is holding it back. That gives me an idea.

Just before the next time it pops out, I aim my gun at the cable and fire. With a spark, it's cut in two, and a second later, the mummy pops out of its plastic sarcophagus, arms raised and jaw hanging open.

"Fuck!" comes a shout from down the hallway, and there's a gunshot, and part of the mummy's head comes off from the gunshot. I take the distraction and pop out of cover myself.

Just as I planned, the man's wide eyes are fixed on the mummy, and by the time his face turns to me, my gun is trained on him, and I squeeze the trigger.

Two quick shots, and the man falls to the ground, dead. I race forward with my gun pointed at him, and I make sure he's down for good before I take the bags and sling them over my shoulder.

That went well, but I don't have any time to celebrate: Nico's still out there.

I race out of the haunted house and listen for the sound of fighting. It doesn't take long before I hear the gunshots of the other man. Nico's using a silenced pistol like me, so I can't figure out his location by listening.

I reach the gravity-spinner ride and move carefully around it before I finally see movement. Nico is blind-firing, ironically pinned down in the shooting gallery booth. Judging by where he's shooting, I can get an idea of where the Cleaner is.

I should be able to flank him. I move around the opposite side of the gravity-spinner, and I can make out motion just beyond a merry-go-round. I clench my jaw. I can't deny that the big, badly painted plastic horses will make for good cover if I want to approach quickly. I can see the shooter crouching behind an overturned popcorn stand.

No time to think of alternatives. I rush forward, still close to the ground, and before I can give the other man a chance to react, I use one of the fake horses as both cover and a rest for my arms to take aim, and with the squeeze of the trigger, the man goes down, slumping over his bag.

Nico and I are both still for a moment, as if expecting something else to happen, but after a few beats, we both stand up, grinning at each other, and

Nico shakes his head as we make our way to the corpse to get the bag.

"Shit, man, I'm glad we didn't tell the others about this after all," he says, taking the bag and slinging it over his shoulder while I check the dead man. "All this? Nobody would believe this bullshit."

We get the bags together and make our way back to the car as silently as we came in, and in a few minutes' time, we're driving back into town.

"Goddamn," Nico says as he looks over the insides of the bags. "Don't think I've ever seen this much money in one place. Even if it is in rock-form," he jokes, not daring to touch the glittering stones even now.

"Jewel thieves have the right idea," I chuckle, glancing at the payload. "You should just skip buying a ring and use one of these rocks for the engagement ring. Find a nice jeweler to do it for you on the down low."

"No shit," Nico laughs. "Nah, Rafaela would kill me." He glances at my arm and notices a dark patch in my black sweater where I'm bleeding. "Hey, you get hit, man?"

"Nothing serious," I say, shrugging my shoulder. "Got a little more muscle to absorb the sting there now. You all good?"

"He couldn't get a shot in on me," he says proudly, "but you still saved my ass back there. Reminds me why I keep helping your ass out."

We chuckle, and I jab him with my elbow. When he stops laughing, Nico looks over at me with a thoughtful look on his face.

"You've been pretty quiet about all this, though. Just what are you thinking about doing with all this cash? 'Keep Serena safe' is a little vague."

"I'll worry about that," I say, smiling. "I've got something special in mind for my share of the cash."

It's a beautiful day, with the kind of crystalline blue skies and puffy white clouds that would look more natural on a painting than in reality. The sun shines down cheerfully over the winding road in front of us, and a delicious earthy breeze filters in through the rolled-down car windows.

Luca has his elbow resting on the window frame, gripping the steering wheel with one hand while the other reaches over to hold mine. He turns to smile at me, looking absolutely gorgeous in his shining aviator shades and just a hint of a prickly five o'clock shadow. He's wearing a white t-shirt with the sleeves slightly rolled, blue jeans, and brown boots. He looks like a rugged, sexy woodsman heading out for a day of tromping through the forest. And I guess that's not too far off from what we're about to do.

The drive up here from Riverdale has been amazing; perfect weather the whole time. Ever since I was a little kid I've loved road trips, and I always dreamed of going on a long drive like this with a handsome man who made my heart flutter. I smile and think, *wow, young Serena would be so happy if she could see us now.*

Of course, everything isn't roses and sunshine. Luca more or less disappeared for about a week after that day at my house in Riverdale. He kept in touch this time, sending me updates from a burner phone, just like old times. Only now he doesn't keep me waiting in such dreadful suspense.

I don't know what kinds of shenanigans he got into, and I didn't dare ask (honestly, I don't know if I even want to know), but when he turned up to collect me for this trip upstate, he did look a little worse for wear, like maybe he's been in some kind of fight. I know he leads a dangerous life, and now that he's a fugitive, danger lurks around every corner. But I have to swallow down my fear. After all, you can't love a dangerous man without expecting some rough patches, right?

Besides, he's with me safe and sound now, and that's what matters to me: collecting these precious little moments together when they come along. I used to think I wanted stability, calmness.

Now I know I just want Luca, regardless of what that might mean.

"God, it's a gorgeous day," I remark, gazing out the window at the trees and other vegetation starting to thicken around us as we drive.

"Perfect," Luca agrees. "I can see why your family used to vacation up here."

"It's been so long since I came here last, but it doesn't even look any different. Well, some of the trees look bigger, but otherwise it's all the same. It's weird to think about how much I've changed, how different my life is now, but it's like time didn't touch this part of the planet," I muse aloud, dangling my arm out the window for a moment to feel the breeze.

"Like stepping back in time," he says.

"Exactly."

The car rumbles over a rough spot and I notice the paved road has given way to gravel now, the tires crunching as we roll along. "Sorry about your tires. I forgot about the gravel."

"This car has definitely seen worse times than this," Luca laughs. "Besides, I'm an excellent driver."

I raise an eyebrow and glance at him, amused. "Well, you're not lacking for confidence, are you, Mr. Tokyo Drift?"

"Trust me, when you've worked the kind of job I have, you quickly learn to be an expert with all the tools of the trade. Tactical driving is just part of the necessary skill set," Luca explains.

"Oh, up ahead! Look!" I exclaim, scooting

forward in my seat and pointing toward a small wooden structure just barely peeking out from behind the trees down the path.

"Is that it?" he asks. "Where do we go to check in?"

"Oh, it's not that complicated. There's kind of a scout's honor type system up here. You just leave the money in an envelope in the mailbox when you leave," I tell him. "Come to think of it, I'm starting to understand why my dad liked this place so much. Privacy and convenience. A property owner who doesn't ask questions and couldn't be bothered to care anyway."

"A Mafioso's paradise," Luca agrees, grinning.

"So many things are starting to make sense looking back now," I sigh, shaking my head. "But whatever the purpose was, I have a lot of great memories here. It's so nice to be back. I can't wait to show you around and frolic in nature with you."

I squeeze his hand and he laughs. "This is definitely more your speed than mine, but it will be interesting to say the least."

"Oh, you'll love it, I promise."

Luca pulls the car up to a spot next to the cabin and as soon as he turns off the engine and the doors unlock, I burst out of the car and take off toward the dense woods, unable to keep a grin off of my face. Luca takes off after me, but when I look back I notice he still looks a little tense, glancing over his shoulder like he's afraid someone might randomly appear behind us. Like he's still worried that we might be watched or followed, even all the way out here in the middle of nowhere. I decide to make it my mission to distract him and get him to relax by whatever means necessary, and I already have a few ideas in mind.

"Come on!" I shout back at him, heading down a barely-there path in the forest. I'm navigating more by instinct than logic, hoping my memory will lead me in the right direction. Just as I stop short at a little babbling creek, Luca catches up to me and grabs me in his arms, swinging me around as I cry out in mock fear. He sets me back down and kisses me, cupping my face in his huge hands as we stand on the mushy bank of the creek.

"Are we going to cross this thing?" he asks, gesturing toward the water.

I take note of a few smooth, large boulders in the creek and nod. "Of course! We're just going to step across those rocks there." I break away from him and deftly hop across to the other side of the creek, beckoning for him to follow. Luca looks a little skeptical at first, but then he easily leaps across.

"Fun, right? Hopping around the streams was one of my favorite things to do here as a little kid. It's easy to do nowadays, but when I was small it was way more intimidating, I swear," I admit, laughing.

"I bet you were the cutest little girl," Luca says. "I

can just picture you tiny and courageous, crossing a creek like some brave adventurer."

"I definitely felt like that's what I was," I say, smiling widely. "Well, let's keep going. I think we're on the right path."

"To where?"

"You'll see!" I exclaim, bolting through the trees again with Luca close behind. My heart is racing, my lungs filled with fresh forest air. The sun reaches down in golden-white streaks through the canopy, illuminating patches of earth. I feel happier than I've been in a very long time, like I'm finally free. Despite growing up as mostly a city girl, with my Manhattan apartment, designer clothes, and trust fund friends, I think I've always been a country girl at heart. Or something like that. I feel so at home here in the woods, running free and wild where nobody is around to judge me for my lack of composure. I can be myself here, and only the trees and lurking wildlife can watch.

Luca darts up behind me and scoops me into his arms, carrying me for a few minutes. We're both laughing openly, grinning from ear to ear as we race along down the narrow path. If you weren't looking for the trail, you wouldn't notice it, because the grass and weeds have begun to reclaim it. I imagine business must be pretty slow for the cabin owner lately. On the one hand, it makes me sad that this place seems to be largely forgotten, but on the other hand, it's nice to know that it's almost like my own personal private world. Like I alone know the secrets of this magical forest.

Luca sets me down and we start walking briskly, hand in hand, down the way as the sound of rushing water grows louder. He looks at me in confusion. "What is that?"

"Be patient. You'll see," I tease him, poking my tongue out at him.

A few more minutes of walking and we arrive at our destination: a small but beautiful waterfall tucked away behind a thick patch of trees we nearly have to squeeze through to reach. Luca's face changes from confusion to full of wonder, and I can't help but beam at how happy he looks. I can tell he never expected to come across something like this, and I'm overjoyed that I got the opportunity to put that look of awe on his face.

"You like it?" I pipe up, biting my lip.

Luca turns and kisses me passionately, holding me close. When he breaks away he says softly, "This is beautiful, Serena. Thank you for taking me here. I — we — needed this."

"Agreed. That's what I love so much about being out in nature. It's like hitting refresh on your whole life, like all your problems stay behind in the city and you can finally breathe again," I say, shaking my head in amazement at how lovely it all is. "I can't believe I waited so long to come back here. I could've really used a visit here during all those difficult years."

"I never got to do things like this growing up," Luca says, standing with his hands on his hips as he surveys the scene appreciatively. "Back home in Italy I ran around the countryside sometimes, just causing trouble with my equally delinquent friends. But it wasn't like this. And when I came to America, my childhood was over. I went from a scrappy little kid to a man overnight, becoming my uncle's apprentice, learning the carpentry trade. Sometimes I wonder how different I would be if I had stayed in Italy. Or if the mafia had never threatened my family."

"I'm sorry," I tell him earnestly, taking his hand. "I can't imagine what you've been through. I wish you'd had a chance to grow up like any other kid, instead of having those years stolen away from you."

Luca shrugs and gives me a peaceful smile. "It is what it is. And besides, the way I see it, all those shitty things only led me down the path to you. And that makes it all worth it."

He pulls me close and kisses me again, his hands stroking my hair, sliding down to grab my ass as he pushes against me. I feel that familiar flicker of tingling warmth pass down my body and makes me shiver. I know exactly what I want. Right here, right now.

Luca leads me over to a huge patch of soft moss

on the dry rocks off to one side of the waterfall, where every now and then a stray fleck of water flies over to land on us. He guides me to the ground, his fingers tangling into my hair as he stares into my eyes. I'm transfixed, held captive in the perfect, blissful moment.

There's no sounds of the city, no fear in my heart, no sorrow. It feels like I've shed myself of all the baggage I've been carrying for so long.

For the first time, I feel totally reunited with my long lost lover, without all the worries and fear marring every emotion. Ever since he's returned, I keep having the feeling that it's fleeting. That soon, he'll be caught. That he'll be taken away from me once more, and I'll have to face life without him all over again.

But in the peace and serenity of the forest, no one can touch us.

Luca's fingers work along my skin, snaking up beneath my shirt as his lips press against mine. His tongue is soft but exploratory as it swipes across my lower lip, leaving his taste on me as he easily unhooks my bra.

He makes quick work of my jeans and panties, as well, folding all my clothing into a neat little stack beside us before he strips out of his own clothes. Goosebumps prickle up on my skin, our bodies both totally exposed to the cool, fresh air.

"You know, this is strangely similar to a dream I

had one night while I was locked up," Luca says softly, kissing his way down to my breasts. "I dreamed that you and I were making love on the edge of a massive waterfall. Of course, in the dream there were also talking trees, but that's beside the point."

I giggle at that image but my laughter is interrupted by a sigh as Luca gently bites and sucks at my nipples, his hand trailing down to cup my mound. "Well, I'm glad these trees don't talk because I'd hate for them to tell anyone about this. Two people fucking in the woods, surrounded by nothing but nature."

"Yeah, I would hate for them to tell anybody about how wet you are when I touch you, how you shiver when I stroke your sweet little clit," Luca growls, his fingertip swirling around that tight, sensitive bud while my hips rock back and forth involuntarily.

"Oh fuck," I moan as he slides down between my thighs to lick and suck at my pussy. I reach down and tangle my fingers in his dark hair, gently pushing him down into my cunt. The waterfall pounds away, the constant white noise of rushing water only adding to the symphony of sensations I'm feeling. Just before I come, Luca pulls away.

I whimper plaintively, disappointed.

But he quickly pulls me up and lies on his back, moving me to straddle him. I bite my lip, eager to ride his cock. I position the head of his shaft at my slick opening and slowly slide him inside of me, groaning with pleasure as I sheath him completely.

"Fuck, Serena. I want you to ride my cock hard. I want to fill you up and make you ache," Luca instructs, his voice husky and low. I begin rolling my hips, slowly and carefully at first, then more frantically as my climax approaches. It doesn't take long for me to explode, crying out as I start bouncing up and down on his cock, feeling him strike my g-spot over and over again.

"Ohh, it feels so fucking good," I murmur, closing my eyes as I ride him harder and faster. Luca's hands slide up to cup and massage my breasts, his fingertips passing over my nipples and making me tremble, starting to lose control. I don't want to go slow. I want to fuck him hard and fast, give in to my animalistic desires.

Luca sits up and pulls my legs around him so that we're facing, my knees hooked around his waist. He kisses me, reaching down between us to rub my clit while I ride his cock. I moan into his mouth as he takes control, bouncing me up and down and thrusting up into my pussy.

"Good girl, good girl. Come for me," Luca murmurs in my ear, his warm breath sending shivers down my neck. Almost as though by magic, I come immediately, my whole body shaking with the waves of intense pleasure. Luca leans me backward, holding me up with his free arm so that I'm nearly horizontal, still speared by his cock as he thrusts up into me and strokes my clit.

He picks up the pace, slamming into me with loud, wet smacks, and I can tell he's getting closer and closer. "Ready for me to come inside you, *dolcezza?*" he says, circling his thumb over my clit so that I'm almost overstimulated to the point of exhaustion.

"Yes! Oh God, yes!" I manage to choke out, my heart hammering away beneath my ribs.

"Fuck!" he bellows, seizing up and shooting his sweet seed deep inside of me as I come at the exact same time, my whole body going limp as my pussy clenches around him. He thrusts a few more times, his hands still on my back, holding me still. His gaze holds mine, both of us recovering from our orgasms.

He kisses me as he withdraws, both of us falling on our backs, panting and sweaty. The fine mist of the waterfall is welcome, cooling our skin as we lie there totally spent and happy. Luca grabs my hand and squeezes it.

"If I die and go to heaven and it isn't exactly like this, I'm going to feel so cheated," he says, laughing. "I genuinely cannot imagine anything better than this."

"Everywhere is paradise with you," I tell him, glancing over to meet his vivid green gaze with a smile. "What's that song? Heaven is a place on earth?"

"That's the one," he agrees, kissing my hand. We lie there in silence for a few more minutes, both coming down from our shared high.

Finally, I can't keep those questions at bay anymore and I ask hesitantly, "Luca, where were you this past week? You just kind of went off on your own. And when you came back, you had all that money. What happened? What did you do?"

He looks over at me with a pained expression. "I didn't want to worry you."

"I know. But I would rather have some idea of what's going on. That scares me way more: the unknown," I explain truthfully. I thought it would be easier not knowing, but it's clear to me now that the secrets scare me more than the truth possibly could.

"Okay. I was involved in a theft. A big time. A heist, you might even say."

"What?" I burst out, sitting up and looking at him with wide eyes. Luca sits up, too.

Calmly, he explains the whole operation, and I listen intently, my mind racing in a million directions.

"I can't believe you would take a huge risk like that just after breaking out of prison. Luca, you're a fugitive. That raises the stakes for everything."

"I know. But Serena, you have to understand that taking risks is part of my job. It's just the way I have to live my life. I promise that I'm as careful as can be. I take risks, but they're calculated risks," he says. "And I knew you would be afraid, so I kept it from you."

I bite my lip.

"Luca, listen to me. I know you think I'm some delicate little flower you have to protect from all the dangers of your world. But remember that I grew up around the mob, too. Even though I didn't know much about it then, and I didn't know any different, my dad was involved in some pretty illicit stuff. And after he died... " I shook my head. "Luca, not knowing what was going to happen to me, if I was going to... if that man was going to be able to touch me... I didn't know if that was my life. And not knowing, I imagined all the worst scenarios. That's what it's like when you leave me, without telling me. My imagination runs wild. Besides, I'm in love with you. Anything you have to deal with you should be able to share with me. Okay?"

Luca shakes his head in amazement, smiling at me warmly.

"Most women would shy away from a guy like me. How are you so brave?"

I shrug, leaning over to kiss him.

"Love makes you brave. From now on, I want to know what's going on. Even if it's dark. Even if it's dangerous. I want to have a say."

"I'll do my best to include you," he concedes,

kissing me again. "I could never deny you anything, you know that? You've got some kind of crazy hold on me."

"It's my superpower," I joke, grinning. "But if we're going to be on the run, undercover and underground and all that, I think we need new aliases."

"Aliases?" Luca repeats, giving me a dubious look.

"Yeah! You know, like code names or something. Fake names."

"That's not usually how we operate, but I'm intrigued now. What name would you give me? Or yourself?" he asks, amused.

I squint at him, thinking hard for a moment.

"Hmm. We need a theme or something. Shakespeare, maybe. Like, you could be Horatio. Or Lysander."

"Oh, those are terrible," Luca laughs. "And what would you be called? Juliet?"

"Juliet? So mainstream! I take it you didn't study as much Shakespeare as I was forced to read," I giggle, pondering female character names. "I could be Rosaline or maybe Olivia."

"Your names are way better than mine," Luca points out. "I sense some unfairness here."

"Fine, you can be something normal like Alexander," I tease, nudging him with my shoulder. Then, I sober up and add, "But seriously, Luca, I don't want there to be any more secrets between us. If this is going to work, we need to be honest with each other. No surprises. No hiding things. You trust me, right?"

"Of course I do. Trust was never the problem," he answers seriously.

"Okay. Good. It's settled then," I declare, grinning. "You and me, we're a team."

Inwardly, I make a different promise: that I'm going to take life by the horns from now on. If I'm going to be on equal grounds with Luca, I need to be brave. Not reckless, but definitely courageous. I need to be strong and assertive. I need to take charge.

"No more trying to 'protect' me by keeping things from me. After all, I always find out sooner or later anyway," I say, shrugging.

"Sounds fair to me. If you think you can handle it, I won't hold back," he says. Then he adds, "Seems like as good a time as any to break out of my usual routine."

I look at him confused as he gets up and offers me his hand.

*What the hell does he mean by that?*

*D*owntown Ithaca is not a world I'm familiar with in the least, even with Serena around my arm at my side. It was my idea to come out here, but with every passing second, I'm feeling more like a fish out of water.

There's none of the bustle of the city here, none of the rush and looming buildings that I was just getting used to calling *home* back in the Bronx. It's almost too quiet for my taste, but I have to admit, I feel like I can breathe here. There's plenty of green, and fewer people look anxious or stormy.

That doesn't help my situation, though. I'm clad in the same old clothes I had before we left, and while I'm not one to worry about fashion, I can tell I stick out here. As we walk down the wide brown sidewalk flanked by shops on all sides, Serena notices how often I'm adjusting the hood and sunglasses I'm wearing to hide my appearance. She finishes off the mint gelato I bought for us a few minutes ago and throws the napkin into a public trashcan, coming to a stop as she does.

"Relax," she says, stroking my arm as I smile down at her. "We're miles away from, well, everything. NYC may as well be a whole different country up here."

"That's part of the problem," I say, looking around at the hipster couples with big hairstyles and sweaters. That gives me an idea, though. A thoughtful smile on my face, I look over at some of the outlet shops nearby, then down at Serena, who tilts her head to the side.

"Whatcha thinking?"

"That we didn't bring enough clothes," I say, smiling a little more broadly at Serena, whose eyebrows go up.

"I... never thought I'd hear you say that," she admits.

"No, but you've been through a lot. I don't get enough chances to spoil you like a proper Italian girl." That makes her blush and smile, and I take her hand to tug her along into the nearest designer clothing store to start spending some of that money I worked so hard to get.

Serena's eyes light up as soon as we enter the place. I can see her mind going back to when she was a teenager on her father's big budget, because I don't have to look at the price tags on some of the clothes in here to know they're above what she usually gets.

"Ohhhh, this is good. This is very good," she says, wandering in ahead of me and looking at the various odds and ends of the fall line of clothes. She looks back at me with glittering eyes and an eager smile.

"Are you sure about this? If you really turn me loose in here, I think I can put a dent in that paycheck of yours." She winks, half-joking, but even if she were dead-serious, I couldn't deny her anything.

"Don't think about the price," I assure her, stepping over to her and planting a kiss on her forehead. "I'll take care of that part."

That's all it takes to get her going on a tour of the store that seems to warm her soul. After about an hour of trying things on, getting new sizes, and even experimenting a little, Serena finally comes out of the dressing room with an ensemble she looks like a regular local in: an oversized, unreasonably cozy green sweater that still makes her body look irresistible. She picks out an equally oversized tan-brown scarf that goes with it and matching tall boots and black leggings.

Even though I've been getting odd looks the whole time I've been in here, my stony expression splits into a grin when I see her, partly because of how cute she looks in her outfit, partly because her happiness is so infectious.

"What do you think?" she asks, holding her arms out and twirling in place, and before she finishes, I wrap my arms around her and pick her up, to her delight, kissing her on the neck.

"Perfect," I say, setting her down and giving a smile to the dressing room attendant, who stands awkwardly nearby. "We'll take it. All of it."

That changes the attendant's mood quite a bit. A few minutes later, I've convinced the store owner to let Serena wear the new outfit out of the store with her old clothes in the bag. Something about the way Serena's eyes widen when I hand the cashier a big wad of cash fills me with pride. I like providing for her, even if it's on things that aren't totally essential.

When we walk out of the store, I can't help but laugh at the new spring in Serena's step.

"I never knew you had such a thing for new clothes."

"It's one of those things I kind of reward myself with when it's been a really good week at the shop," she says, wiggling a little when I hug her to my side. "I mean, nothing this nice or this much, but a little thing here and there is good." But it isn't long before her eyes get thoughtful as she looks my outfit up and down, smiling mischievously.

"What?" it's my turn to ask.

"Your turn, obviously," she says, and before I can

protest through my chuckles, she's tugging my big arm toward the closest men's apparel store.

This is as much for Serena as it is for me.

My tastes are usually simple. I went through most of my life in the Bronx in jeans, a white t-shirt, and a leather jacket. Apparently, I need to get a little more creative than that to fit in up here in Ithaca. Fortunately, I don't have to leave my style behind too much to do that.

After a few minutes, I come out of the dressing room with an outfit that Serena seems to like very much. Even though the hand-knit tan sweater is the biggest size they have, my muscles are still visible underneath, making it a snug, warm fit. Over it, I get a big coat in a darker brown with a flared collar, and I finish the ensemble with a simple crimson beanie and a new set of aviator sunglasses. I get a new set of jeans and boots, too, just in case I wasn't fitting in with the outdoorsy style enough.

I like it mostly because it keeps my appearance a little less than obvious, but the smile from Serena and the big thumbs-up from the attendant tell me it's stylish enough that I won't stick out like a sore thumb anymore.

One big fat receipt later, we step out onto the street again like new people. I have to admit, it feels good to be wearing a new set of clothes. Serena can't stop looking up at me, either, which gives me a quiet sense of pride.

"See something you like?"

"A lot," she says, a silly grin on her face, but then she narrows her eyes, reaching up and touching my beard. "Just one more thing to freshen up, and you'll be a new man."

Another hour later, we step out of a hipster-y barber shop, and I've got a new haircut and trimmed beard. You'd never guess I spent the past two years locked away in prison. I started to protest the haircut since I'll be wearing the beanie anyway, but Serena insisted.

I can't argue with the results, either.

"So, I've never been this far north," I say as it starts to get closer to the time to get an evening bite to eat. "What does a perfectly normal, definitely-not-fugitive couple get to eat in upstate New York?"

"Good question," she giggles, playfully slapping me on the chest, "but maybe don't google 'what do fugitives eat,' ok?" We laugh and wander around a little more, but it isn't long before we spot a place that looks good to both of us. When price isn't an issue, those kinds of things get a lot easier.

We step through the doors of a local brewpub, a building with exposed brick and a cozy interior, complete with a roaring fireplace toward the back of the building and wooden tables all around. There's a good mood in the place I can't quite put my finger on. Maybe it's what Americans call *good vibes*.

A little while later, both of us are sitting side-by-side at a corner table, backs to the walls so I can see the whole place, and the waiter brings us the beer and cheese soup we ordered, complete with breadsticks and some rich, dark beers.

"Carbs on carbs on carbs," Serena says as I wet my lips and take the bread basket to start loading my plate. "You really know how to spoil a girl, huh? Good to know prison didn't change that."

"After prison food," I say after a long drink of the outstanding beer, "you learn to love the little pleasures in life like good food."

"You won't hear me complaining," she says with a smile, and she takes a drink of her beer and blushes after setting it down. "Wow, little stronger than I was expecting."

"It's not Italian, but I think I can appreciate American drinking," I say, and we dig into our food. It's hearty and hot, exactly what you'd want on a fall day that's just starting to get cool enough for sweaters and boots. The cheese is rich, the beer helps us relax, and the atmosphere of other young people chatting and enjoying themselves makes us feel... comfortable. It's not something I'm used to, I realize.

Just *being* somewhere with Serena is a special pleasure I missed dearly.

"You look thoughtful," Serena says as she sets down her beer, going through it a little faster than I am. It's making her cheeks rosy, and the whole picture of her looking a little tipsy in that sweater against the brick wall makes my heart feel all the warmer.

"I just forgot how much luxury there is in the world," I say, looking around at the place with a smile on my face. "I know this place doesn't look like much, but it's these little things you forget when you're locked away."

"Like beer and cheese soup?" she asks with a playful smile on her face that I return.

"Yes, like beer and cheese soup," I say. "Really though. Little things. Walls and floors that aren't gray concrete. The feel of a warm fire. Clothes that aren't the same thing every day." I look back to her. "Spending time with you."

I kick her gently under the table, and she crosses her leg with mine, resting her chin on her hands and beaming at me.

"Those letters really did keep me going in there," I say to her, leaning forward. "I would have lost sight of the real world and all its pleasures. They were like... little breaths of fresh air before going back down under again. I can't believe how much I took for granted out here."

She nods thoughtfully, swirling her beer around. "I've thought about that too. There's so much I don't even think about in my day to day life."

"One thing I could never take for granted, though," I say in a low, husky tone, and I lean forward to kiss her on the lips which she meets with a soft, surprised moan, made all the warmer by the beer.

When we break apart, I pull out a few bills and set them on the table. I nod over to the couches by the fireplace as another group gets up to leave. "I've got the bill. Want to get a few more drinks?"

Serena hesitates a moment, biting her lip and squirming in her chair. I know that look: she's not used to spending that much, not for a long time. But I put a hand on her smaller ones and give her a reassuring smile, and that old excitement comes back to her eyes. "Oh, sure, why not?"

Serena goes to 'save' the seat while I go and get more drinks: a beer for me and a mixed drink for her, one of the fancy cocktails she picked out from the menu with cinnamon and whisky. When I walk back over to her, I can see she's already curled herself up by the fire, looking at me with the firelight dancing off her hair.

She looks radiant. Every time I see her, I'm reminded of how lucky I am to have her with me, and it reminds me what I'm fighting for. It's not just me anymore. A lot of young men forget that. I'm not so foolish.

I sit down, making the couch groan in protest under my bulk as I wrap my big arm around her and hug her to me while we clink our glasses together softly in the fire's warmth. We're almost too close to the fire that it burns, keeping just barely out of harm's way, still enjoying ourselves together. It's just like our everyday life, but so much richer.

"I think I could get used to a place like this," I say, running my hand up and down her arm as she sips her drink through the tiny straws they gave her.

"Are we turning into upstate hipsters now?" she giggles, wiggling her hips into me.

"Not quite," I chuckle, "but I have to admit, I missed the quiet life."

"Was your hometown quiet?" she asks.

"Kind of. Taranto isn't a quiet place. But my home was on the outskirts of town, and it's a lot more peaceful out there. Not nearly as rich as you are here, but there's something to be said for the... rustic charm," I say, smiling down at her before planting a kiss on her lips. I feel my manhood growing between my legs, and even though I can't act on it here, it makes me feel even closer to Serena.

"I could get into that," she says.

"You might like it around here more, I think," I say, "but I'd like to take you there sometime. Here, though," I say, pointing to the tables around the place, "I can tell some friend of the owners must be a carpenter. These are good tables. Chairs, too. They make some of these things in factories to look like they're handmade, but any real carpenter can tell the difference."

She nestles her head into my shoulder and gives a contented sigh. "I suppose I could see us up here. My shop could do alright in a place like this, and everyone needs carpenters."

"True," I say, squeezing her thigh, "I could go just about anywhere you think you'd like to set your business up. Not that the Bronx is too terrible."

"It's alright," she says, wistfully looking into the fire, "just... a lot of baggage, you know?"

"I do know," I say, staring into the fire with her. We're quiet for a few moments, but she looks back up at me and smiles.

"I'd rather make new memories with you."

I bring my face down to hers, and we lock lips, a deep, long kiss. I don't care that we're in public. I love the feel of her melting into me as our tongues explore each other briefly, and we break apart. I'm about to kiss her again when the sound of music reaches our ears, and I turn my head to see a band playing live music up on stage. It's folksy, and to my surprise, the singer is Italian, singing in my mother tongue. I have to admit, they're not bad, and I smile at them.

Serena nudges me.

"Hey, it's kinda like the old world music you and your friends used to listen to."

I blink and give her a confused look, laughing.

"Wait, do you think this is what that sounded like?"

"Shut up, it is!" Serena says, giggling yet blushing, self-conscious.

I laugh and hug her close to me, peppering her in kisses as I set my finished drink on the table and start to stand up. "Okay, now I *have* to bring you back home and show you the real music. But at least I can remind you how we dance back home."

"Luca, this is a restaurant!" she laughs as I pull her to her feet, but I don't care.

"Good, we can show them too," I say, and we start dancing to the lively tune in front of the fire. The band catches on and keeps the good vibes going, encouraging us to keep going as we move to the rhythm and Serena nearly falls over from laughing so much, the alcohol and the mood getting to her.

Works every time.

But soon, the song winds down, and I don't want to attract *too* much attention to ourselves. I admit, it was a little irresponsible to start dancing with my girl in a crowded restaurant, but nobody's going to recognize us here.

Besides, a life not taking risks for your loved ones isn't a life worth living.

I open my eyes to the sight of golden sunshine streaming in through the window, through the pale green privacy curtains Luca always keeps pulled shut. They're sheer enough to let the light in, but provide just enough coverage to be worth closing. I know for a fact there isn't going to be anyone all the way out here watching us, but Luca is still paranoid, understandably. He's a dangerous man on the run, and I know there are so many different factions of equally or more dangerous men looking for him. Still, I wish he would relax a little here at the cabin.

I check my cell phone tucked under the pillow charging and see that it's already after eleven. With a yawn, I hold my arms up over my head and stretch, reveling in the slight achiness of my body. I smile to myself, knowing exactly why I'm so sore today: last night we had some seriously acrobatic sex. Amazing acrobatic sex. Luca bent and positioned my body in ways I didn't even think I could manage.

I turn over in bed, instinctively reaching out for Luca, but to my confusion, he's not there. The spot beside me in bed is empty and cold, and my heart sinks. Despite my desire for Luca to relax, in moments like this I can't help but panic a little myself. I quickly sit up, holding the sheets to my neck to cover myself, and look around the room. His stuff still appears to be in the same places: his jacket hanging over the corner chair, his bag on the floor by the bathroom entrance. So he couldn't have gone far. Unless he didn't go willingly.

I swallow hard, feeling the hairs prick up on the back of my neck.

"Luca?" I call out, my voice scratchy and rough as it always is first thing in the morning. There's no reply, and my pulse quickens as I gingerly, quietly scoot out of bed and pull a robe around my body to go search for him. Just as I start to walk across the bedroom, there's a soft *thunk* from the other side of the cabin and I freeze in place. Then I hear footsteps, rather heavy, like a man wearing boots. Someone is whistling cheerfully. I feel like I'm going to faint for a second, my heart is racing so quickly, but then it occurs to me that the intruder is whistling a familiar tune: Sinatra's "Strangers in the Night." Luca and I played that last night on the cabin's ancient entertainment center (the thing had to have been bought in the eighties) while we cooked dinner together.

"Luca?" I ask hopefully. The footsteps get louder as the intruder comes through the doorway and I let out a sigh of relief to see that it is, in fact, the man I love, and not some murderous hit man breaking in to kill me. Although, considering Luca's history, I suppose maybe I should reserve judgement on hit men from now on. He looks a good deal different from how he did when we first arrived here at the cabin a month or so ago, with his hair grown out and his beard full and bushy. He always looks so rugged and woodsy nowadays, and while it's a much different version of him than I'm used to, I can't say I don't love the lumberjack look on him.

"You're up," Luca says, smiling as he leans in to kiss me gently. "I thought after last night you would want to sleep in a little longer. Maybe I didn't work you as hard as I could have," he adds with a wink. My cheeks burn pink.

"It's after eleven. This is sleeping in for me. In fact, I can't remember the last time I woke up after nine. I think the sunlight woke me up. Or the birds singing outside," I guess.

"This place really is idyllic," he says. "Isn't it better to wake up to the sound of birds instead of an alarm clock?"

"Oh, definitely. I don't know how I'll ever go

back to that stupid beeping after this," I agree. "What are you doing up so early, though?"

Luca looks away, a small gesture that most people wouldn't catch, but I know him better than anything. He's big on eye contact, always holding my gaze when we speak. So whenever he averts his eyes I know something is up. I notice that he does look a little weary, a little sleep-deprived. But then he just shrugs.

"I was just setting up a couple more cameras around the premises," he admits, taking off his coat and hanging it over the chair with his thicker jacket.

"Oh," I say simply. Then I can't help but step up to him and take his face in my hands, looking up into his gorgeous face. "Luca, don't get me wrong, I know the stakes are really high for us right now. Especially for you. And I get that you want to be cautious, but… I don't think you need to be this paranoid."

I feel a tiny bit hypocritical lecturing him on this directly after I mistook him for an intruder coming in to murder me, but still. It needs to be said.

Luca smiles warmly and turns to kiss each of my hands before pulling me in for a tight hug. His beard is scratchy against my forehead and I wrinkle my nose at the ticklish feeling.

"I will try my best to relax," he promises. "I just want to be as sure as possible that we're safe here. I could never forgive myself if you got hurt just because you're with me."

"I don't even remember you buying extra cameras," I laugh. "When did you do that? The last time we were in Ithaca—"

"You went to the frozen foods section and I just took a little meander through the electronics department," he answers, a little sheepishly.

"Damn. You're sneaky," I remark, raising an eyebrow.

He shrugs. "Well, considering the profession I've worked for the better part of a decade, that really shouldn't be much of a surprise."

"Speaking of surprises," I begin, "you did kinda scare me this morning when I woke up and you weren't here. I know I just got finished telling you to relax, but I was a little worried. I think we could all do with fewer surprises around here, don't you think?"

Luca kisses my forehead, a mischievous light in his eyes. "Well, how about just *one* more surprise? It's a good one, I swear."

"Uh, okay. What is it?" I ask, taken aback.

"Get dressed and I'll show you. It's outside."

I quickly put on jeans, a thick sweater, a coat, and my well-worn boots. Luca puts his jacket on and leads me out of the house into the brisk December air. The sun shines down, warming us even as the breeze makes me shiver. I'm not as accustomed to upstate New York winters, having only ever visited here during the warm summer months. The other day we actually had a flurry of snow, which was beautiful to watch from the warmth of the cabin.

"Where are you taking me?" I pipe up, crunching through the dead leaves on the ground.

"Just down the hill toward the pond."

We walk for several minutes until we arrive at the squelchy, muddy bank of the pond and Luca tells me to close my eyes. I oblige, standing there feeling a little bit foolish until he announces that I can look. I open my eyes and see him beaming at me, standing next to what looks to be a hand-built two-person canoe.

"What is that?" I ask, grinning.

"It's a canoe, obviously," he replies, gesturing to it. "Can't you *tell* what it is?"

I detect just the slightest note of concern in his voice, like he's second-guessing his ability to make an instantly recognizable boat-like structure, and I burst out laughing. "Yes, yes, I can tell it's a boat. I just mean, where did it come from?"

"I built it myself. For you. Well, and for me. Two people can ride in it."

"Again, when did you find the time to do this?" I inquire incredulously.

"Here and there. Mostly while you were cooking meals or taking naps. You know, for such an ambitious, detail-oriented woman, you are shockingly unobservant sometimes," he chuckles.

"This is amazing, Luca. Seriously, I can't believe you just happen to know how to build a boat. Are you sure it's sea-worthy? Well, pond-worthy?" I ask, biting my lip.

"I'm sure. I am a carpenter, after all. I've been itching to try a project like this for a long time. And if it makes you feel any better, I did read about a hundred articles on how to build the perfect boat. So I have the great experts of the internet to back me up," he jokes. "So, how about it? Want to take this baby for a ride? Don't worry, I only bought one set of oars because I'm going to do all the work."

I hesitate, looking nervously at the little boat. It's not that I don't trust Luca's craftsmanship, I've just always been kind of wary of large bodies of water. I mean, I have spent most of my life living in New York City. It's not like I've encountered all that many opportunities to ride in a boat. Even when I used to go swimming and fishing with my dad here growing up, it would always take about half an hour of coaxing and reassurance before I would get over my fear. And that was with a professionally-made fiberglass boat rental, not a little wooden canoe made by an admittedly talented guy who usually builds house frames, not boats.

"Come on, I even packed us a picnic," Luca urges

me, pointing to a little woven basket sitting at one end of the boat.

"This is so cute," I laugh. "You're so prepared."

"Always," he says, grinning. "I promise it'll be fine. I won't let you fall out of the boat or anything. I've got you."

"I know you do," I tell him, nodding. I heave a sigh. "Okay. Fine. I'll do it. But only because you worked your ass off to make this beautiful little boat. Plus, I'm starving."

Luca helps me settle into one end of the canoe, then takes the oars and pushes us off from the shore, sitting at the other end of the boat. I can feel my stomach turning a little as I look back and see the banks of the pond drifting back away from us as we move out into the open water. It's a small enough pond that you can see shore from all points, but just big enough to be passable for fishing and swimming.

"What are you thinking about right now?" Luca asks. I giggle.

"Just remembering how my mom used to get so angry when Dad and I came back to the cabin dripping wet and muddy after hanging out at the pond all day. She's always been such a clean freak, but back in the city we had a maid when I was growing up. Here at the cabin she had to do her own cleaning, though, and we definitely didn't make it any easier on her," I explain.

"A maid?" Luca repeats incredulously, raising his eyebrows. I nod, blushing.

"Yeah. Yeah, I know. It's embarrassing now. My mom didn't have a job or anything except for occasionally checking in at Bathing Beauty, but she still refused to do housework or cooking most of the time. It's how she grew up. The Gasparis always had house staff, too, so I guess she just never learned to do any of that stuff on her own," I go on, shrugging.

"Wow. Your childhood and mine couldn't have possibly been more different," he says.

Shivering in the cold air combined with wind across the water, I answer, "I know. So weird that fate brought us together from such different worlds."

"Are you cold?" he asks. I nod.

"A little bit. I should've put on leggings under these jeans."

Luca opens the picnic basket and hands me a bottle of Campari. "This will help you warm up, if you're interested. I swear there's actual food in there, too."

"Well, I'm sure it's five o'clock somewhere," I say, gladly taking a swig of the bottle and blanching a little at the bitterness. "And what about you? Are you going to drink and row? What if some pond cop pulls you over?"

Luca laughs. "I'm not too worried about that. Besides, I know how to hold my booze."

I take out the neat little prosciutto-and-mozzarella sandwiches and freshly-chopped pineapple out of the basket, distributing the food between us. Luca stops rowing, letting the boat float freely out in the middle of the pond while we have our little picnic. We laugh and joke about our respective childhoods, sharing memories, learning more and more about each other. I want to know everything there is to know about Luca: the good, the bad, and the dangerous. Even the ugly parts are beautiful, all part of the magnificent package that is the man I love.

Out here on the pond, surrounded by the stillness and silence of open water, Luca looks so happy. Those teeny-tiny little crinkles at the corners of his eyes appear when he laughs, when he smiles big. The cool air has whipped his face, making his cheeks ruddy and his hair ruffled. I can see that this is what he needs: a quiet place to unravel and forget about the horrors of his former life as a hitman and his current life as a fugitive. Underneath those awful labels, he's just a handsome man with a huge heart, the carpenter from southern Italy who came to this country to find a better, safer way to live.

I want to give him everything, fulfill that hope he had coming here.

As much as I try to get him to talk about his past, he still manages to steer the conversation back to me. As always. "So, Bathing Beauty. What are we going to do about it?" he asks.

"I've been thinking over it, trying to figure out how to keep it afloat with this massive setback. I need to get those cops off my back and reopen. I won't just roll over and let them take everything from me," I say vehemently, feeling warm and buzzed from the Campari.

"Well, I'll fight with you, tooth and nail. We're going to get the shop back open and running, I promise. I don't know how, but we'll make it happen," Luca promises.

"Sometimes I just look around this place and wonder what it would be like if I had a different life. Somewhere far away from the hectic environment of the city. It gets so tiring, fighting off attacks from every angle. I wonder if any of the towns outside of the forest here would welcome a shop like Bathing Beauty. Artisan goods. Humble craftsmanship," I muse aloud. "And not too far from a city, with Ithaca just an hour down the road."

"You really love this place, don't you?" Luca says. "I would've assumed you were the never-leave-the-city type back when we first met."

"Oh, back then I was just doing what all my high-society friends were doing. They were all obsessed with city life and looked down on anyone who didn't live in the five boroughs. Hell, when one of my friends moved to Staten Island, even that wasn't good enough. So I guess it had to be one of the *four* boroughs. Competition was steep and everybody was so neurotic and over-concerned with what everybody else was doing and thinking. My mom got caught up in that kind of style, always pushing for the next big status symbol. It's a vicious cycle," I explain.

"We are having a good time out here in the middle of nowhere," Luca agrees. Then, he adds wryly, "Way more fun than you would expect from two people hiding from the authorities."

I grin.

"Yeah, I mean, under normal circumstances this would be hell. But anything with you is heaven. I can't imagine being anywhere else, even with all the trouble following us."

Luca leans forward and kisses me, and I can taste Campari on his lips. The kiss deepens as his hands move down my body, sliding down to cup my breasts through the thick fabric of my sweater. I can feel my body responding warmly to his touch, the thrill of a buzz heightening all my senses. Luca gazes into my eyes, something like fire flickering in his eyes.

"What do you say we bring this boat to shore?" he murmurs, and I think I know exactly what he's getting at. I nod, biting my lip.

"Yes, please."

Luca's powerful arms get to work, rowing us to the muddy banks off to one side of the pond quickly. He helps me out and carries me across the shore to the dry earth, leaves crunching under his boots. He sets me down and we kiss, his arms folding around me. Just as I'm melting into his embrace, we hear the distinctive sound of a twig snapping somewhere nearby. We break apart and freeze, both of us glancing around nervously.

Suddenly we hear a man's voice.

"Hey, you there."

A man dressed in what looks like a forest ranger's uniform comes out of the woods holding a clipboard and walking stick. He's an older guy, probably in his fifties, and he has a very suspicious look on his face. My heart races. I never expected to run into someone way out here. The cabin, the pond... it all feels so isolated, but I guess not!

"You kids doin' okay out here? Pretty far off the trail," the ranger says.

Luca smiles, jumping into character. "Yeah, just doing a little exploring."

"That your boat?" the ranger asks, pointing to the canoe.

"Yes, sir. We've been itching to take it out for a spin," Luca explains.

"It's a little cold out, but the sun is shining so we thought today would be a good opportunity to hit the water before the snow starts up again," I pipe up.

The ranger nods and smiles. "No worries. Just be careful out here, alright? Cell service isn't so good in the forest and I wouldn't want ya gettin' hurt."

"We'll be careful. Good to meet you," Luca says. The ranger tips his hat and carries on his way, leaving us standing there silently. Once the ranger is out of sight, I look up at Luca worriedly and he gives me a light squeeze.

"We'll be okay. But that was a close one," he whispers, but his face says everything his words don't: we need to leave. Soon.

Snow falls softly on the windshield as I drive the big black sedan back down the curving woodsy roads to the cabin. I'm on my way back from a quick shopping trip in Ithaca, getting some groceries we desperately needed. It's nice to be out in the middle of nowhere — feels a lot safer than being in the middle of a crowd, especially with my fugitive Mafioso boyfriend — but it's not the most convenient situation. Still, I don't mind it very much, having to make solo trips to Ithaca. I love driving on the lonely country back roads, as long as the weather isn't too terrible. I would much rather be making these little trips with Luca, but we've recently gotten more nervous about his being out in public. I'm always worried that someone will recognize him somehow, even way out here upstate, and turn him in.

Today I was especially glad he stayed behind at the cabin, because it's Christmas Eve, and the crowds were out in full force today in Ithaca. The grocery store was packed with families buying gigantic turkeys and tins of holiday cookies, parents racing down the toy aisles to buy last-minute gifts for their kids. I went in with a simple list of groceries, planning to have a low-key Christmas with Luca, hand-making pasta and antipasti tomorrow. It was difficult to resist going down the street to the cluster of specialty shops to look for a Christmas present to give him, but he made me promise not to get him anything. A low-key Christmas. No gifts, no fuss. Just quietly spending time together by the fire.

I mean, I can't complain. I love the holidays, but for so many years it's been just my mom and me, so I've gotten accustomed to *not* going all out for Christmas. I do miss my mom, and I worry about her being all alone for the holidays. Cell service is still virtually impossible out in the sticks, but on my drives into Ithaca I usually give her a call once I'm in range.

I'm worried one of these days she's going to swallow her pride and plead with me to come back, or worse, start asking questions I know I can't truthfully answer. But she's promised that she is doing just fine on her own, and even hinted that she might be spending the holiday with "someone special." I know how secretive she is about that kind of thing — I've never spent much time with any of her social circle — so I didn't press her for more information. Besides, if my mom has finally joined this decade and made herself a Tinder account or something, I *definitely* do not need to know about it.

On my own end, romance is truly in the air, floating around our little cabin hideaway just like the soft flurries of pure white snow. It's hard to believe that just months ago I was alone in the city, fully expecting to never see him again, and worrying that even if I did get to see him, he would be irrevocably changed by his time in the clink. And he has changed, of course. I see the faint worry lines on his face, the hint of sadness in those beautiful green eyes, the way he sometimes grinds his teeth at night when he's sleeping. It's a tension I hope someday he'll be able to release, but for now it's perfectly understandable.

Especially since he's now dealing with being on the run. Anyone would be tense and a little paranoid in this predicament. But apart from that edge, he's the same man. Maybe even more of a man than he was before. Granted, it makes sense that he's changed over time. After all, he was only a teenager when we first met. And so was I. It seems like both of us have changed, becoming both tougher and softer at the same time. The world has hardened us, but when we're alone together we're soft.

I think we're good for each other. In fact, I know we are.

I pull the car down the gravel road up to the cabin and park. Just as I'm turning off the engine, my stomach twists and I feel a little nauseous. I clap a hand over my mouth and catch a glimpse of myself in the rearview mirror. I look slightly green. I don't know why this keeps happening, but I must have caught some kind of icky bug. I'm not too surprised, since I'm notorious for getting sick over the holidays. My body just doesn't love cold weather.

I walk around to the back of the car and pop the trunk open, but before I can even pick anything up, I hear the front door of the cabin click open and in a few quick strides Luca is beside me. "You're back," he says, grinning as he easily loads up his arms with all the grocery bags.

"Yep," I answer. "You're awfully smiley. What's going on?"

Carrying what has to be at least twenty pounds of groceries, he gives me a wink. "What? I can't just be excited to see the love of my life returning safely home after her harrowing drive through a blizzard?"

I burst out laughing as I follow him up to the cabin. "A blizzard? Luca, it's barely snowing." As I step through the doorway, my eyes adjust to the dimmer light and I realize that the entire place is strung up with twinkling Christmas lights, white candles flickering on every surface, and there's a pervasive sweet smell in the air. Is it… eggnog?

"Oh my god," I breathe, looking around in awe. Luca sets all the groceries down in the kitchen and starts putting things away, looking over at me happily.

"I know we said 'low-key' Christmas, but I felt like the place needed a little bit of holiday ambiance. I was going to put on some music, but the guy who owns the cabin must have the worst taste in Christmas music imaginable. All I could find was an old *Feliz Navidad* record. You'd think someone with that much Frank Sinatra in their collection would have better taste, but apparently not," Luca laughs.

"Again, when did you possibly have the chance to buy all this stuff?" I ask, shaking my head. Luca saunters over and puts his arms around me, giving me a rather smug smile.

"Like I've said before, you aren't very observant. As soon as you set foot in the snack aisles I know your attention is completely taken up trying to choose between chocolate chip cookies or chocolate graham crackers, so I just quickly sneak away to electronics. You really have yourself to thank for this. You're very easy to surprise," he explains.

"Okay, okay, I get it, I'm oblivious," I laugh, rolling my eyes. "But in my defense, chocolate is *very* distracting."

"Hey, I'm not complaining. All the sneakiness is

worth it just to see the look on your face when I get to surprise you with something," he says, kissing me on the forehead. "Plus, I do have an ulterior motive here. The fairy lights might be for Christmas cheer, but the candles are supposed to set a different kind of mood, if you get my drift."

I smile and lean in to kiss him, standing on my tiptoes. "Oh, you don't need to light a bunch of candles to get me in the mood for that."

Luca scoops me up in his arms and carries me down the hall to the bedroom, gently tossing me onto the gigantic bed. I can tell the sheets have been freshly washed and dried — another surprise he took care of while I was out — and there are more candles lit up around the room. I lie back and stretch out, watching greedily as Luca strips off his long-sleeved Henley and jeans, then his boxers. It's a delicious sight, his muscles rippling in the flickering candlelight as he climbs onto the bed beside me. He leans down to kiss me, his hands sliding down to grope my breasts as I feel warmth spreading between my thighs. Even his simplest touch sets me on fire, my body waking up instantly. He reaches down to pull my thick blue sweater up over my head, peeling away my undershirt, bra, jeans, and panties quickly. I can tell he's eager for it, his patience limited.

I love it when he's like this, when I can tell just how difficult it is for him to take his time with me.

Slow and sensual is good, too, but there's just something so satisfying about seeing him unable to resist me for another second that really turns me on and makes me feel special. He bends to pull one of my nipples into his warm mouth, his tongue playing over the stiffened point. I groan and arch my back to meet his lips as his hand slips down between my legs to stroke my clit.

"Already so wet for me, *dolcezza*," he murmurs, moving to my other breast.

"You make me wet just by looking at me," I answer breathlessly, my eyes rolling back in my head as he expertly circles my clit with his forefinger, giving me spikes of pleasure. Then he moves his hand down, sliding two fingers inside my slick hole to stroke my g-spot slowly and teasingly. He backs down between my legs, leaning in to enclose my folds in his mouth, his tongue flicking over my clit while his fingers thrust into me faster and harder.

"Oh fuck," I murmur, rolling my hips to meet his touch. I reach out and grasp at the bed sheets with both hands, feeling my pleasure mounting higher and higher. "So—so good."

"Come for me, Serena," he says softly, his fingers curling ever so slightly to push harder against that heavenly spot deep inside me. He sucks at my clit, sending spirals of warmth and tingles up through my body and I clench at the sheets as I climax with a whimper.

My body goes limp as he quickly slides off the bed and picks me up so that I'm straddling him, my legs around his waist. With my pussy still shuddering with the after waves of my orgasm, he walks me over to pin me against the wall and slams his cock inside of me with one fluid shove. I cry out, immediately coming again. I can feel my honey gushing over his cock as he rears back and thrusts into me again and again, fucking me hard against the wall. He has one arm holding me up and the other holding my wrists together above my head as he fucks me, spearing me with his thick, hard cock.

"Yes! Oh god, fuck me," I moan, closing my eyes as I lose myself to the shocks of pure bliss radiating through me. I revel in Luca's ridiculous strength, his ability to hold me up and fuck me so hard with ease, like I weigh nothing at all.

"I know you love it like this," he growls through gritted teeth, leaning forward so that his lips brush against my ear. "You love it fast and hard, don't you, baby?"

"Yes, yes, yes," I murmur, feeling a third orgasm coming on. The head of his cock is slamming into my g-spot while the friction of our bodies pressed up together stimulates my clit, combining into an indescribable pleasure.

"I want to hear you come, *mia passerotta*. I want to hear you scream for me," he commands softly, sending ticklish shivers down my spine. "Tell me how good it feels."

He fucks me faster, the slick slap of his balls against my ass resounding in the quiet room as my pussy clenches tighter and tighter. "Oh my god, oh my god," I moan. "Luca, it feels so fucking good. You're so deep! Oh fuck."

"*Si, dolcezza*," he whispers. "Tell me more."

"Luca, you're gonna make me fucking come. Oh god, it's too much— I-I can't take it. It feels so good. I love it when you fuck me like this. Don't stop, don't stop, don't—" my words break off right as another orgasm shatters across my body and I shudder, my legs shaking uncontrollably as Luca keeps going, not slowing down even for a second. A moment later, he bellows my name and holds me close as his own orgasm explodes, shooting hot spunk deep inside my pussy.

He rests his forehead against mine, both of us breathing heavily as we struggle to recover from the overwhelming pleasure. Then, without a single word, Luca carries me into the bathroom and turns on the shower, setting me down.

"Fuck," I mumble, brushing the hair back out of my eyes.

"Indeed," Luca agrees, an exhilarated smile on his face.

"Merry Christmas," I tell him, laughing breathlessly. We both step into the shower and he starts washing us off, starting with me, as usual.

"That was the best Christmas gift I could ever ask for. Who needs anything else?" he says, lathering soap over my shoulders as he leans down to kiss me.

After we shower off, we eat a quick dinner and get ready to climb into bed, both dressed in warm pajamas. Luca looks ridiculously handsome in his plaid flannel pants, his shirtless chest powerful and glistening with post-shower dew. Just as I'm pulling the sheets up over myself and about to turn off the bedside lamp, Luca comes over with his hands behind his back.

"I know we said we weren't doing gifts, but I did get you something," he says.

I sit up in bed, confused. "Oh, but I didn't get you anything!" I lament.

He shakes his head. "Don't worry. This gift is as much for me as it is for you." He hands me a little golden box about the size of a standard book. I take off the lid to reveal two navy blue passport books. I frown at them in confusion, then look up at Luca, who's smiling warmly.

"What is this? I already have a passport," I ask.

"It's a chance at a brand new start," he begins. "Those passports contain new identities for us to take on. I've been in contact with some of my people, and they're arranging for us to be smuggled out of here. I've done some research and found a quiet, beautiful town just over the border in Canada where I think Bathing Beauty would do very well. We could finally be free and safe to live our lives, Serena. We could stop hiding here in the woods and be regular people again. We could be together without so much paranoia and fear. We can start over."

"Oh my god," I breathe, thumbing through the pages of the fake passport made for me. It looks completely authentic, identical to the one I already have except that it has a different name. I recognize the names as the Shakespearean character aliases I jokingly selected for the both of us weeks ago. "Are you serious about this?" I ask.

"Dead serious. All it takes is one phone call tomorrow morning and we'll be on our way to freedom and safety, Serena," he explains.

A million thoughts race through my head as my logical side argues with my romantic side. However, this time all the questions raised by fear are squashed back down with hope. My mother has a passport. She can visit us anytime. Rafaela and Nico can visit, too, and Raf always talks about wanting to see Niagara Falls anyway. The shop is doing well enough that I could probably afford to open a new location, maybe even keep the New York shop open, too. I can send money home to my mother, and the house should be paid off within the next few years anyway.

We could stop living under the shadow of fear.

We could be free to walk down the streets hand-in-hand, knowing nobody could recognize us. Nobody would know our names.

My heart skips a beat. This dream... it could come true.

"What do you say?" Luca asks, and I detect a slight hint of nervousness in his voice. I give him a smile, climbing out of bed to hug him tightly, pressing my face against his chest.

"I say yes. I say let's do it. Tomorrow," I tell him earnestly.

~

On Christmas morning, I wake up to the smell of bacon frying in the kitchen. As my brain comes awake I remember our discussion the night before, the fake passports, the plan to escape to Canada. I can't help but smile as I bound out of bed and out into the living room. I see fluffy pancakes, maple syrup, a bowl of fruit, and a plate of bacon on the table waiting for me, but no Luca. I walk into the kitchen to find him standing by the pantry, but when I catch sight of the serious look on his face, my smile fades away. He's holding his phone to his ear, and I realize that's why he's hiding out over here by the pantry. Weirdly enough, through a lot of boredom and trial and error, we determined that the only spot in the cabin where we can get any hint of a signal is right by the pantry door. At first, I think that he must be making the call to his people to get us smuggled into Canada like we talked about, but when he hangs up, the pain on his face only intensifies. He looks over at me with baleful eyes.

"What's wrong?" I ask, worried.

He sighs, running a hand back through his hair. "Change of plans. Something awful has happened. I have to go back to the city."

LUCA

It's a risk to get so close to the crime scene, but I can't hold myself back. I have to see this with my own eyes. We pull up to the sidewalk around the corner and down the road, far enough that nobody would suspect us, and I pull out a pair of binoculars to look at the building down the road from us.

My heart sinks at what I see.

"Luca... I'm so sorry," Serena whispers, putting her hand on my arm.

Uncle Carlo's workshop has police tape wrapped around the whole perimeter and over some of the shattered windows. The walls are riddled with bullet holes, there's broken glass all over the ground, and I can see the door has been kicked down. I can even see shells on the sidewalk, and a few uniformed people are walking around the place. They're too busy with their work to look our way. I can just barely make out some of the inside of the shop, and I see splintered wood: signs of a fight.

And there's blood on some of that wood.

I lower my binoculars, and I can feel the color leaving my face. The message I got in the cabin was that Uncle Carlo's place had been hit. I wasn't expecting something like this.

"And Nico didn't say…?"

I shake my head. "He just told me the shop had been hit. I… I don't remember anything else, it got hazy after that."

"Should we go up there and see…?"

"We can't," I say through a tight jaw, clenching the wheel so hard my knuckles turn white. "Even after those investigators leave, there will be someone watching this place. They'll be waiting for us. Disguises won't matter." We're both wearing sunglasses and hats now, but my frame is easy to recognize this close to where I'm being looked for.

"Those bastards," Serena says in a thin voice, and even as she does, I'm looking at the place and seeing glimpses of the past. I see myself running away from that shop my first few weeks here, only to end up back there shortly after. I see my friends and me wrestling in the back. I see Uncle Carlo teaching me how to defend myself, how to be an American, how to work to support myself. I see him being a father to me when my father couldn't be there.

Then the image of him getting shot alone in the darkness flashes into my head. I feel something hot on my face, and I realize a tear is running down my stony cheek. Serena must have noticed, because I feel her small arms wrapping around my bicep and resting her head on it.

We're quiet for a long moment.

Then there's a tap on the car window.

Instinctively, my hand goes to the gun at my side, and my eyes snap to the window, ready to fight whomever it is, but I only see Nico looking down at us, putting his hands up after seeing my gesture.

I let out a sigh, tension leaving my shoulders, and I roll the window down.

"Jesus, try to be here more than an hour before you get arrested again," he says as I relax my hand, and I unlock the door, nodding for him to get in the back. He does, and I roll the windows back up once he's safely inside.

"Hey, Nico," Serena says, smiling apologetically back at him.

"Sorry to get the jump on you," he says, running his hand through his hair. "Wish I could have said more over the phone, but I don't know who's being listened to anymore. We're going through burner phones like water."

"What happened here, Nico?" I say, my voice gravelly. "Where is Carlo?"

"He's alive," Nico says first, and I see Serena

visibly relieved. I am too, but my anger makes my emotions hard to read. "But Luca… he's not in a good way. He's comatose in the hospital. We've got our men keeping an eye on him, but the police aren't making it easy. They keep trying to question our guys."

"This was a setup," I growl.

"No doubt," Nico says grimly. "I heard about what happened here a few minutes after it went down. One of our guys happened to be at the gas station down the road and heard the shots. Weren't any cops around for a mile."

"Oh my god," Serena says, her eyes widening. "They were in on this?"

"Price," I say.

"The cops have been putting on more and more pressure ever since you got out, Luca," Nico explains. "They tried to be subtle at first when you got out: nobody wanted word spreading that someone broke out of Sterling. That's why your face hasn't been plastered on every TV and newspaper in the country. So instead, Price has been leading an investigation that's been twisting *our* arms."

"Have there been arrests because of me?" I ask, turning back to look at him for the first time.

"No," he says, "turns out that you keeping out of Costa business while you were in prison really helped us out. They can't make the connections they need to start making arrests. But they can harass us so much we can hardly move, and that's what they've been doing since you got out. The Cleaners are getting bolder, and the cops are making it easy, since Price is in their pocket."

I rub my forehead, feeling a headache coming on. This is too much. How could everything have boiled over so much so quickly?

"We shouldn't stay here too long, speaking of," Nico says, glancing out the back window. "Let's get to the Room With a View."

~

Nico did good with his share of the heist money. He and Rafaela have fully rebuilt and renovated the Room With a View to look better than it ever had been before. While Serena and Rafaela throw their arms around each other and hug warmly, Nico and I take a seat by the bar.

"Cleaners were *beyond* mad about the heist we pulled off," Nico says in a low tone. "They needed that money bad. They can't prove we're involved, but they can throw a fit."

I clench my fist and feel my teeth grinding. "This is my fault. I should have planned better."

"None of that bullshit," Nico says, pouring us a couple glasses of limoncello. "You and I both know what those fuckers are capable of. If it hadn't been this, it would have been something else. You killed Lorenzo Abruzzi."

It feels like a lifetime ago that I killed that wretch. Mafia royalty in his own right. "Wonder how he's enjoying his little corner in hell."

"Not as much as we'll enjoy ours," Nico says, and we clink our glasses together and drink.

Serena and Rafaela come over to join us after their quick reunion, and we all sit together at the bar. For a moment, it feels like old times.

"Luca, one of the boys sent me a picture of your uncle from the hospital to let me know he's still hanging in there," Rafaela says gently. "If you want to see, for peace of mind…"

"No," I say, shaking my head. "I don't want to see him like that. *He* wouldn't want to be seen like that."

"No problem," she says with a quick wave of her hand. "Anyway, good to see you both. Life's treating you two alright, I see," she adds, looking our outfits up and down.

"Helps to blend in," Serena says.

"Not anymore, though," I say. "Someone found us up there. I took care of it, but we can't keep running like this. If we go further, more people will just keep getting hurt here."

Serena nods in agreement. "Now we just need to figure out where to start."

"We could try to mobilize some of the Costas,"

Nico says, leaning on the bar. "You've still got a lot of friends here, Luca, not just me and Rafaela."

If I'm honest, I want even less to do with the mafia now than ever. I want to leave that life behind me, and I plan on making that happen. But now isn't a good time to try and burn that bridge, not while we're recouping here with two good friends who still have close ties to the Costas.

Much like Italy, the mafia here is a complex web that isn't always so easy to work around.

"This is personal," I say simply, "and I don't want to fan the flames of another war. Enough blood is getting shed without my help. Besides, we know now that things are going the way they are because of Price and his lackeys in the NYPD."

The others nod in agreement. "The police are untouchable, though," Serena points out, "it's not like another gang where you can go in and just start fights until things go our way. How do you go up against a detective?"

A confident smile crosses my face. "I have a good idea of where to start."

"Are you sure about this?" I whisper to Luca as we walk up to the nightclub. The bass is booming, making the very pavement outside vibrate to the beat. I'm wearing a tight black dress, dark hosiery, heels, and a black leather jacket, and I'm shivering in the cold winter air. The city is wide awake and pulsing with life, from the neon signs to the honking horns and shrill laughter of a bachelorette party group filing clumsily into a bar across the street. It's strange to be back in New York after our stay in the cabin, to be surrounded by so much noise again. Back to the real world, where all our fears still live, waiting for us to walk back into focus.

I would be lying if I said I wasn't afraid. I'm definitely scared.

"I'm sure. This is the way we have to do this," Luca answers me in an undertone. The bouncer stands up as we approach, crossing his arms over his broad chest. He's a big guy, but still not as tall as Luca. However, he looks infinitely meaner, with his shaved head, scowling eyes, and face tattoos. He seems a little rough to be working the door at a nightclub like this, but I suppose the more exclusive the club, the more aggressive the door guy has to be.

He opens his mouth to inevitably tell us to fuck off, that the club is at full capacity, but then he stops short, his eyes falling on me. He gives me a quizzical look for a second, like he's trying to figure out who I am. My heart starts racing, worrying that maybe he recognizes us somehow, that maybe I'm known as an accomplice to Luca the fugitive. But then he smiles.

"S—Serena?" he asks haltingly. "That you?"

"Uh, yeah," I answer, confused. He nods slowly.

"Yeah, yeah. It's me, Damian. We took that comp sci class together in college, remember?"

It dawns on me that I have actually shared a classroom with this guy before. Maybe I can use this to our advantage. I give him a big grin. "Oh yeah! Hi! How—how are you?"

"Great! I'm graduating in the spring, but for now I'm doing this job to get by. Crossing my fingers I get picked up as a CPA somewhere. Just tossin' out a million resumes right now, ya know. Gotta follow the grind, man," he explains cheerily. I remember him as a scrawny computer nerd type, but I guess in the past few years he's either hit the gym five times a day or possibly gone through some miraculous second puberty.

"That's awesome, Damian. Good luck!" I tell him, amused by the spontaneity of this interaction. I mean, who would've guessed it? Sometimes even New York can feel like a small town. Damian moves aside, gesturing for us to go inside.

"Thanks! Well, it was good to see you, Serena. Go on in and have a great night!" he says brightly as we walk into the club. I can feel Luca's eyes boring into my head and I look up at him, stifling a laugh. He's shaking his head, eyebrows raised.

"That was lucky. Good thing you've got a memorable face," he says, grinning.

"Yeah, talk about kismet," I laugh. We make our way over to the bar and Luca orders a couple shots. I shake my head, and he doesn't push me, taking both of them in quick succession. The seriousness of what we're about to do tonight is flooding back into my mind. Luca obviously notices my tension, and takes me by the hand, leading me out onto the crowded dance floor. The last thing I want to do right now is dance, but he's insistent.

"We need to play it cool. Be convincing," he whispers in my ear. "We're just a young couple here for a casual evening of dancing. No big deal."

"How will we know when he gets here?" I ask quietly as Luca takes hold of my hips and starts to sway with me.

"I'm keeping an eye on the front entrance and the employee's entrance toward the back. He doesn't work here but he's a regular, so he might come in through there to go undetected. But he knows what I look like, and I know what he looks like. We'll find him, no problem," he explains.

"What if he doesn't show?" I ask, biting my lip.

Luca shakes his head. "He will. Trust me. This guy might be the only person on the planet who hates Price as much as I do."

We dance together for what feels like hours. I'm beginning to feel hopeless when finally Luca puts a hand on my arm and nods in the direction of the back of the club. Even though I didn't know what he looked like before tonight, I recognize him instantly by the world-weary look on his face. He's a relatively tall man, but he walks with a slight stoop, like he's perpetually ashamed of himself, trying to make himself look smaller. He has thinning salt-and-pepper hair and deep frown lines on his paunchy face. He looks over and locks eyes with Luca, both men nodding once in acknowledgement before the ex-cop walks over to a booth against the wall and sits down.

Luca orders a beer and we head over to the booth where our contact is waiting. I can feel my heart beating fast, but for some reason my mind is totally cool and collected. After spending all this time with

Luca on the run, I think my tolerance for high-stakes situations has gotten a little higher.

We settle into the booth across from the ex-cop and Luca slides the beer across the table to him. The guy gladly accepts it and takes a long sip before speaking.

"Sorry, I wasn't expecting you to have company," he says quietly, his voice a little rough. I can tell he's probably been a lifelong smoker. Luca nods.

"This is Serena. And you already know who I am," Luca says.

"Hi Serena. I'm Hank. Ex-cop, ex-success story, ex-productive member of society. Nice to meet you," the guy says flatly, taking another drink of his beer.

"I'm sorry... can I just ask a question?" I begin, leaning forward and lowering my voice. "What made you quit the force?"

Hank sighs and answers, "An operation went foul at the fairgrounds a while back. Found my own neck on the chopping block. Could've made some serious waves if I spoke up, but Price would have my head before I even got the words out. So I decided it was best to just cut and run."

"So, you worked closely with Price?" I press on.

He nods, rolling his eyes. "Oh yeah, Price and I go way back. We were at the Academy together, rose up in the ranks side by side. He got accolades, I got accolades. He got promoted, I got promoted. We were on parallel tracks to greatness, you know.

Colleagues working our asses off on the same team for the greater good. Or so I thought."

"Price used to be on the straight and narrow once upon a time, then?" Luca suggests.

Hank shrugs. "I don't know how far back his dirty business goes. He could've been scheming since day one at the Academy for all I know. I had no idea for the longest time. I guess that's part of why I wasn't cut out to be a cop after all: I just kind of assumed the best of everyone. You can't do that in my former line of work. Ain't nobody one-hundred-percent clean. Price was a good cop, don't get me wrong. He made arrest after arrest after arrest. He shut down gangs and crime syndicates, threw a bunch of small-time dealers in the clink. If the chief had been handing out gold stars, he would've been a goddamn constellation. But turns out, he was double-dipping. Got one hand on the badge and the other digging into places he got no business in. Jewel smuggling, gambling rings, even sex trafficking."

He shakes his head, his fists tightening on the table in front of him. "That fucker was moonlighting for both sides all along, but really it's not about good or bad. Price doesn't work for anybody but himself."

"Are you the only one who knows about this?" Luca asks.

Hank chuckles, but the laughter doesn't warm up his cold expression one bit. "Nah. I can think of a half dozen guys on the force who could give evidence about Price's shady business dealings. I got evidence of my own. But nobody's gonna speak up."

"Not even you?" I pipe up. "You're already off the force. What do you have to lose?"

He stares at me for a moment with narrowed eyes. "You don't get it, do you? This is bigger than just a stupid job. I got the hell out of dodge because that was the only way I could at least kind of hold onto what's left of my damn conscience. Price has friends in high places, but it's his friends in low places you really gotta watch out for. Everybody hates him, but he made damn sure they're afraid of him, too. We all know what that rat bastard is capable of, and nobody's willing to risk life or livelihood to take him down. He's too powerful."

"The bigger they are, the harder they fall," I interject. "And if you came out to meet us here tonight, that must mean you haven't totally given up all hope yet."

Hank gives me a weak, almost wistful smile. "Hope? Nah. I'm way past hope. Nowadays all I got left is desperation and spite."

"Well, then maybe you're just desperate enough to help us," Luca says. "You said you have evidence. Good enough to put him away?"

"I don't know. Maybe. But it wouldn't make a difference unless we got everybody on our side, and that'll never happen," Hank laments. "Look, I feel for you, man. I get it. Price has taken so much away from me, from you, from a lot of people who didn't deserve it. I admire what you're trying to do here, but it's never gonna work out."

"We can pay you," Luca says. "We can get your job back. We can take Price down."

"Man, it's not that I don't wanna help you. It's just that I can't. I already lost everything when I quit the force. That job was everything to me, all I ever wanted to do with my life since I was a little boy playing cops and robbers. But that department is all in Price's pocket nowadays. Ain't nothing you or anybody else can do about it. The stakes are too high."

He gulps down the rest of his beer and starts to slide out of the booth, trying to leave. Desperately, I blurt out, "What if we could promise you a new start? A do-over, somewhere far away. Y-You could get away from all this. Pretend it never even happened."

Hank turns back to look at me with his brows furrowed. Luca looks at me, too, confused at what I'm talking about. "A new identity. Untraceable," I go on, glancing at Luca meaningfully. "We can do that, can't we? We can get him out of the country."

Luca catches on, realizing that I'm talking about the fake passports he had made for us, the ones with the pictures missing. He nods, gesturing for Hank to sit back down.

"Yes. We can promise you safe passage out of

here. Consider it a guerrilla-style witness protection service," he explains. Hank slowly slides back into the booth, looking apprehensive.

"In exchange for your evidence and your assistance, we can get you a new life. A new chance to make something of yourself, without all this baggage weighing you down," I tell him.

Hank looks back and forth between us, clearly torn. Luca and I wait silently, impatiently for him to say something.

*I* feel like I can hear my heartbeat getting slower and steadier as I bring the car to a stop and turn off the engine. It's a skill I learned in prison. I forced my body to calm down and be ready for anything when having to deal with the police.

Most of all when dealing with Price.

Some close contacts and I set up a meeting with him under the pretenses that he's meeting his the ex-cop we met at the club. It's a run-down bar just off the highway on the outskirts of the city where bikers tend to pass through. Not the kind of place you'd expect to be finding a cop, but Price has an understanding with the owner, and from what I understand, the two have a tenuous alliance, of a sort.

That's going to be a problem. But this is the one shot I have at getting Price alone, maybe even off-guard. It's a risk I need to take.

But it isn't a risk I'm willing to put on anyone else. That's why I'm out here alone tonight.

I lied to Nico. I told him I'd meet him at the Room With a View to plan a proper setup with all the support I really need for a job like this. But to do that would be to ask too much of a man who's already given me too much. And besides, if this goes sour, I don't want him to get his name implicated in something as big as this. It's a miracle he's kept himself out of too much hot water so far.

As for Serena, she thinks I'm meeting Nico too. It pains me to keep her in the dark more than anything, but she's the one person above all I can't risk getting hurt. Right now, nobody knows she's been an accomplice to a wanted fugitive. I want to keep it that way.

I feel the little disk in my jacket pocket. It's one of many copies I made, of course. Our ex-cop friend really pulled through: there are more people willing to move against Price than I ever expected. Most of them are beat cops who are too young to get jaded, but there are a few mid-level people running desk jobs in the force who have been paid to cover up Price's paper trail of corruption. Just enough to knock him off his high horse.

I push the door to the bar open and step inside to the smell and thick haze of smoke. Old rock is playing while rough-looking bikers hang out around the pool tables or at the bar. I don't stop as I move in.

I'm not planning to stop and chat with the bartender before heading upstairs.

Price's usual meeting place is the rooftop. The sign on top of the front of the bar makes sure anyone up there has a little privacy from the street view, even though the building is only a story high.

Unfortunately, I see the stairs leading up to the roof are past the bar. I'll be noticed heading upstairs. No matter. Price still can't get away.

I head toward the bar, and I'm about halfway there when a voice behind me makes me freeze.

"Hey, think I'd let you go in there alone?"

As I stop, I can't help the feeling of a smile tugging at the corners of my mouth. "You tailed me. Well done."

"Learned from the best," says Serena as she steps up beside me and I look down at her. "Don't worry, I didn't snitch to Nico."

As I see her standing there beside me confidently, I don't feel any impulse to tell her this is too dangerous for her or too much for her to handle. She has her family's blood in her, after all. She's my girl. I should have known that any girl of mine wouldn't accept anything less.

"Be ready, then," I say in a low tone, barely audible over the sounds of the bar. "I don't expect this to go so good."

"I'd be disappointed if it did," she says with a wink.

I step up to the bar, and as I start to head to the stairs, the bartender's eyes snap over to me. He's a squirrelly little guy with a chin-strap beard and a shaved head.

"That's staff-only," he says with a suspicious look.

"I have business upstairs," I growl, moving past him and taking Serena's hand as I go.

I don't hear him shout after us, which tells me something's up.

"He was texting something on a burner phone last I saw him," Serena says as we hurry up the stairs. That confirms my suspicions.

"He must be in Price's pocket," I say, pulling out a gun and holding it at the ready. "We've lost some of the element of surprise, then."

"Not all of it," Serena points out.

"No, not all of it," I say with a smile as we reach the door to the roof. I stop, turn to Serena, and pull her into me to press my lips to hers briefly.

"I love you," I whisper.

"I love you," she says back with a smile. "Let's handle this, together."

I kick the door down.

My gun is out and ready, but instead of hearing the gunshots I was expecting, I hear the sound of someone blowing smoke.

Furrowing my brow, I look at the figure standing at the edge of the roof toward the rear of the building, his back to me, a glowing cigarette in his hand.

"You move fast, Luca," says Detective Price, not turning around to face me. He's staring out into the woods behind the bar, and I see him slip his phone back into his pocket. "Gotta say, I wasn't expecting my man to turn me out like this. Well done."

"What, were you hoping your winning personality would keep him in line?" I ask as Serena steps up beside me, her fist gripping her switchblade.

"Good point," he says with a quiet, humorless laugh, turning around to face us, "but when he's found dead in his apartment, I'll make sure the report says that he was a loyal friend of yours."

"If you were calling for backup, I'd call them off," Serena says, and Price raises his eyebrows, amused. "We've got something you don't want them seeing."

Showing my hand, I carefully remove the disk from my jacket pocket, holding it up for Price to see. A thin smile comes across his lips.

"Get a little dirt on me, did you?" he says, lighting up another cigarette. The smoke swirls around his face as he breathes in and out, cold eyes flitting between us. "Looks like I have some housecleaning to do when we leave here."

"There's enough info on this disk to put you away a lot longer than I would have been in prison," I say, twirling the disk around before putting it back in my pocket. "I would guess there are a lot of boyscout-types on the force who'd like to get their hands on this." Price is keeping his cool, but I can tell it's a thin veil. His eyes follow the disk as I put it away, and he isn't as calm as he was when he would talk to me in prison. We're getting to him.

Still, he keeps a poker face that would fool most people.

"Come on, you don't think I'd call the boys in blue to back me up at a place like this," he says, gesturing down to the bar itself."

"No," I agree, "there's a lot of things here that would be embarrassing to explain."

"Y'know," he says, "I'm sure you're new to the whole 'whistleblowing' thing, but usually, you keep things a little more uh, subtle than this."

"I'm here because this is personal, Price," I say, stepping forward, my fist clenched. "This is more than just you chasing me down. You've made Serena's life hell. You went after my associates. You tried to kill my uncle!" I bark, and I have to fight the urge to fire my weapon into him right then and there. "We're past you just stroking your ego or building your spider's web of corruption in the NYPD. This has become between you and me. Why?"

"Are you serious?" he laughs, flicking his cigarette to the ground and snuffing it out. "Listen, Luca, you've been a lot more pain than you're worth, but you've got guts, so I'll level with you. Organized crime? That shit is *fantastic* for me. You mafia families have your factions and your blood feuds and your politics. You're like little governments flying under the radar. And it just so happens that some of us cops realize, 'hey, this can work out for us, if we open our minds up a little.' So I help some Mafioso out here, they help me back. When one family loses power, I shuffle my priorities around, and at the end of the day, I get a nice paycheck. It ain't pretty, but it *works*, get it? People like me are what keep the city running. The mafia keeps the streets cleaner than they would be, and I just help the right Mafioso do their jobs and stay in their place."

He takes a few steps forward, raising a finger and gesturing between the two of us with a hardening face.

"But you two? Some upstart rebel without a cause with a chip on his shoulder and the bratty daughter of a mafia don who should have been killed off with him a long time ago? You two are a threat to all the good stuff we've got going on. You outlived your usefulness a long time ago. The Abruzzi family, those guys you call Cleaners? *They're* the future of the Bronx."

He turns his eyes to me, narrowing them. "And if I've gotta kill some useless old man to make that point, nobody's gonna cry, and it'll be a lot cleaner than dragging out a bloody mob war."

"I never asked for any of this, you fucker," I growl, stepping forward and gripping my gun, but he just smiles.

"Ah-ah-ah, let's not add cop-killing to your track record now."

"I don't have to kill you," I say, controlling my temper, for Serena's sake, though each word is laced with anger. "As much as I want to. I want you to disappear, Price. Back off my family, and that includes the Costas. Get a transfer somewhere quiet, and I'll leave your reputation intact. It's cleaner that way, like you say. Cross me, and you'll rot in the prison cell you had set up for me," I say with finality.

Price stares into me for a moment, then licks his lips and scratches his head. "Hate to burst your bubble, but I already decided how this was gonna go down before you even got up here."

Before I can ask what he means, I hear the sounds of crashing glass and breaking wood from downstairs.

"Hear that?" Price says with a chipper smile. "That'll be the bikers downstairs. My bartender friend knows how to get a fight going, and man, some of these gangs get *violent*."

In the blink of an eye, Price draws a gun, and mine snaps up to him... but he aims his at Serena, and we both freeze.

"So when they find your bodies," he explains in a cold, even tone, "you'll just be two fugitives who were in the wrong place at the wrong time, and by the looks of things, there'll be nobody else to handle that blackmail of yours."

We're frozen for a moment before I hear a creak behind me. Pierce's eyes move to the door for half a second as the bartender emerges from the stairs with a lead pipe in hand, and I take my chance.

But I don't shoot. I can't risk that.

I dive for Serena, and just as my body wraps around her and pulls her to the ground, Pierce fires, and I feel my side burning.

"Kill them!" Pierce shouts, and he dives for cover behind an AC unit as I get off Serena and fire at him.

Adrenaline surges through my body as my bullets make sparks on the unit, and I realize Serena has rolled away from me, blade flashing.

"Serena!" I shout, but she's already rushing toward the bartender, who looks just as surprised as I am. But I don't have time to watch their fight: a bullet whizzes by my ear as Price blind-fires.

Gritting my teeth, I fire twice more at the unit he's hiding behind, and as I fire, I barrel toward it. Faster than I knew I could move, I leap up on top of the unit and fire down toward where he is, and I see his crouching form turn with wide, white eyes in surprise. He tries to raise his weapon to me, but I descend on him so fast that when he fires, his wrist is already on the ground under my hand, and the bullet ricochets off the sign.

I have him nearly pinned, and I bring my head down to his nose to disorient him. He grunts in pain as I make contact, but he lands a hard blow to my side where I was already bleeding from the gunshot wound, and I'm forced to release him.

He staggers to his feet, but I'm back up the next second. He squares up with me, fists raised, and we trade blows like boxers. Our guns have fallen to the side, and I don't think either of us notice until we're already swinging at each other, our hatred runs so deep. He lands a blow on my jaw, and it's got more force behind it than I knew he had in him, but soon I have the chance to move in close and grapple him.

I bring him down to the ground with all my weight, and as I wrestle him, I catch sight of Serena fighting with the bartender.

I can't avoid watching her for a moment, my heart leaping into my throat as I see him lunge, his brutish moves careless, but I swell with pride at the sight of Serena handling herself perfectly: she moves as nimbly as if we'd been training just yesterday, and I watch her dodge the heavy swing of the lead pipe and move up close to the bartender, grabbing him by the wrist with one hand before she brings her knife up under his arm.

At the same time I hear the blade go into his flesh and hear him scream, Price lands a solid punch across my face, then grabs it, trying to get his thumbs up to my eyes.

I roll with him, putting my knee to his stomach and wrenching him hard, and we're deadlocked, our pressure points putting each other in intense pain.

"I... I was there, you know," he snarls as we struggle, "at the shooting. I saw the whites in the old man's eyes when the bullets flew into his house."

I start to turn him around and wrench his arm behind him, but the knees me in the stomach and rolls away, and we're on our feet again, both breathing heavily. There's a wild look in his eyes as he gets ready for me again, and he wipes away a little blood from his lip.

"Don't worry," he says, "when you're dead, I'll make sure Serena isn't lonely this time."

It's then that I notice he's standing beside one of our guns, and he dives for it. I start to run forward, but as his fingers wrap around it and he lifts the weapon…

… There's a solid *whump* as Serena swings the lead pipe across the side of his head, and Price falls to the ground, clutching his head as his mouth is fixed in a silent scream.

"Luca!" Serena calls as she tosses me the pipe, and I catch it solidly as I stride forward, flashing a smile at her, the bartender dying behind her.

"The gang fight isn't a bad cover," I say as I loom over him, knuckles white as his reddened eyes glare up at me, still dazed. "I think it'll do for you." I lift the pipe above my head and take aim.

"Say hello to Lorenzo for me."

I swing down.

"Serena!" rings out a clear, excited voice from down the hallway. Rafaela comes rushing toward me to give me a hug. Luca steps aside for a moment to let us reunite, watching with an amused smile. Rafaela looks at me with her big brown eyes twinkling and her cheeks flushed and I can tell she's already a couple drinks in. "I heard about what happened. Holy crap, *chica*, that's some seriously fucked-up shit."

She then turns to Luca and gives him a hug, too, surprising both of us. Rafaela is a huggy person, but she's usually a little more reserved than this. I laugh at the shock on Luca's face as he hesitantly pats her on the back. Raf looks up at him and says very gravely, "I can't thank you enough for keeping Serena safe. That's my best friend, you know. If anything happened to her I would fall apart."

"As long as I'm around, nothing will happen to her. I promise you that," Luca replies warmly. Rafaela nods and turns back to hook her arm through mine.

"How many drinks have you had tonight?" I ask her, stifling a snort. She flips her hair over her shoulder, trying her best to look offended, but she's still smiling.

"Not enough. *Vámonos!* We're celebrating tonight and you two are the guests of honor!" she declares, leading the way down the corridor.

We're on the top floor of a swanky corporate tower, one of the buildings I used to marvel at as a teenager, thinking that one day I was going to be a super-powered businesswoman in a pencil skirt, heels, and a white button-up starched and ironed by my home staff. It seems like a million lifetimes ago that I nursed that dream, and it couldn't be further away from what I dream about now. I used to long for fortune, notoriety, all the typical status symbols my parents taught me to lust after: fancy high-rise apartment, designer wardrobe, expensive car, maybe even a yacht. But now I just want the simple things: peace, freedom, stability, and most of all, love.

My heart flutters as I look over and lock eyes with Luca. He gives me a fond smile, warming the hard features of his handsome face as soon as he looks my way. I reach out and take his hand even as Rafaela leads me by the other arm. In a way, this is the best I could ever ask for. Walking side by side with my man and my best friend.

"So, who owns this building? I mean, this seems like an unlikely choice for this kind of crowd," I ask curiously. Luca chuckles.

"You would be surprised how far the strong arms of the Costa family reach. The top three floors of the building belong to a shell corporation. A front. Don't get me wrong, they do regular business, as well. Trades, marketing, all that. But it's also a Costa head-quarters, owned by one of the highest-ranking guys in the family," Luca explains.

"Ah," I say, nodding. "Big-wig type. Should I be worried about meeting him? I mean, with my dad's history and everything?"

Rafaela interjects, "Everyone there is so friendly! Those people know how to party. They got hors d'oeuvres, champagne, an open bar, good music—"

"Don't worry. The Costa family will welcome you back just as quickly as they'll ostracize you. They're a mercurial bunch, but for now, things should be settled smoothly. Besides, you were never really to blame for your father's actions. These people can hold a grudge like no other, but even they have to admit at some point that you weren't involved. You were taken advantage of and duped just like they were. I mean, you were still a kid," Luca explains reassuringly.

"I hope so. The idea of walking into a room full

of dangerous people who despise me is enough to make me wanna turn around and run back down to the car," I lament. Rafaela gives my arm an encouraging squeeze.

"If it helps, remember that you were also the one to assist in the disposal of Officer Price. He was one of the Costa family's most hated enemies. And the mafia tends to follow the rule that the enemy of their enemy is their friend," Luca adds.

Sighing, I straighten up and prepare myself to walk into the room. We walk up to a set of double doors at the end of the corridor and Rafaela goes in ahead of us, cheering excitedly. Luca kisses the top of my head.

"Everything will be alright. These people are happy to see you. I promise," he whispers.

I nod and force myself to smile. "Okay. Let's do this."

We open the door and step into the spacious, airy room amid the cheers of a big crowd of well-dressed people holding champagne flutes. They all look genuinely overjoyed at the sight of us, and Luca raises our arms up together in a gesture of victory, making them all cheer louder.

"Welcome, friends!" calls a pot-bellied man at the front of the crowd. He has thick dark hair, a bristly mustache, and he's wearing an expertly-tailored suit.

"Come in, come in! Get yourselves a drink!" says another man.

"Join the party!" says another. Luca looks at me grinning.

"Well, you heard them. Let's hit the open bar," he suggests. My stomach turns at the mere thought of a drink, but I follow him to the bar counter anyway, and order a ginger ale.

"Luca! *Mio amico!*" booms a deep voice from behind us. We both turn around to see a huge bear of a man stride up to us and pull Luca into a manly embrace. With a heavy accent he says, "You look good, *fratello*. And is this is the girl who helped you take down that *bastardo*, Price? She's a beauty! Well done!"

"Oh, thank you," I laugh nervously, but then the man hugs me, too, before heading off down the bar to mingle with some other people. Luca shrugs, looking amused.

"I knew him as a teenager back in Italy," he explains quietly. "Some of these guys I have not seen in a very long time. But mafia family is tight. They make it their business to recognize their fellow man."

"And what about you? I thought you had one foot out the door?" I ask, whispering.

Luca takes a long sip of his drink. "We'll play it by ear. Tonight, as far as anyone knows, nothing is amiss. Let's keep it that way. Besides, tonight we really should be celebrating. Are you sure you don't want something a little more... festive than ginger ale?"

I laugh. "Yes, I'm sure. Just, uh, not feeling very well. But I'm fine."

"Okay. We have a lot to celebrate tonight, *mia passerotta*. Let's join the party. Take my hand. It'll all be fine, just follow my lead," he says, kissing my hand before he leads me back into the fray so we can mingle with everyone else. Every single person we encounter seems over the moon to talk to us, everyone congratulating and thanking us for what we've done. I'm still feeling just a tad bit conflicted over my involvement in such a dirty mess, but it's a little easier to feel better about it when every single person in the room is thankful for it.

And we *do* have a lot to be thankful for. We're both alive and well, for one thing, and Price is not. That man can no longer terrorize the people of this city, mafia or civilian. I keep reminding myself that taking out Price is probably an example of extinguishing one life in order to save countless lives. Room With a View is almost completely rebuilt by now, using the money from the jewel heist, and the grand re-opening is scheduled for next week. Rafaela and Nico are safe and sound, and they seem happier than ever. With Price out of the way, the cops have released their chokehold on Bathing Beauty, and I've scheduled its re-opening the same day as Rafaela's so we can have a combined celebratory drink that night. I just have to get some of the accounts back into order after falling into disrepair for so many weeks, and I need to re-hire my former employees.

My mom has met and started dating some mystery guy she hasn't let me meet yet, but either way I'm jumping for joy at this news. She's not going to be all alone in that old house anymore. She has someone to look after her and love her. So I'm moving out of the Riverdale house as soon as Luca and I find an apartment in the city that we both agree on. It'll be bittersweet, of course, leaving the house where I feel closest to my father's memory, but I can always visit anytime I like. And besides, I'm old enough now that it seems silly to live at home.

And the thought of moving in with Luca and having him all to myself with all the privacy in the world 24/7? Well, that's motivation enough to get me all packed up and ready to go.

Luca and I move from group to group, mingling and chatting with different rough-looking men and bejeweled women, all of whom are happy to see us. Luca speaks Italian with a lot of them while I just sort of nod and smile, but it doesn't matter that I can't tell what they're saying. The celebratory vibe in the room is infectious, and soon I'm feeling down-right giddy. Periodically, Rafaela and Nico pop over to talk to us, with Raf excitedly chattering away about how awesome it will be when our respective businesses open back up again. She's probably hugged me about twenty times in the past hour or so, and it's all Nico can do to keep her upright and walking straight, she's had so many cocktails.

Finally, someone announces that dinner is being served, and we all file into another adjoining room with a massive, long table set up for everybody. The table is laden with a ton of delicious-smelling foods and countless bottles of wine, both red and white. My stomach growls as we hurriedly take our seats, with Luca and I being directed to the head of the table, taking our places as the guests of honor. After a brief speech from the same paunchy dark-haired man who first greeted us upon entering the party, we all dig in. I heap my plate with pasta and salad and olives.

About ten minutes into the meal, Luca suddenly stands up and taps his glass with a spoon, calling us all to attention to make a speech. I look up at him, surprised. Everyone sets down their utensils and falls silent, looking at Luca expectantly.

He looks down at me and smiles, his whole face lighting up.

"Friends, brothers, everybody... I cannot thank you all enough for this fantastic evening. The Costa family knows better than anyone how to celebrate good news when it comes, and so it is my pleasure to deliver some more good news for us to toast," he begins. He pauses, and the room is dead silent. He turns to me, those green eyes vibrant in the dimming sunset behind us through the big glass pane of the windows.

"Serena. You are the love of my life. In fact, before I first met you as a teenager, I had no idea what love could even feel like. I assumed I would walk this world alone, following a solitary path. But from the very first moment I laid eyes on you, I knew there could be no greater dream to reach for than to make you mine. I would cross any ocean, climb a mountain, fight any enemy for you. I would change the world a thousand times over just to make you smile. *Mia passerotta*, you have always been the guiding light, the beacon that has led me back to shore when I thought I might be eternally lost at sea. Any success, any good fortune that I might achieve is all because of you, and nothing else can ever compare to the way I feel when I'm standing beside you. Serena, with your love I am invincible. Unbreakable. You make me stronger. You make me proud. You make me a better man. And I will do anything and everything in my power to keep you by my side for the rest of my life."

He kneels down next to my chair and I feel my heart skip several beats as the room erupts into gasps of surprise. "Oh my god," I murmur breathlessly, staring down at Luca. He smiles at me, eyes shining, and takes a little velvet box out of his coat pocket.

Luca opens the box to reveal a white gold band with a gorgeous, sparkling diamond. My jaw drops and I feel my lungs seizing up, like I've suddenly forgotten how to breathe at all.

"Serena De Laurentis, would you do me the ultimate honor of becoming my wife?"

Tears burn in my eyes and spill down my cheeks as I break into nervous, joyous laughter and throw my arms around him. "Yes! Of course! Absolutely!" I sob happily. Luca hugs me tight while everyone bursts into deafening cheers and applause all around us. My heart beat has gone from zero to a million in a moment, and I can't seem to wipe the smile off of my face as Luca kisses me again and again, his hands stroking the hair back out of my face as we embrace.

Suddenly, it becomes absolutely imperative that I share with him the secret I've been holding back from him for the last few weeks. He needs to know. Right now.

While the whole room continues to pour celebratory glasses of wine and chat happily about how amazing the night is, I lean in close to Luca's ear and whisper, "Luca… I-I'm pregnant."

He pulls back and looks into my face with wide eyes, shocked. Then he grins, laughing as he kisses me. "Are you sure? Really?"

I nod vigorously, a giggle escaping my mouth. My whole body is trembling, overwhelmed with the joy of the moment. "Yes. I'm totally sure. Luca... we're going to be parents."

"*Mia passerotta*," he breathes, shaking his head in awe and happiness, like he just can't believe his good luck. "This is all I've ever wanted. More than I ever could have hoped for."

"I love you so much," I tell him.

He slips the engagement ring onto my finger, and miraculously, it fits perfectly.

"I love you, Serena. Until the day I die," he replies.

As we stand up, Rafaela and Nico come rushing over, Raf throwing her arms around both of us. There are tears streaming down her face and she kisses both of my cheeks. The rest of the evening is spent in impossibly high spirits, everybody wine-drunk and joy-drunk as the hours fly by like mere minutes. Finally, around one in the morning, the party starts to wind down, and my pregnant body is begging for me to go home and get some sleep. We haven't found an apartment together yet, so we've been staying at Room With a View in one of the finished rooms. It's been pretty great, actually, since the place isn't officially open yet. We have perfect privacy to do whatever we want... which is usually just each other.

Luca and I take several minutes to say goodbye and thank you to everyone before heading down the elevator with Nico and a very, very intoxicated Rafaela. Luckily, Luca stopped drinking about three hours ago, so he's stone-cold sober by the time we reach the street outside. I offer to drive, since I'm pregnant and therefore absolutely sober, but he insists.

"I'll go get the car and drive it around to you. Just wait here with Nico and Raf," he tells me, giving me a kiss on the cheek.

"Fine, fine. But you know I'm not *that* pregnant yet. I can still walk just fine," I reply teasingly. He gives me a shrug, grinning widely as he heads off down the street to collect the car.

"Nope. No excuses. You're not going to lift a finger for the next nine months if I can help it," he calls out. "Might as well get used to it, *mia passerotta!*"

I shake my head and roll my eyes while Rafaela sings loudly beside me in Spanish. She's had way too much to drink and I know she'll be feeling it in the morning, but if there was ever a good reason to drink way too many celebratory toasts, tonight would certainly qualify.

Life is a dream. Nothing could ever be better than this.

Suddenly, there's a deafening crack and Nico yells, "Get down!"

He tackles Raf and me to the ground as a hail of smaller bangs crack through the air.

Bullets.

I roll over and stare down the street, my eyes going wide as I take in the bright explosion of flames licking upward toward the night sky. Down the road. Where Luca went to get the car.

"Luca!" I scream, scrambling to my feet and making a run for it. Nico grabs me by the arm and pulls me back.

"Serena, no! Don't go down there!" he shouts. By now, many of the other partygoers are down on the street, too, and the crowd becomes a mass of panicking, screaming people. Everyone is running, many people falling to the ground as another hail of bullets rain through the air.

I hear somebody shout, "Car bomb!"

No. No, no, no. This can't be happening. This is just a nightmare. I try to break out of Nico's grasp and run down the street. I have to know. I have to see which car exploded. I need to look at it with my own eyes, even though I already know.

It was Luca's car.

I know it in the deep, painful ache of my heart.

"Luca!" I scream, my voice cracking as Nico and Rafaela drag me back away down the street to their own car, forcing me into the back seat. "No! Let me go to him! Let me go!"

"We have to get out of here," Nico explains, throwing the car into gear and peeling out down the road in the direction of the explosion. "The Cleaners must have known we would all be here. Somebody leaked it. We're not safe, Serena."

Rafaela is crying hysterically, huddled in the

front passenger seat while I turn and gaze wide-eyed out the back window of the car as we pass the explosion. The car is in flames, with hunks of metal and glass strewn all across the road. There is no sign of Luca.

My voice freezes and disappears in my throat as I press my hands to the back window, watching as we drive away from the smoke and flames. I hold my eyes open for as long as I can, not even daring to blink in case I miss the sight of Luca escaping the fire.

But he doesn't.

He's nowhere to be found. He's gone.

As Nico's car hurtles down the road, the flames shrink away into a mere blinking light in the distance, and I close my eyes just as the tears start to fall.

~

Thank you so much for reading! I hope you enjoyed <3 If you have a moment, please leave a review. Other readers are dying to know what you thought.

Make sure to buy Killer on Fire now so you can read the conclusion of the Killer Trilogy!

~Alexis Abbott

ALSO BY ALEXIS ABBOTT

**<u>Romantic Suspense:</u>**

**HITMEN SERIES:**

Owned by the Hitman

Sold to the Hitman

Saved by the Hitman

Captive of the Hitman

Stolen from the Hitman

Hostage of the Hitman

Taken by the Hitman

The Hitman's Masquerade (Short Story)

**THE KILLER TRILOGY:**

Book 1: Killer for Hire

Book 2: Killer Desire

Book 3: Killer on Fire

**SEXY SEALs**

Sweetheart for the SEAL

Sights on the SEAL

**HOSTAGES:**

Stealing Her

The Assassin's Heart

Killing For Her

Abducted

**STEPBROTHERS:**

Ruthless

Criminal

**STANDALONES:**

Betting on Love

Hunter's Baby

I Hired A Hitman

Vegas Boss

Rock Hard Bodyguard

Innocence For Sale: Jane

Redeeming Viktor

## Romance:

Falling for her Boss (Novella)

Most Wanted: Lilly (Novella)

Bound as the World Burns (SFF)

## Erotic Thriller:

**THE DANGEROUS MEN SERIES:**

The Narrow Path

Strayed from the Path

Path to Ruin

Alexis Abbott is a Wall Street Journal & USA Today bestselling author who writes about bad boys protecting their girls! Pick up her books today if you can't resist a bad boy who is a good man, and find yourself transported with super steamy sex, gritty suspense, and lots of romance.

She lives in beautiful St. John's, NL, Canada with her amazing husband.

facebook.com/abbottauthor

twitter.com/abbottauthor

instagram.com/alexisabbottauthor

bookbub.com/authors/alexis-abbott

pinterest.com/badboyromance

youtube.com/AlexisAbbott

# CONNECT WITH ALEXIS

Get an EXCLUSIVE book, **FREE** just as a thank you for signing up for my newsletter! Plus you'll never miss a new release, cover reveal, or promotion!

http://alexisabbott.com/newsletter

facebook.com/abbottauthor

twitter.com/abbottauthor

instagram.com/alexisabbottauthor

bookbub.com/authors/alexis-abbott

pinterest.com/badboyromance

ACKNOWLEDGMENTS

Thank you to my amazing Patrons. I'm constantly humbled and grateful for your support.

*Ramona Cabrera*
*Melissa Hedrick*
*Virginia Swanson*
*Dawn Daughenbaugh*
*Don Doss*
*Stacie Currie*

If you'd like to join them — and get my ebooks or paperbacks — you can find me here on Patreon.
https://www.patreon.com/alexisabbott

www.ingramcontent.com/pod-product-compliance
Lightning Source LLC
Chambersburg PA
CBHW051212190726
48288CB00006B/1929